Gone by Dark

Carolina Moon Series, Book 2

By Christy Barritt

CHRISTY BARRITT

Gone by Dark: A Novel
Copyright 2015 by Christy Barritt

Published by River Heights Press

Cover design by The Killion Group

This ebook is licensed for your personal enjoyment only. This ebook may not be re-sold or given away to other people. Thank you for respecting the hard work of this author.

The persons and events portrayed in this work are the creation of the author, and any resemblance to persons living or dead is purely coincidental.

Other Books by Christy Barritt

Squeaky Clean Mysteries:
#1 Hazardous Duty
#2 Suspicious Minds
#2.5 It Came Upon a Midnight Crime
#3 Organized Grime
#4 Dirty Deeds
#5 The Scum of All Fears
#6 To Love, Honor, and Perish
#7 Mucky Streak
#8 Foul Play
#9 Broom and Gloom
#10 Dust and Obey (coming in 2015)

The Sierra Files
#1 Pounced
#2 Hunted
#2.5 Pranced (a Christmas novella)
#3 Rattled (coming in 2015)

The Gabby St. Claire Diaries (a tween mystery series)
#1 The Curtain Call Caper
#2 The Disappearing Dog Dilemma
#3 The Bungled Bike Burglaries

Holly Anna Paladin Mysteries
#1 Random Acts of Murder
#2 Random Acts of Deceit

Carolina Moon series
#1 Home Before Dark

#2 Gone By Dark
#3 Wait Until Dark (coming late 2015)

Suburban Sleuth Mysteries:
#1 Death of the Couch Potato's Wife

Standalone Romantic Suspense:
Keeping Guard
The Last Target
Race Against Time
Ricochet
Key Witness
Lifeline
High-Stakes Holiday Reunion
Desperate Measures
Hidden Agenda

Standalone Romantic Mystery:
The Good Girl

Suspense:
The Trouble with Perfect
Dubiosity

Nonfiction:
Changed: True Stories of Finding God through Christian Music
The Novel in Me: The Beginner's Guide to Writing and Publishing a Novel

GONE BY DARK

Special thanks to Chris Baker, Sue Smith, and Deena Peterson for their help on this book.

Author's note: Though Hertford is a real town, certain liberties have been taken in the novel for story purposes.

CHRISTY BARRITT

PROLOGUE

"Do you want to walk through the woods?" Andrea asked.

Charity stared at her best friend. They'd been inseparable ever since they were eight years old. Today, they were sixteen, and they had a bond that was unmistakable, almost like sisters.

"Well?" Andrea's brown eyes remained on Charity as she waited for an answer.

Charity surveyed the thick trees in front of them, noting how the sunlight disappeared from sight the deeper she stared into them. Miniature channels of water traversed between the trunks of oaks and cypresses and pines. Sometimes the water traveled in straight lines, sometimes in patches of puddles. The river wasn't far away, and the ground always seemed wet and moist the closer one got to the mighty Perquimans. "You know I don't like the woods, Andrea. They're . . . creepy."

"It will take off thirty minutes from our walk. If we just cut through right here, we'll get home and be able to have some hot chocolate sooner. It's cold out here anyway. I say we get inside as soon as possible." She offered an affirmative nod and put a hand on her hip. Andrea had always been the more dominant of the two, a natural born leader. She was smart and decisive, and everyone knew she was destined for bigger things than the small town of Hertford, North Carolina, where they lived.

Charity shivered as she stared at the thick trees in front of her. Her friend was right; the walk would be shorter. And it was so cold outside. But the woods . . . they seemed so isolated. Wild animals and thick underbrush and snakes hid in the shadows.

"We should have just waited for your mom," Charity finally said, rubbing her arms despite the thick coat she wore. "It's getting dark."

"Even more reason to make this as short as possible." Andrea tugged at the knit hat on her head, proudly emblazoned with an Eagleton logo. Eagleton was a factory in town that employed two of Andrea's older brothers.

Charity and Andrea had stayed after school for drama club and had missed the bus. Charity's mom was single and currently at work, so she couldn't pick them up for another two hours, at the earliest. Andrea's mom had a fund-raising committee meeting until five. Neither Charity nor Andrea was very patient, so they'd decided to walk home.

Charity's throat tightened as she looked at the sinking sun. There was something about the dark that she'd never been comfortable with. Truth was, fear liked to dominate her life, liked to control her decisions.

Andrea always pleaded with her to break away from that pattern. Andrea said her fears were keeping her caged, preventing her from flying away.

Her friend was right. Her fear had held her back—from big things and small things. Even just last month, for example. Charity hadn't auditioned for the lead role in the school musical out of fear of failure, and Andrea, of course, had both auditioned and gotten the role. Charity knew she was a better singer and actress than Andrea. Plus, *My Fair Lady* was her favorite musical ever. She would have loved the role of Eliza

Doolittle.

But it was too late to change anything about that now.

Somehow that thought jostled her into action. "Okay, we can cut through the woods, but just this once," Charity finally conceded.

"I'll protect you," Andrea said, raising her chin and heroically putting one hand on her hip and flexing the bicep of the other arm. "If anyone nefarious appears, I'll go all She-Ra on him."

Andrea was such a goofball, and Charity loved her for it. She could always be counted on for a laugh. But she'd also been the one source of stability in Charity's life. Her existence so far had been a series of ups and down—mostly downs, it seemed sometimes. She could always depend on Andrea's friendship, though.

Her friend held out her hand. "Come on."

With a deep breath, Charity walked with Andrea toward the large swath of trees that separated their school from the lonely stretch of road where they both lived. Freshly cut grass stuck to their shoes, a result of the downpour last night. That also meant the woods would be particularly damp.

Their walk would be short, and the darkness of the woods would only surround them for a few minutes. Then the thickness of the trees would break with light as the fields of cotton behind their houses came into sight.

Charity was overreacting. There was nothing to be scared of.

The first few steps weren't that frightening. The sunlight still permeated the canopy of tree branches overhead enough to reach them. The underbrush wasn't as thick. There was no murky water. But Charity knew that the deeper they traveled, the more likely it was that the elements would sneak up on them. Stagnant water filled with parasites and other critters would be hiding on the other side of logs or beneath low-lying shrubs. Spanish moss would tickle their faces, and spiderwebs just waited for new prey, human or otherwise.

None of that was to mention the fact that the two of them could easily get turned around. One wrong move, and they could be lost in this patch of woods.

There it was again. Fear. If Charity weren't careful, the emotion really would consume her.

"I think this is kind of nice," Andrea said, holding down a branch and glancing around in curiosity. "It's enchanting."

"Spooky," Charity corrected, noting that it was getting darker already.

"It makes me feel like I'm in a fairy tale or something."

"Bad things always happen in fairy tales." Charity frowned.

"Bad things happen, but they're only as a launching pad for great things that are ahead."

Charity would settle for just living a good life. It didn't have to be great; she'd accept that if it meant there'd be an end to what she felt like was one tragedy after another.

Suddenly, Charity's skin crawled, and she grabbed Andrea's arm. They both paused by an old cypress tree, one absent of any foliage. It was spindly and bare, almost like a skeleton in a graveyard of dead trees. The thought made Charity tremble. "Did you hear that?"

"Hear what?"

"A branch snap."

Andrea tilted her head with almost comical compassion. "We're in the woods, Charity. It was probably nothing. A squirrel."

Charity swallowed, her throat tight as troublesome

thoughts closed in. "I just want to get home. I feel really strange right now, like something's not right."

She expected Andrea to make fun of her. Instead, her friend took her arm, all teasing gone. "You should trust your instincts. That's what my dad always says. Let's walk a little faster."

Relief filled her. Her friend had understood. Thank *goodness* she'd understood. When a girl had a friend like Andrea, she held on tight. With the barrage of heartache Charity had experienced, most people would have left. In fact, most people *had* left.

Another snap sounded in the distance. This time Andrea heard it. She paused.

In sync, they both looked over their shoulders.

Charity screamed when she saw a man standing behind them.

He wore some kind of black mask that only showed his eyes. And he stared at them, his large arms projecting menace. His stance seemed bulked up, like he was a soldier preparing to destroy any semblance of life around him.

"Charity, run!" Andrea shouted.

They took off through the thick underbrush. Tree limbs slapped their faces. Logs tried to trip them. Mud suctioned their feet to the ground.

But they kept going. Andrea kept a firm grip on Charity's arm.

Charity dared to take a glance over her shoulder. Curiosity, self-preservation, terror, maybe, had propelled her to do so.

The man . . . he'd quickly closed the space between them. He was practically close enough to touch them, to grab them, to . . . kill them.

She sucked in a breath at the thought. Who was he? Why was he after them? Would they reach the field behind their homes in time?

Dear Lord, please help!

She hadn't prayed in a long time, but now seemed just as good a time as any to start again.

Just then, her foot got tangled in something.

She lunged forward.

Andrea caught her before she hit the ground.

But so did the man.

He grabbed Charity's ankle, his grip like a vise.

Charity screamed so loudly she was sure people all the way in town could hear her. She *hoped* they would, for that matter.

Up close, the man looked even more terrifying. What she couldn't see scared her the most. All his features were hidden behind that mask, behind the clothes that covered every inch of his skin. Even his eyes just seemed to be a black abyss.

He said nothing, just clutched her ankle with a grip tighter than any she'd felt before.

She kicked, trying to get away. Panic enveloped her.

It was no use.

This was it. She was going to die.

Andrea suddenly released her grip on her arm and scrambled away. She grabbed a fallen branch and swung it toward the man. The stick hit him squarely on the head.

The man grunted and, in that split second, released Charity.

She scrambled away, crawling on all fours, her instinct taking over, reacting, in survival mode.

Once the man regained his footing, anger seemed to ignite in him. He surged forward and tackled Andrea to the ground. Andrea hit the dirt hard and let out a grunt.

Charity saw the fear in her friend's eyes. The emotion caused grief to clutch her heart. She stepped toward her friend when the man looked up and growled. He started to grab Charity, but she pulled back, torn between what she should do.

Grab Andrea. Find help.

Grab Andrea. Find help.

The man pulled Andrea to her feet and wrapped an arm around her neck.

"Andrea!" Charity gasped, indecision tearing her apart.

"Go, Charity! Run. Get help!" Andrea shouted.

Her hands balled into fists. "I can't leave you."

"You have to. "

Just then, the man covered Andrea's mouth with his large, gloved hand. Only there was something clutched there. A syringe.

He plunged it into Andrea's arm, and her friend went silent.

Charity panicked, freaked out, didn't know what to do.

So she ran.

She left her friend behind and went to get Andrea's father, praying that he'd be able to help.

CHAPTER 1

Ten years later

Charity White's hands trembled as she attempted to start the rusty old lawn mower. She'd lived in an apartment for so long now that she'd forgotten the basics of lawn care. But the grass at her childhood home was overgrown, and this seemed as good a place to start as any.

The house had been abandoned for years. Three years, to be exact. That's when her mom had died, and the last time Charity had been here in North Carolina was for her funeral.

She'd sworn then she was never coming back again after that day. She no longer had any reason to return.

Yet here Charity was, already in over her head and questioning her decision to come here, and she'd been in town less than twenty-four hours.

Funny how one unexpected, unsigned letter had turned her plans upside down. The twelve powerful words inside had been enough to lure her here again.

I have answers for you in Hertford, but you must come now.

She instinctively knew that the sender had been talking about Andrea. Charity only had to think about her options overnight. There was no way she'd be able to stay away, not when the possibility of finding answers dangled in front of her.

Besides, her friend had always encouraged her to stop living in fear. Coming back to Hertford was one way of doing that. All these years, fear gripped her. Its hold on Charity had tightened and tightened until she could hardly breathe. Until panic tried to rule her life. Until worry churned in her stomach. Charity couldn't live like this anymore.

She'd taken a leave of absence from her job, knowing she needed to put closure to this chapter of her life once and for all. As long as questions lingered over her, she'd never feel any sense of peace. Wasn't that what she constantly told her clients—that, to the best of their abilities, they needed to tie up loose ends and move on? It was time that she applied her own advice.

Now she just hoped that whoever had sent that letter would reveal himself or herself, because Charity had no plan on how to find answers on her own. She'd had ten years to think about ways to track her friend, but none of them had offered a smidgen of hope. She'd sketched out timelines, followed news articles, and even started an anonymous website. She'd even tried praying.

But nothing had happened.

Maybe that letter was her last hope of gaining her life back. Until then, she needed to tidy up her affairs here. She'd get this house in shape and put it on the market. Finally, she'd cut all ties with this town that brought back so many bad memories for her.

Charity jerked on the cord attached to the lawn mower again, but nothing happened.

With a sigh, she hung her head. The heat was stifling, and even such a minute action caused sweat to sprinkle across her forehead. She lifted her hair from her neck, trying to cool off.

"Can I give you a hand?" a deep voice asked.

Startled, she jerked her gaze toward the man behind

her and sucked in a deep breath—both at his nearness and his striking good looks. The man was tall and well built. He had a defined face—perfectly chiseled, actually—and short light brown hair. He wore jeans and a grass-stained T-shirt that fit snug around his muscular torso. Where had he come from?

She looked down at the lawn mower, suddenly flustered. Flustered at her cluelessness, at the realization of how she must look with sweat pouring across her skin, her blonde hair a tangled mess, and her old cutoff jean shorts and tank top. "No. No, I'm fine."

He nodded behind him and extended his hand. "I live next door. Joshua Haven."

Next door? That was Andrea's old house. The family had moved about five years ago. Charity supposed that was when they'd accepted that Andrea was never coming back and that the memories of being there were too strong.

Last Charity had heard, there had been some renters living there, and when they'd moved out, it was abandoned. She'd thought the house was still empty. She hadn't seen anyone there since she arrived yesterday afternoon, and she'd been listening for any more cars coming up the lane.

Of course, it was hard to hear anything over the box fans running in the house. Her childhood home had never had central air conditioning and had relied on window units, none of which worked anymore. Charity was thankful she'd been able to get the power and water back on, for that matter.

"I'm Charity. Charity White." She might as well get that out in the open.

Her neighbor didn't even flinch, though. He didn't recognize her name. That could be a good thing.

Instead, he pointed to the old, neglected house in the background. "You buy this place?"

She shrugged, not wanting to give too much information. Soon enough, everyone would know she was back in town. She didn't recognize this man, which meant he'd probably moved here sometime after she left. The town was small, and everyone seemed to know everyone, unless something had changed in the last decade, which she doubted. Certainly the gossip chain would reveal her story soon enough.

He'd asked her a question. *You buy this place?*

"Not exactly," she finally said, swiping a wayward hair behind her ear.

He stared at her another moment, and she realized how illegal what she said might have sounded.

"The house used to be my mom's," she explained, already sharing more details than she'd desired.

She watched his face carefully for a reaction, but there was none. Most people around here knew about her mom. Knew about the family. Knew about the tragedy that always surrounded them.

"It will be good to have someone else nearby. This road is pretty quiet. As a cop, I usually appreciate that fact. Peace and quiet."

A cop? Great. She didn't have much respect for cops, and she had a list of reasons why. Still, she nodded. "Well, I promise that I'll give you that peace and quiet."

"Wasn't trying to imply otherwise." He offered an apologetic smile before glancing at the lawn mower. "You sure you don't need a hand?"

"I'm just . . . I'm just trying to start this thing."

"Did you prime it?"

"Prime it?"

He grinned. "You have to press this button here to force the gasoline into the lines. There is gasoline in the mower, right?"

She nodded. She had remembered to check that.

Her neighbor pressed the button a few times. Then he held the starting lever down and jerked on the handle, pulling a cord back. The lawn mower roared to life.

"So that's how you do it," she said above the hum of the mower. She grabbed the handle, afraid if he let go, she'd never get it started again. "Thank you."

"No problem." He drew his hands back and hesitated a moment.

Charity just needed for him to go away. She needed to compose herself, to build her little fortress of self-preservation where she felt safe and untouchable. Being around Joshua Haven already made her feel off balance.

"Thank you again," she told him over the rumble of the mower. She took a step forward but could hardly push the machine through the thick, overgrown grass. Her cheeks heated at the thought of having an audience here to witness her absolute failure.

She gave the mower another shove, but the machine wouldn't move through the thick grass. She released her grip on the handle, and the motor went silent again, filling the air with uncomfortable, awkward silence.

Charity hated feeling off-kilter. She'd worked hard to overcome her past, to remain in control of her persona. It had worked, too. She was a professional woman, respected in her field of work. She was known as quiet and private, but compassionate and trustworthy.

She had to stay in Hertford and hold her own, even if it meant feeling out of her comfort zone. Even if it required facing her worst nightmares.

Facing memories of . . . Andrea.

Her heart lurched at the thought of her best friend. Even after all these years, the pain still hadn't subsided. It was always there still, lingering just beneath the surface. Maybe she wouldn't ever be able to put it behind her, with or without closure.

"Do you want me to bring my riding mower over?" Joshua asked, eyeing her with a touch of concern in his eyes.

"I couldn't ask you to do that. I'll manage."

"It's really not a problem. I could have your yard cut in less than an hour. It's going to take you all day."

She ran a hand through her tangled blonde hair, wishing she'd taken a moment to fix it. The humidity of the late August day blanketed the area, causing her hair to curl more than usual.

Before she could respond, her phone buzzed with an incoming text. She hoped it was her friend Lucy texting her an interesting tidbit from work.

Judge Matthews had lunch on his mustache during a trial today. Tuna salad. Not pretty.

Defense attorney Al Hastings got the case files mixed up and called his client by the wrong name.

The sheriff's deputy at the courthouse flirted with me again today.

All those texts would be classic Lucy.

Charity pulled her phone from her back pocket and glanced down at her screen.

As soon as she read the message, Charity gasped.

Do you want to walk through the woods?

Was someone playing a twisted game with her?

***

When Joshua saw the color drain from Charity's face, some kind of protective instinct stirred in him. He started to reach for her but stopped himself. "Is everything okay?"

She quickly shoved her phone back into her pocket and let out a weak, not quite believable laugh. "Yeah, everything's fine. Just a bad joke."

Joshua watched her expression and saw her cheek twitch, a sure giveaway she wasn't telling the truth. Everyone had tics—subtle indications they weren't telling the truth. Charity wasn't very good at hiding her lie. Joshua's instincts had been trained from his days as a cop.

Charity looked away, obviously feeling self-conscious. As she turned, Joshua's gaze traveled from her cheek to her collarbone. A scar stretched across the skin there.

His throat tightened. How had she gotten that? The mark looked big enough and painful enough that there had to be a story behind it.

She must have noticed Joshua studying her, because she tugged the strap of her tank top over the scar. At least she tried to. The mark was too large to conceal.

"Well, it was nice to meet you," she said, offering what appeared to be a forced smile. "I'll only be in town for a short time, long enough to get my affairs here in order before I go back to Tennessee."

He nodded. "Well, if you need anything while you're here, let me know. The offer to cut your grass still stands. I don't know if your old mower here is going to cut it—literally."

Charity offered what looked like a dismissive smile. "I'm sure I'll manage just fine. Thank you, though."

Joshua walked back to his own yard so he could continue pulling weeds from his small but ample flower bed. It had been a long shift with the police department, and he was glad to be home and outside doing something semi-relaxing. He'd spent his shift as a mediator between two neighbors squabbling over free-range chickens, had pulled someone over for a DUI, and had worked with social services in a custody dispute case.

But his conversation with his new neighbor still remained foremost in his mind, no matter how hard he tried to push it aside.

What had that been about? Charity had seemed so skittish. Her eyes had widened, her hands shook, and her breaths came in hurried little gasps. Something on that phone had shaken her up.

Even with her stubborn—perhaps foolish—determination, Joshua had to admit that the woman was appealing. She had a pleasant, heart-shaped face and a pert nose, and was so petite that she almost looked like a teenager. Tendrils of silky blonde hair clung to her neck, and dirt was smudged across her face.

Not that any of that mattered. Any attraction he felt had to be nipped in the bud. Though he was a changed man now, different than he'd been two years ago, the effects of his last relationship still lingered heavy in his heart. He was better off remaining single and focusing on his job.

Just then, he spotted his friend's truck bumping down the gravel lane, coming toward his house. Ryan Shields hopped out and strode toward him.

"Hey, man. What's going on?" Ryan called.

Ryan owned the local car repair shop in town, and the two had bonded over their love of vintage cars. Later, they'd started going to the same church. They'd been fast friends since then.

"I just had the strangest experience," Joshua muttered.

He glanced over at his neighbor and saw her steal an uneasy glance his way. "Do you know her?"

Ryan followed his gaze and frowned. "I can't say for sure, but she looks like Charity White."

"Should I know that name?"

Ryan shook his head and pressed his lips together again. "No, I haven't seen her in years. Since she graduated high school, probably. Never thought she'd be back, but I heard a rumor she was in town."

"I tried to help her with her lawn mower, but she acted uncomfortable," Joshua finished, collecting various weeds he'd thrown on the sidewalk and stuffing them into a lawn bag. "Something just isn't sitting right with me about our conversation."

"Yeah, well, she's had a tough time, to say the least. She was younger than me, and when everything went down, I was already up in New York. I never really knew her well, but I don't envy what she went through. It would test the strongest person."

"A tough time?" Joshua's curiosity spiked.

"That's a conversation for a day when I have more time." Ryan held up the paper in his hands. "I need you to approve these flyers so I can get them to the printer before they close tonight."

"Sure thing. Sounds great." Joshua and Ryan had put together a car show and concert featuring Ryan's fiancée, Daleigh McDermott. The show was a fund-raiser for Ryan's nephew, who was in a wheelchair.

Even as they discussed the car show, Joshua's mind lingered on his mysterious new neighbor. He just needed to stay focused on his job in this new town and on helping with the car show. But as he glanced over at Charity one more time, he realized that would be easier said than done.

***

Do you want to walk through the woods?

Charity couldn't breathe as she remembered the message on her phone. Who had sent her that text message? Why would someone do that?

She downed her last sip of ice water and leaned against the porch railing. The drink had cooled her off but not enough. She rubbed the cold glass against her forehead, her cheeks, and her neck, even.

Was it the late August heat that made her sweat or the text message?

Probably it was both.

She glanced around, half-expecting to see someone watching her from afar. The only person she spotted was her neighbor, Joshua Haven, as he waved good-bye to someone pulling away in a truck.

He was a police officer, he'd said. That was just great. She'd had a string of bad experiences with police officers, most recently when she'd dated one.

She found them all hard to trust, though she would never admit it. She worked as a victim advocate, so she had to work one-on-one with police officers almost daily. That was how she'd met Bradley.

Bradley had destroyed the last bit of faith she had in humanity. She'd waited for so long to truly trust a man with her heart. And all she had to show for it now was regret.

She put those thoughts aside and drew in a deep breath of pure country air. From where she stood, she could see the gravel road stretching along beside a fortress of woods. The road led to a stretch of lazy highway that cut through eastern North Carolina.

Beside this property was Joshua's house. Andrea had grown up there, and the two girls had instantly bonded as children. They'd made mud pies, and picked cotton from the neighbor's fields, and had watermelon-eating contests between just the two of them.

Those memories had been so powerful in her life for so long. Now they brought so much pain.

Joshua had done a good job keeping the place up. There were neat little flower beds, a nicely mowed lawn, and clean paint on the exterior walls. To the right was a field full of cotton. Last Charity knew, a man in town leased the property for farming.

Behind the house was a small shed where she'd found the lawn mower. Even farther back were the woods where Andrea was abducted.

She frowned. Who even knew that Andrea had said those words to Charity before their jaunt in the woods that day so long ago? No one did; no one but Andrea.

But it couldn't have been Andrea who sent the message . . . that just wasn't possible. Besides, only a few people had Charity's number, and most of them were back in Tennessee.

So how had someone gotten it?

Oh, God, what's happening?

She looked to the sky, as if that's where God watched her from—a distance, only watching but not really caring. Almost as if human life amused Him. Like people's lives were simply TV shows. *Maybe that's what we all are: God's soap opera.*

Her heart beat out of control, her chest was tight, and she could hardly breathe.

When she finally got herself under control, she pulled out her phone again. Thankfully it hadn't broken. As she read the message there again, fresh terror washed over her, as if she'd just seen the message for the first time. She forced herself to look beyond the words to the phone number.

It was unlisted.

She had to think this through. If not Andrea, then who could have sent the message? The man who'd abducted Andrea, maybe. But why?

She had so many questions. Coming home had already only proven to offer more puzzling mysteries and less of the answers she so desired.

She wanted to run, to leave.

But she couldn't do that. She'd been running for the past ten years. She couldn't do it anymore. She had to face her fears . . . even if her fears killed her.

CHAPTER 2

The next morning, Joshua reported for his shift at the police station. He wasn't supposed to work today, but the other officer, Isaac, had to take a trip to visit his mother, who was recovering from minor surgery. As of now, it was only Joshua, Chief Rollins, and their dispatcher, Lynn.

Joshua hadn't been able to stop thinking about his new neighbor since their encounter yesterday. Though it was none of his business, curiosity burned inside him and made him want to know more about her, especially after the cryptic conversation with Ryan.

If he'd had more time last night, Joshua would have done some research himself. Instead, he'd gone to see his four-year-old son, Rider, and taken him out for pizza and ice cream. Rider was leaving for vacation today with his mom and stepdad. They'd be gone for two weeks on a cruise and a trip to Disney. Joshua wasn't sure what he'd do with himself not seeing his son for that long.

"Good morning," Chief Rollins called as she walked into the station, her perfunctory cup of chicory coffee from the Have a Nice Day Café in hand. Everyone said the chief reminded them of Reba McEntire. She was a pint-sized, redheaded spitfire.

"You have a minute?"

Chief Rollins raised a thin eyebrow as she crossed to the other side of the desk and sat down. "I have about an hour before I have to be in court. Come into my office."

Joshua sat across from her and lifted a prayer that he'd remain respectful. The chief was a nice woman, but he didn't always agree with her tactics. She acted like being police chief was equivalent to being an elected official, which made sense when considering her background was as a sheriff's deputy. She too often made decisions based on how people in town would look at her or what they would think. Overall, she did a good job, he supposed.

He cleared his throat. "I wanted to ask if you knew anything about a woman named Charity White."

"Is she your date this weekend or something?" The chief's eyes sparkled.

"She's actually my neighbor. I have the impression she has some kind of history here."

The chief leaned back in her chair, wrinkling her lips in thought. "Charity White. Of course. It's been a long time since I've heard her name. You said she's back in town?"

"She is. What's her story?"

"I wasn't the chief when everything happened. I was working as a deputy over in Beauford, as a matter of fact. But everyone in North Carolina knew about the case. It made national news."

National news? Now he was really eager for answers. Was it because he'd moved from the busy metropolitan area of Atlanta to sleepy little Hertford? He supposed there was a part of him that missed the excitement of the police work he'd done back in Georgia. Hertford wasn't even close to the same.

"Charity White and her best friend, Andrea Whitaker—"

"Whitaker? Any relation to Ron Whitaker?" Ron Whitaker was the former police chief. The town had gone through a string of officers in chief over the past decade. But Joshua had had numerous run-ins with Ron. Though the man was a hothead, he still held an incredible, almost unexplainable influence in the town. Since leaving law enforcement, he'd opened a bar called Kicking Cotton. Trouble always seemed to brew there.

"Andrea was Ron's only daughter. Youngest child. Her disappearance is what broke the man. Then he lost his wife two years ago in an auto accident. I don't like the man, but I feel sorry for him."

"That's a lot of loss."

"Anyway, the girls decided to walk home from school. It was cold outside and getting dark, so they cut through the woods in order to shave some distance off their walk."

His skin pricked at the foreshadowing of what would happen next.

"Long story short, a masked man appeared and abducted Andrea. Charity barely got away."

"Did anyone ever find Andrea?"

The chief shook her head. "Never did. To this day, no one has seen her. Of course, we all assume she's dead. It's the most logical conclusion. But her family has never been the same."

"I can imagine. That would be horrible." He thought of his own son. His wife had gotten remarried and decided to move out of state. It was one of the reasons he'd moved from big city Atlanta to Hertford: he wanted to be closer to his son, Rider.

Rider had been the real one who'd lost out in the midst of the problems between Justina and himself. Joshua wasn't willing to give up his relationship with his son just because he and Justina had problems. Moving here was just one more way of trying to make things right.

"The whole town felt the loss," Chief Rollins said.

"What happened to Charity?"

"I'm not sure. As soon as she could, she moved away. Went to college. I don't know if she ever came home again after that. From what I've heard, it sounds like she blames herself and thinks everyone else in town does, as well."

That would be a huge burden to carry. No wonder she'd stayed away. But that also raised the question: Why did she come back? "Were there any suspects?"

Chief Rollins sighed in thought. "From what I remember, Buddy Griffin was the main suspect. No one could ever find any proof to tie him to the crime, though."

Joshua had met Buddy a couple of times. The man worked for animal control and Joshua had been called on scene to help out in a couple of circumstances. "Why was he even a suspect?"

"He was accused of abduction about four years before Andrea went missing. You know Buddy. He's a strange bird, an eccentric. Couldn't find any evidence, though, to connect him to the crime."

"He was the only suspect?"

The chief let out another sigh. "From what I understand, there were hundreds of leads. Like I said, I wasn't here when any of this went down. All I know is that Andrea was never found and no one was ever arrested. The family—this town—never got their closure."

Joshua let her words sink in. An unsolved mystery. A key player in the crime back in town. Suspicions that still flared.

Maybe things in this sleepy community were about to get interesting.

***

As the morning sun rose higher in the sky and soaked in through the front windows of the living room, Charity sat on the ugly brown couch and stared at the picture in her hands. A sad smile brushed across her lips as memories flooded back to her. Being here in Hertford, her emotions felt even stronger and more vivid.

The photo was of her and Andrea. They'd both participated in a Christmas parade downtown. In the picture, they were wearing Santa hats and red sweaters. Their arms were around each other, and huge grins were stretched across their faces.

That had been such a fun day. The two of them had planned on being in the parade again the year Andrea disappeared. But that never happened.

She traced the outline of them with her fingertip. Andrea was tall and thin—but not so thin that she looked fragile. She was the picture of healthy and vibrant with her long brown hair that was naturally highlighted by the sun. Her eyes were big and brown, and her features full. She'd been beautiful.

Charity, in this picture, had blonde hair to her shoulders. She looked slightly awkward, like she hadn't come into her own yet. She was super skinny, almost painfully so. The fact was only emphasized by a sweater that could have fit better and jeans that were a little too faded to be stylish. She still preferred to look natural rather than overdone, but she'd figured out which clothes worked on her petite frame and which hairstyle was more flattering.

The memories of Andrea were so bittersweet. There'd never be anyone like her again.

Since Andrea disappeared, Charity had put a lot of distance between herself and other people. Charity knew she had relationship issues. She had very few close friends and rarely dated. In fact, she was pretty content to be alone for the rest of her life. Maybe it was better that way. Maybe that was the punishment she deserved for leaving the one person who loved her behind.

Charity sighed and put the photo down.

Coming here was painful. More painful than she'd imagined. The memories were raw still, even after all these years.

She let out a sigh and looked toward the ceiling.

"Okay, I'm here. Now what?" she mumbled, as if Andrea could hear her.

Did she expect answers just to drop into her lap? If the FBI hadn't been able to find Andrea's abductor, what made Charity think she could?

She didn't know. She hadn't formulated a plan. But she felt like she needed to be here, that somehow she'd instinctively know what to do. She hoped that would happen sooner rather than later, because she only had two weeks of vacation time before she needed to be back at her job in Tennessee.

She'd come here to get answers. That meant she couldn't stay locked up inside the house for the entire time she was here.

Even though she'd gotten groceries last night, she'd opted to travel to a town twenty minutes away so she could remain hidden. Again—that would get her nowhere.

Gathering all her wits, she decided she would go into town. She'd stop by the town's pharmacy and get a sandwich at the deli counter in the back.

It was a baby step, but maybe that was all she could handle right now.

She pulled her hair back into a sloppy bun, checked to

make sure her cotton sundress was in place, and then stepped out. She paused on the crumbling porch and scanned the area.

Was the man who abducted Andrea out there watching her? Had he been living for this day, when he could finish what he started? Rattled now, Charity hurried to her car, slipped inside, and locked the doors.

Her hands trembled on the entire trip into town. It only took ten minutes to get there. As soon as Main Street came into view, her trembles intensified to the point of nausea.

But she couldn't avoid facing people forever.

A café, a travel agency, and several gift shops composed Main Street. There was also a court building and the police station. Finally, what she'd been seeking came into view. A vertical black-and-white sign for a local pharmacy appeared on the corner. Apparently, the place had a new owner, but it still retained all the old-fashioned coziness it always had.

As soon as Charity walked into the old-fashioned pharmacy, she was swept back in time. The scent of—what was that? Ice cream, she supposed—along with creamy milk and gooey hot fudge filled her senses. In the background she could hear the swish of whipped cream being doled out on sundaes and banana splits.

She had a few vague memories of her grandmother bringing her here as a preschooler. When her grandmother died, all the good memories had died with her. Charity firmly believed her past had made her who she was today; she only wished there wasn't so much pain in the process.

Suddenly, Charity froze. There at the counter talking to the cashier was none other than her neighbor Joshua Haven, dressed in his official law enforcement uniform, one he filled out very nicely.

He spotted her at the same time she spotted him.

"And we run into each other again," he said with a grin.

She paused, eyeballing the ice cream and sandwich counter in the back and weighing her options. "The joys of small town living, I suppose."

"I hope you're adjusting well."

She shrugged as she attempted polite conversation. "I'm just trying to tidy up the property so I can put it on the market. No adjustment needed."

"I see."

Something in his gaze seemed to indicate he knew more. Had he already heard her story since they met yesterday? It wouldn't surprise her. Yet he'd been kind to her. There was no need to be abrasive toward him now.

She shrugged again. "Coming home is . . . it's hard."

"I can imagine."

She nodded toward the back, almost desperate to get away. "Well, I'm going to grab a bite to eat. Have a good day."

Joshua was definitely attractive, but Charity didn't date cops. The one she had dated back in Tennessee had decided to dig into her past. It almost became like she was a case study for him. In the end, he hadn't been interested in her at all; she'd been a potential stepping-stone for his career.

No more.

It was better if she just kept her distance. From Joshua and from the rest of the town.

***

Joshua turned away from Charity before he got caught staring. Instead he grabbed a bottle of soda from the cooler and started toward the front of the pharmacy. It was his lunch break, and he'd stopped by to pick up a couple of things. He liked to make himself visible around town, especially since he was the new guy. People needed to see his face, needed to know he was trustworthy.

Two older ladies were gathered near the register in front of him. He saw the women cast secretive glances at Charity before whispering to each other. They were obviously gossiping about the past.

He bristled. Was this what Charity went through whenever she came into town? There was little he could do, he reminded himself. He couldn't change the social dynamics in the small town, and gossip wasn't exactly a crime.

But he wanted to know more about what had happened ten years ago. An unsolved abduction in such a small town had gotten a lot of attention. He even vaguely remembered hearing about the case. Had it been recreated on one of those TV crime dramas a couple of years ago?

From his brief research this morning, he'd discovered that even the FBI had gotten involved. He could only imagine how the crime had turned the community upside down.

One of his first cases when he worked as a detective in Atlanta had been a teenager who'd disappeared. They'd searched for her for ten days. On the eleventh day, they'd found her body. He remembered how agonizing it had been for the girl's family. At least they finally had answers and were able to move on.

That case had solidified Joshua's calling as a detective. Through careful police work, Joshua had been able to track down the man guilty of the crime. He'd arrested him and taken a sicko criminal off the street before he could do more harm to society.

Before Joshua had taken the job here, he'd considered applying for the FBI and their missing persons unit. That had changed when his wife had left him for another man. Somehow the judge had granted Justina full custody, and she'd packed up his son and moved to this area with her new boyfriend—the man she'd cheated on Joshua with.

Maybe that's why this cold case involving Charity's friend continued to linger in his mind. He'd always had an interest in missing persons cases. It *wasn't* because he was drawn to Charity.

He offered one last glance at Charity before stepping outside into the sunny summer day. His steps slowed as a man across the street from the pharmacy caught his eye. The stranger wore a baseball cap and sunglasses, and he leaned against a tree near the courthouse.

There was nothing illegal about the man lingering there. But something struck Joshua as odd about the man's mannerisms—he just seemed out of place, though Joshua couldn't pinpoint why exactly. Maybe it was because the man's gaze seemed fixated on the pharmacy.

Joshua took a step toward him, deciding to say hello, when the man suddenly straightened and shoved his hands into his jean pockets. He started at a quick clip down the street.

Joshua watched the man until he disappeared from sight. That was probably nothing. But Joshua would keep his eyes open in the future, just in case.

***

Everyone wishes it were you who'd been taken and not Andrea.

As Charity's mother's words came back into her mind, she flinched. The memories always had that effect, even ten years after Andrea disappeared. They still caused her heart to thud and ache.

She grabbed her club sandwich and paid for a few various items. The women whispering around her brought back so many bad memories. Maybe Charity shouldn't have come back here.

Besides, what kind of mother would say something like that to her daughter? Sure, Charity's mom had been drunk at the time, but her mom had always been an honest drunk. Andrea was the town's golden child. Hardly anyone would have missed Charity if the roles had been reversed. They wouldn't have tied colorful ribbons all over the county or held prayer vigils or pleaded on the national news.

Charity made it out the door and all the way to her car, her first fear conquered, when she heard someone behind her. Immediately, she tensed, anticipating the worst.

She twirled around, not sure who or what to expect—only knowing the confrontation wouldn't be pleasant. She'd had death threats after Andrea disappeared. Certainly there were still people here who hated her.

"You!" a man said. "What are you doing back here?"

Charity put a hand over her racing heart. It was Ron Whitaker, Andrea's dad. The man had blamed her for everything that happened and didn't make a secret of it. She'd kept tabs on Andrea's family over the years, hoping they might move away. But they didn't. They'd stayed here, a verbal attack always ready and prepared. He'd even found her after her mom's funeral, just so he could lash out.

Mr. Whitaker looked the same, only older. Much older. He had pronounced wrinkles now, a receding hairline, and gray hair. He still appeared tall and strong, but the tautness in his muscles had lessened. Still, the man was intimidating, just as he'd been when Charity was a child.

Everyone in town knew that he wasn't someone to be messed with. That apparently hadn't changed.

"I repeat: What are you doing back here?" He leered at her, simmering anger heating his gaze.

"That shouldn't concern you," she muttered, holding her bag of groceries closer, almost like a shield between herself and the man.

"I can't believe you'd show your face around here. You have some nerve."

"I'm going to go." She tried to turn to her car and fish her keys out of her purse.

Before she could, Mr. Whitaker jerked her back around to face him. In the process, her bag dropped and her eggs cracked against the asphalt below. "My Andrea would still be here if it hadn't been for you."

Charity shook her head, hot tears rushing to her eyes. She didn't even care about her groceries anymore. She just wanted to get to a safe place. Anywhere but here, for that matter. "I really need to go."

He leaned closer, close enough that spittle sprayed on Charity. "I pray every day for bad things to happen to you, that God will find some kind of justice fit for you."

Charity's throat clenched. "I've prayed the same things," she whispered.

Before he could stop her, Charity thrust her sandwich into his hands, grabbed her keys, and quickly unlocked her door. She jumped into the car and locked the door. Mr. Whitaker still stood there as she pulled away.

Being here was going to be one of the hardest things she'd ever done.

It wasn't too late to run. But that would be cowardly. No, it was time to own up to her mistakes. Make peace with herself. Maybe even make peace with this town.

Charity hurried home, ready for the reprieve she'd find there; she needed an escape from people's judgments. Her own judgments of herself were heavy enough to try to endure.

She rushed toward her door, knowing full well she was being irrational. No one had followed her here, waiting to exact God's judgment on her and take justice into his or her own hands. But seeing Andrea's dad had only confirmed her fears: everyone still blamed her.

The town's precious poster girl had been taken, while the town's misfit had survived.

It had seemed like the ultimate injustice for so many people here.

The daughter of a woman who'd had more boyfriends and one-night stands than people could count had lived, while the daughter of the town's revered police chief had disappeared.

As she reached her porch, Charity stopped.

There on the stoop was a blue knit hat.

Just like the one Andrea had been wearing when she disappeared.

CHAPTER 3

Joshua had just gotten back to the station when Lynn, the dispatcher, handed him a slip of paper.

"The chief asked if you could take this," Lynn said. She was in her fifties with platinum blonde hair and lots of makeup. She proudly told anyone who asked that she had ten grandchildren, and she hadn't let age slow her down. Joshua always called her the glue that held the department together.

He took the form and looked down at it, mumbling, "Sure thing" before he even read any details.

"It's from Charity White," Lynn continued, her voice tinged with curiosity. "I heard you and the chief talking about her earlier. Charity thinks she found some evidence tying in with the old case."

His pulse spiked. Charity. Again.

Was God trying to tell him something? How many times within twenty-four hours could two people be thrown together?

"The old case? You mean the abduction of Andrea Whitaker?" Joshua clarified.

Lynn nodded, a little more bounce in the motion than usual. "That's right."

Joshua crossed his arms a moment, sensing Lynn was eager to share what she knew. "Were you in Hertford when that happened?"

Lynn sobered. "It was awful. Just awful. Andrea was such a wonderful girl. The town hasn't been the same since then. And her poor family. They fell apart, especially Ron. He only lasted as police chief for about a year after Andrea was abducted. Then he was asked to resign. He lost all his good judgment, though you could never tell him that."

"So you were working here when Andrea's father worked for the department?"

She nodded. "That's right. Andrea and Charity used to come in sometimes. Charity was just the sweetest little girl. I remember one time a woman came in to file a report because her little boy had gotten lost in one of the cornfields. Charity was probably only ten at the time, but she came and sat beside this grieving woman. The girl didn't say anything: she just held her hand and let her cry. That's just the way Charity is."

The mental image warmed Joshua's heart. "So you don't have any hard feelings toward her?"

"Toward Charity? No. Of course not. I just wished she had a better home life. Her mom was pretty worthless, and I don't say that very often. But there were so many men in and out of the home, so much substance abuse and neglect. I even called social services one time, but nothing ever came of it."

Joshua's heart squeezed as the new facts were revealed. There was more to his neighbor than he knew. He wanted to ask more questions, but before he could, he noticed Lynn squirm and swipe a piece of blonde hair behind her ear.

"What?" Joshua asked.

"Speaking of which, I thought you should know that someone reported a confrontation in the parking lot off Main Street."

"Okay . . ." He waited for her to continue.

She shifted as if uncomfortable again. "It was Mr. Whitaker. He and Charity were talking, apparently. It was heated."

"Is everyone okay?"

What he really wanted to know was: Was Charity okay? He wasn't sure why he was so concerned about a woman he barely knew. Maybe it was the trauma she'd endured as an adolescent or the way people had treated her in town today. Whatever the reason, he sensed she needed someone to be in her corner. He wasn't saying that person should be him; he wasn't saying it shouldn't be, either.

Lynn nodded. "From what I understand."

He didn't want to waste any more time. "I'm going to go check on Charity, see what's going on."

He took off down the road. This should be interesting. Even for a small town, the amount of run-ins he and Charity had with each other was uncanny. And what kind of possible evidence could Charity have found in the time since he'd seen her at the pharmacy?

He pulled up to her house, and when she opened the door, he immediately noticed she was pale. Her hands trembled, and her eyes had that blank expression that only grief and shock could cause. He'd seen it too many times. It reflected how she'd looked yesterday when she'd gotten that message on her phone, as well.

"Thanks for coming," she murmured, pushing the screen door open. "Come on in."

He stepped into her home, instantly noting how stifling hot it was inside. A single box fan sat in the window, attempting to move air through the room. It didn't help.

He turned back to the woman. "You had evidence of a crime that you wanted to report."

She nodded, her arms pulled tightly over her chest. She nodded toward a plastic bag on the coffee table. "It's right there."

He picked up the bag and stared at the blue stocking hat inside. "A hat?"

"I need to sit down." She fanned her face.

He caught her elbow, afraid she might pass out, and he kept his hand there until she reached the couch. He sat down in the chair near her and waited until she composed herself. Finally, she nodded to the hat again.

"It was my best friend Andrea's," she started. "I'm sure you've probably heard the whole lurid story by now. She wore it on the day she disappeared."

"I've only heard bits and pieces. I know she disappeared and that the case went cold." He wanted to hear Charity's interpretation of everything.

She glanced his way, a fleeting emotion in her blue eyes, and finally nodded. "That's right. Ten years ago."

He studied the hat a moment as he gathered his thoughts. "What makes you think this is her hat?"

Charity kept her chin raised and her shoulders back. "Because it is. It's blue, and it has the Eagleton logo on the front—the old logo. It changed the year after Andrea disappeared."

As much as she seemed convinced, Joshua had to stay objective and think this through. "But still, there could be others just like that around here, right? Other people work for that company."

"But Andrea's had a tear on it, right below the logo. She got it caught on the swing out back one time, and it pulled the stitching out. If you examine that hat, you'll see that the rip is still there. That hat is Andrea's."

He needed to buy some time as he processed that information. "I'm new in town, but I understand that no evidence has turned up for a very long time."

"Believe me, I know how this sounds. But I had to report the hat, just in case there was any hope of finding her . . . I couldn't hide what might be potential evidence." Her voice broke under the strain of her words.

"I'd like to hear what happened that day, Charity. Would you mind talking about it?"

She sucked in a long breath. "A man snatched my friend as we walked home from school. That's everything in a nutshell."

"Did he try to grab you also?"

"He grabbed me first, but I got away."

He softened his voice. "What happened after you ran, Charity?"

"I went to go get help. But when I reached the field, I tripped. I hit my head. I didn't come to for another thirty minutes. By the time I called the police, Andrea was long gone." Her words cracked with unspoken emotion. "Darkness had already fallen, both literally and symbolically."

Joshua shifted, realizing the guilt Charity probably felt. "Charity, did something happen in the parking lot of the pharmacy after I saw you there?"

When her eyes widened with surprise, he had his answer. Yes, it did.

"Word travels quick around here," she finally said. "Some things never change."

"What happened?" It didn't matter if she tried to brush the incident off; Joshua took matters like this seriously.

She raised a shoulder in a poor attempt to look nonchalant. "It was nothing I didn't deserve."

"I heard Ron Whitaker grabbed your arm, made you drop your groceries."

Her eyes widened again. "And when word got around

town, no details were spared." She dropped her carefree act, and her shoulders slumped. "Yes, he did. He's angry. He's had ten years to be upset with me, so when he saw me after all this time, everything obviously boiled to the surface."

"Do you want to press charges?"

"No, of course not. The last thing I want to do while I'm here is to stir up trouble."

He stared at her another moment, trying to decide how hard to push. Finally, he stood. If she wanted his help or advice, she would ask. Besides, there'd been no crime or direct threat. "We'll have this hat tested, see if there's any of Andrea's DNA on it. How's that?"

She rubbed her hands on her dress, looking ill at ease. "Before you go, there's more."

He remained where he was, more curious than ever.

"Okay."

Her face grew even paler. She didn't say anything for a moment, and instead just sat there looking incredibly uncomfortable. She didn't want to say whatever it was, yet she seemed to feel obligated, he realized.

Finally she drew in a shaky breath. "I got a text message yesterday. It said: 'Do you want to walk through the woods?'"

"I'm not sure I'm following."

"That was what Andrea asked me on the day she disappeared. No one else besides Andrea would know that. It was never important to the investigation. I never told the police or anyone, for that matter. But I've never forgotten that conversation with Andrea. It's burned into my mind."

He sat down again, trying to let what she'd said sink in. "So, you think Andrea texted you and then left her hat at the door?"

She rubbed her hands on her dress again. "I know it

sounds crazy. I don't really have any idea what's going on. I'm just reporting what happened."

"Has there been any other contact through the years?"

"No, not really." She looked at him again, her big eyes almost childlike in their innocence. "Look, I know how this looks. I come back into town, and all of this starts happening. Believe me, the last thing I want is to draw attention to myself. People already hate me enough without all this stuff coming to the surface again. I just wanted to be unseen while I was here."

The weight of what she said pressed on his shoulders. It must be a terrible burden to carry. No wonder she acted like a nervous wreck. Being back here must be painful and intimidating at the same time. So why had she come?

That was a question for another time.

"Can I see your cell?" he asked.

She nodded, reached into her purse, and pulled out her phone. She hit a few buttons before handing him the device. "That's the text."

He read the words there, and the message was just like she'd said. *Do you want to walk through the woods?* Alone, the message might sound creepy. In context, the words were chilling.

Was someone trying to scare her? But it was like Charity said: Who would have known about their conversation besides Andrea?

Unless Andrea had told someone else. Her abductor, maybe?

The theories raced around in his mind, but without more research and investigating, nothing would really make sense.

He didn't know what to make of everything Charity had told him. But he'd do his best to investigate this with an open mind. For Charity's sake, as well as the rest of the town's.

***

As soon as Joshua was gone, a sense of loneliness gripped Charity. It had felt good to talk to someone about what she'd discovered.

Charity closed her eyes, and visions of the hat filled her mind. What happened today would haunt her for a long time. Just as what had happened ten years ago still haunted her, like a ghost that wouldn't leave her side.

As the day began flashing back in her mind, the phone rang, effectively saving her from reliving that awful day. Her heart skipped a beat, but when she looked at the number, her panic subsided. It was her best friend from Tennessee.

"Hey, Lucy." Charity leaned back into the couch, trying to stay cool, both physically and mentally. She didn't want her friend to know just how hard all of this had been. Lucy worried about her coming back here enough already. Her friend had seen the effects of her childhood on her adult life. That was the problem with having friends who were also counselors: they could see past the facades and lies.

"Charity! I haven't heard from you, and I was starting to get worried." Her friend's warm voice always made her feel better.

"It's been crazy since I've been here. I've thought many times about packing up and going back to Tennessee." Take today for example . . .

"You're always welcome to do that. It's not the same around here without you."

Charity's heart longed to be back there, but she knew she couldn't do that. Not yet. "I can't even describe the internal urging I had to come back here to North Carolina. I couldn't ignore it anymore. I don't think I'll ever be able to move on until I have peace with my past."

Lucy's voice changed from lighthearted to dead serious. "You making out okay?"

Everything that had happened raced through her mind. Charity shut her eyes, wishing it was that easy to shut out her memories. "I want to say yes, but . . ."

"What's going on?" Concern and compassion etched her friend's voice.

She told Lucy everything. There were few people she could talk to like Lucy. They'd met right after college when they both began to work as victim advocates. Their friendship had been slow to develop, but it had lasted through the years.

"Sounds scary, Charity. Even more reason for you to come back. Sometimes confronting our pasts isn't the answer. Sometimes we just have to accept them and move on." Her words sounded like the counselor she was: always perfectly measured and well thought out.

"I don't know, Lucy." Charity absently twirled a piece of her hair, her mind still racing. "Why is all of this happening now that I'm back? It can't be a coincidence."

"It's almost like someone was just waiting for you to return."

Charity shuddered at the thought. The idea had lingered in the back of her mind also, but she hadn't dared voice it aloud. The notion seemed too crazy. Even more than that, it seemed frightfully scary, like something from her nightmares.

"I just don't know what any of this proves," Charity said, trying to sound logical. "Did the person who snatched Andrea wait for ten years to bring the case back into the spotlight? Why didn't he just track me down in Tennessee and terrorize me there? Nothing makes sense."

"I don't know what to tell you except be careful. Is there anyone there who can watch out for you? If there is some kind of psycho out there, I'd hate for you to be alone. Someone needs to keep an eye on you."

Charity frowned. "No, there's no one. Not anymore."

"You haven't talked to anyone since you got back, you mean? What would you tell one of the clients on your caseload if she was in your shoes?"

"I'd tell her it was important to have people in her life she could depend on." Charity sighed as Joshua's face flashed through her mind. "I have made contact with a police officer, who just happens to be my neighbor. We've run into each other several times."

"Well, at least you've interacted with one other person while you're there. Don't be a hermit. Remember, there comes a time when we all need other people. Sometimes our survival depends on it."

Lucy knew her all too well. Charity had a tendency to draw into herself and become secluded from other people. It was a by-product of everything that had happened in her life. Her trust in other people had been shattered. It took her a long time to allow herself to open up to anyone now.

"Girl, as much as I'd like to talk more, I have to run. I have a counseling session coming up," Lucy said. "But I will be calling often to check on you. Maybe I am a mother hen, but I won't sleep at night if I'm wondering if you're okay."

After they hung up, Charity paced over to the back door and stepped outside onto the deck, hoping some fresh air might calm her down. The old wooden structure was dilapidated and green, and the land stretching behind it was a tangled mess. Random trees—oak, pine, and apple—were scattered here and there, surrounded by both patches of dirt and layers of weeds.

An old swing was almost impossible to see through the unkempt nature between the house and the woods that started about an acre beyond that. There was also a shed that had been painted a lovely shade of red at one time. She and Andrea had taken to fixing it up once for a summer project. Today, the paint was peeling and faded, a grim reminder of the fact that time could heal or it could bring further destruction.

This piece of property really could be lovely with some TLC. So many people craved this kind of peace and solitude.

If only Charity didn't have so many bad memories here.

Charity's gaze traveled to the woods at the back of the property.

What she saw there between the trees stopped her cold.

Someone stood at the edge of the woods.

Andrea.

CHAPTER 4

Charity blinked, certain her eyes were deceiving her. That *couldn't* be Andrea.

Yet her friend stood there, by a tree, staring right at her. She was taller now and just as slender as ever. Her hair was longer, and she wore jeans and a plaid shirt. Her hands were tucked into her pockets, and a blank expression remained on her face.

"Andrea," she whispered. Charity took a step closer, her knees close to buckling.

It couldn't be . . .

But . . . that really was her. It was Andrea.

She was alive. She was okay. She was here!

Charity's heart leaped with joy, with surprise, with relief.

How could this be? After all these years? Andrea was here now.

Charity took another tentative step forward.

Andrea continued standing at the edge of the woods staring at her. Was she silently asking Charity to come? Why wasn't her friend making an effort to approach her, to come any closer herself? Why was she here now after ten years?

Charity didn't care. She had to talk to her friend, to know for sure that she was okay. She'd dreamed about something like this happening, but it didn't seem possible.

Her mind swirled as she started across the grass, her

steps quickening.

When Charity was halfway across the yard, Andrea moved for the first time. At first, she shifted. The action was so subtle that Charity almost thought she'd imagined it. But then, in the next second, her friend darted into the woods as if running for her life.

Charity started to rush toward her, to try and catch her before she got away. But just as Charity reached the edge of the woods, she stopped.

Panic kicked in. Her heart raced. Her throat tightened. Her lungs squeezed.

She couldn't go into those woods. She couldn't go back to the place where Andrea had been lost.

But now her friend had been lost again to those very woods.

Tears rushed to Charity's eyes. What was she supposed to do? Why had her friend run? What was going on?

She hated herself for doing it, but she took a step back. Then another. And another.

Finally, her heels hit the last step of the deck. She fell backward, cascading into the wood planks behind her.

Then she began sobbing for everything she'd lost—then and now.

**

Joshua didn't know what to make of the information Charity had shared with him about the text and the Eagleton hat. He turned it over in his mind as he drove back to the station. Was someone trying to shake Charity up by leaving a hat similar to Andrea's on her porch? What effect would the perpetrator be shooting for—maybe trying to run Charity out of town? Or was there more going on here than met the eye?

By the time he reached the station, he had even more questions: How would someone have known about Andrea and Charity's conversation? Was Charity really just back here to sell her mom's old house, or was there more to the story? Why exactly did people feel so much animosity toward her?

She'd only been sixteen when the crime occurred. In some ways, she was just as much a victim as Andrea.

He nearly collided with the chief as he started toward his desk.

"Everything okay?" Chief Rollins asked, arching one of her thin eyebrows. "Did you just get back from talking to Ms. White?"

He nodded. "Yeah, something strange is going on."

"Come on into my office and give me the rundown. I'm intrigued."

He plopped down into the seat across from her, hoping that if he voiced some of his thoughts out loud, they'd start to make sense.

When Joshua finished sharing the facts of the case with her, Chief Rollins leaned back in her chair, laced her hands across her thin midsection, and grunted pensively. "Interesting that all of this is coming to light after so many years and right when Ms. Charity White comes into town."

Something about the way she said the words got his attention—and not in a good way. "What are you implying?"

She shrugged. "I wonder if this Charity woman is trying to stir up trouble?"

"Why would she do that?" A surge of defensiveness rose in him, for no apparent reason. He was supposed to remain objective in this. Then again, so was the chief.

Chief Rollins shrugged. "Why do people do anything? It

could be a variety of reasons. For attention. For sympathy. If I remember correctly, some people thought Charity staged all of this herself. Maybe she's just trying to start trouble."

Charity staged it all herself? That was the most ludicrous idea he'd ever heard. "That's an awful lot of trouble to go through to get a few minutes in the spotlight. Besides, I have the impression she doesn't want any attention, that she'd just disappear if she could."

"Then why did she come back?"

He shook his head. "To sell the house and move on. Besides, ten years is a long time to keep up a ruse. I still can't comprehend why people might think she had something to do with her friend's disappearance. She doesn't strike me as the type." He'd been in law enforcement for a long time; he was no rookie. He had a good gut instinct for these kinds of things, and he couldn't imagine Charity being behind something like Andrea's disappearance.

Chief Rollins unclasped her hands and leaned toward her desk. "Since we talked yesterday, I've been chatting with a few people in town about all of this. Charity was the last one seen with Andrea, and there was no evidence that anyone else had been in those woods. It's Charity's word that the entire case hinges on."

He shook his head, trying to let all of that sink in. Something just didn't sound right. "No other evidence? You're telling me there were no footprints in the woods, even?"

"It was hard to say. Hunting season and all. There were a lot of footprints. Plus there was the fact that about four hundred volunteers scoured the woods looking for Andrea."

"So any evidence would have been trampled," he concluded.

"If we're talking about footprints, then yes. But why was

there no ransom note? No body? There was just nothing after she disappeared. Zilch."

He needed to play devil's advocate for a moment and prove to himself that he was being objective and not afraid of asking the hard questions. "Okay, let's say Charity had something to do with it. What would she have done with Andrea?"

"People speculated for a while that Charity buried her."

The thought seemed ludicrous. "Why would they think that?"

"She waited an hour to report Andrea was missing."

"She fell and bumped her head. That's her story. People think she's lying and that during that time, Charity killed Andrea, buried her somewhere, and inflicted wounds on herself so she wouldn't get caught?"

The chief nodded slowly.

"That's a big charge. And if you think it through, Charity would have had to do a lot of planning, even to do something like that in a one-hour period. She would need a shovel, a means of killing Andrea. She would have had dirt all over her clothes, under her nails. Besides, based on her size, I doubt she could have dug but so deep."

"I agree. I think the idea is far-fetched. The girl's mom was never right in the head. Maybe it runs in the family. That's what people assumed, at least."

Joshua didn't want to believe that. It sounded to him like people were grasping at straws. "What about the search-and-rescue dogs?"

"They lost the scent."

He sighed. It wasn't unheard of. Dogs lost the scent all the time. But the total lack of evidence in the case was astounding.

"Anyway, I do think that hat is interesting," Chief Rollins said, obviously not as disturbed as he was at the facts of the case and its reappearance.

"Do you really think Charity saved Andrea's hat all these years and put it out on her porch herself?" He tried to get a read on what the chief's body language was saying.

"I'm not sure. Right now, all I want to know is if it's really Andrea's. Send it to the state crime lab. Let's see what they find out."

"It will take months to get results," he argued.

"What else can we do?" The chief shrugged. She obviously didn't think this was going anywhere.

A plan of action solidified in his mind. "I'd like to revisit the facts of the case. You okay with that?"

The chief twisted her head before nodding as if impressed. "I know this town would love some answers. Just proceed with caution. You never know exactly what kind of skeletons you might dig up."

CHAPTER 5

The next morning, Charity felt a new determination to find some answers. Maybe going back to where this nightmare had begun would stir something in her.

After throwing on some shorts and a tank top and pulling her hair into a sloppy bun, she climbed into her sensible sedan—a ten-year-old model, but it was paid off—and started down the road. She crossed the bridge over a creek branching from the Perquimans and followed the road. Finally, she pulled off onto a gravelly patch of earth beside the woods.

Dread filled her as she stepped out. Flies buzzed around her, and the dank smell of the nearby stagnant water filled the air. Grass tickled her ankles, and the sun beat down on her shoulders, promising to scorch her skin if she wasn't careful.

Shielding her eyes from the sun, she stared at the school in the distance. It seemed like a lifetime ago she'd been a student there. Despite how hard life was at home, she'd enjoyed the reprieve of being at school; she felt safe there.

It was a shame that a girl didn't feel safe at home, but her mom's choices had ensured that. Instead, Charity had excelled at academics. She'd been active in the drama club and vice president of the school's service club. She didn't get approval at home, so she'd worked hard to receive it at school.

After Andrea disappeared, that had all changed.

Her grades slipped. People looked at her differently—even her teachers. She couldn't handle the responsibility of being VP of anything.

Charity let out a long sigh.

Turning away from the school, she glanced at the woods. A shiver ran up her spine and her throat went dry at the sight of this spot. This was where all her nightmares had begun.

She'd wished a million times that she could do it over again. She would have insisted she and Andrea wait for a ride. She wouldn't have left Andrea when the man grabbed her. She would have paid more attention so she could have given the police more clues.

But it was too late to do any of that.

She stepped closer to the tree line. The landscape hadn't changed much, except now the terrain seemed both thicker and murkier. Apparently, they'd had a rainy summer here in Hertford, and the woods proved it. Huge puddles lingered between the trees.

Charity closed her eyes a moment, traveling back in time.

She could clearly see Andrea. Her friend had that carefree look on her face that was always there. Her eyes had glimmered with adventure. Nothing had scared her.

"Do you want to walk through the woods?" Andrea asked.

The same sick feeling gurgled in Charity's gut now as she remembered the proposition.

Why, oh why, couldn't she have said no?

Charity still remembered her first step into the woods that day; she still remembered the fear she'd felt.

She felt it now.

Instantly, the man in the mask flashed into her mind. The image was so vivid it felt real. Charity pictured him standing behind them. Just staring.

Then, in that horrifying instant, he'd attacked.

So who was that woman Charity had seen yesterday? It couldn't be Andrea. Certainly she hadn't been hiding out in the woods just waiting for Charity to return.

But then who had sent that text message?

Nothing was making sense.

Charity sucked in a deep breath as something pulled her from her thought vortex. The sound was subtle—so quiet she thought she'd imagined it.

But she hadn't.

It was a footstep.

Behind her.

CHAPTER 6

"Charity White?"

Charity whirled around, trying to place the voice. A tall man with close-cropped dark hair, startling blue eyes, and a trim build came into view.

Instinctively, she stepped back. Reached for something. There was nothing but air.

"Charity, it's me. Brody Joyner." He shoved his hands into his pockets. "It's been a long time."

She released the breath she held and narrowed her eyes. "Brody?"

He grinned slightly. "The one and only."

Her shoulders relaxed as she let out a feeble laugh. She'd overreacted. Again. She did that a lot. "I'm sorry I didn't hear you come up."

"I was heading down the road and I saw you. At least, I thought it was you. Sorry about that. I thought you heard me pull over."

Her gaze drifted to her car. Sure enough, a truck was parked behind it. How could she have missed that? Had she been that absorbed in her trip down memory lane?

"I was in my own world." She paused, almost waiting to see the judgment in his eyes. When she didn't, she continued. "I didn't realize you were still in this area."

He nodded, his eyes friendly. "I'm Coast Guard now, working out of Elizabeth City. I couldn't believe it when I actually got stationed back here."

Brody and Andrea had dated for two years. He was three years older, though, so he'd been gone during the time everything happened. Of course he'd come home and helped search and done all he could. But eventually he'd gone back to college. What else could he do?

Charity had always thought he seemed like a nice enough guy, but she'd never really known him that well. At times, she had felt second place to their relationship, which was why it was a relief when he went off to college. It had been selfish of Charity, but she'd had Andrea to herself for so many years.

"What brings you back here?" Brody asked.

She shrugged, not sure of the right answer. "I decided to take some leave from my work. I wanted to have some closure here. It's hard when my mom's house is in my name now and everything."

His gaze sobered as he looked toward the woods. Charity knew exactly what he was thinking; Brody was no dummy. He'd put it together why she was standing at this exact spot.

"So this has nothing to do with Andrea?" he asked, his voice soft.

She swallowed, the motion causing her throat to ache. "I've prayed that I would have some closure with her also, but that possibility seems unlikely."

"I've prayed the same thing for years."

An idea suddenly began to grow in her mind. Charity had avoided all her friends after the incident; she'd never bothered talking to them about Andrea or what happened out of fear her mom's words might be true. *Everyone wishes it was you and not Andrea.* But what if one of them knew something she didn't? It was a possibility worth considering.

"Brody, this might sound like it's out of left field, but did you ever have any theories about who grabbed Andrea?"

He let out a long sigh. "I've thought about it nearly every day for the past decade. The best conclusion I've been able to come to is that a random stranger grabbed her."

"That's what everyone seems to think." She stepped closer. "I know this is going to sound weird, but do you know of anyone she was having problems with, Brody?"

Her question seemed to startle him, and his eyes widened. "I don't know, Charity. It's hard to say. She wasn't acting like herself in the two weeks before she disappeared."

"You weren't here. How do you know?"

"I could tell from her voice when we talked on the phone. She tried to cover it up, but I knew."

"Did you ask her about it?"

He nodded. "I did. She said she was disappointed with her dad."

Charity remembered her confrontation with Andrea's dad earlier. The man had a temper; everyone in town knew that. But could he have had something to do with Andrea's disappearance? Charity found that hard to believe. What could his motive possibly be?

"Ron is having a hard time since Roberta died. I think she helped keep him grounded in the aftermath of all of this. Since she's been gone, his temper has really flared up."

Charity nodded. "I heard about the car accident. That had to be really hard on everyone."

"It was. She was a nice woman." He let out another sigh and rubbed his chin. "I wish I could help. I'd love to have some answers also, Charity. What happened still haunts me. I think it haunts everyone who knew Andrea."

Charity smiled out of force of habit. The expression was more an attempt at gratitude than anything else. "Thanks, Brody. It was nice running into a friendly face." He was possibly the first friendly face she'd seen since she'd been here other than Joshua.

"Anytime, Charity." He reached into his pocket and handed her a card. "Here's my contact information if you need anything. I wish you luck."

***

Joshua spent his time between calls studying the old police files on Andrea's disappearance and letting the facts stew in his mind. He reread the reports. Made a list of questions. Compiled a timeline.

As he stared at his notes, he heard the buzzer at the front desk beep and tried to ignore it. Lynn usually greeted anyone who walked in. When the buzzer sounded again, he stood and walked into the lobby.

A woman stood at the desk, wringing her hands together. She wore a colorful, shapeless dress that reached all the way to the floor. She was probably in her fifties, and her hair, black peppered with gray, was pulled into a neat braid. Joshua had never seen her before. Then again, he was new in town.

"Can I help you?"

"I was hoping I could speak with someone. Privately." Her voice was so soft that he had to strain to make out what she was saying.

"Of course. Why don't you come back to my desk?"

She nodded timidly and followed him down the hallway. He pulled out a seat across from his desk and then waited until she was seated before lowering himself into his chair. The woman looked nervous. Her gaze fluttered about the room, her lips parted, then squeezed shut, and she didn't fully relax in the seat.

"Can I get you some water or coffee?"

She shook her head. "No, thank you."

"What can I help you with?"

"I need to know what my options are." She rubbed her lips together, her skin listless.

"For what?"

"If someone is . . . hurting me. Hypothetically speaking. If I report this person, will he or she go to jail?"

"There's a good chance of that."

She blinked silently for a moment. "What do you mean *good chance*?"

"It's hard to say anything for sure, especially not knowing any details. Could you offer any other information?" In the background, Lynn stepped out from the supply room and waved an apology.

The woman in front of Joshua shook her head, unmistakable sadness in her eyes. "Not really."

"Ma'am, if someone is hurting you, you should distance yourself from this person."

"It's complicated."

He softened his voice. He'd had conversations like this more times than he'd like. "You shouldn't be with someone who harms you."

"What if this person who's being hurt has no one else?"

"Then we can find her help. We just need her to file the report."

She suddenly stood. "I can't do that. I need to . . . I need to think. Figure things out. It's not that easy."

Joshua bit back the words he wanted to say. He couldn't make the woman do anything she didn't want to do. But he saw a world of pain in her and wished he could intervene.

"I should go."

Before he could even get her name, the woman darted from his office and out of the station.

Their eerie conversation remained on his mind, though. Just what had all of that been about?

He strode toward the lobby, his gaze remaining on the front door as if he hoped the woman might magically reappear. "Do you know who that was?" he asked Lynn.

She shook her head. "I can't say I've ever seen her. Once in a while we have people visiting from out of town or stopping in as they travel throughout the state."

Lynn seemed to know everyone in town. She'd lived here twenty years and was intricately involved in many groups and causes and anything social. She never forgot a name or a face.

"Everything okay?" Lynn asked.

He shrugged. "I'm not sure. I have the definite impression she's in an abusive relationship. She just came in to ask questions."

"As the saying goes, you can lead a horse to water, but you can't make it drink. It's a shame, too. Sometimes you just want to step in and help people. That's not always possible, though."

"Yeah, you're telling me." He shifted as his thoughts turned to Charity. She was another person he'd like to help. He just needed her permission to get involved, and it wasn't likely she'd give it to him. But maybe if they could forge some kind of trust between them, she'd be more willing to talk. "I'm going to go give someone an update on a case. You know how to reach me if something comes up."

Lynn nodded.

As soon as Joshua stepped onto the sidewalk, he glanced both ways, looking for a sign of the mystery woman who'd come into the station. There was no sign of her anywhere. Maybe she would stop by again before things escalated.

He climbed into his cruiser and took off toward Charity's place. He wanted to talk to her—official police business. At least that's what he told himself. But he wondered if there was more to it.

CHAPTER 7

Joshua pulled up Charity's driveway, and before he could even knock on the door, it opened. Charity stood there, wearing shorts and a tank top, tendrils of hair clinging to her neck, and a sweaty glass of water in her hand.

His throat went dry at the sight of her. Even in stifling heat, the woman looked stunning. Yet she didn't seem to realize how attractive she was.

"I heard you coming up the driveway," she started. "Come in."

He stepped inside and noticed that the fans were off. The house felt heavy with heat, almost like an oven. Why in the world were the fans off? They were her only means of moving air through the room.

"Sorry it's so hot. Can I get you some water?" She fanned her face with her hands.

"I will take one. Thank you."

He followed her into the kitchen and watched as she pulled a glass from the cabinet.

"Wasn't expecting to see you here," she said.

He leaned against the doorframe, his hands in his pockets. "I wanted to give you an update."

She stole a glance over her shoulder as she filled a glass with ice. "Oh yeah?"

"The chief gave me permission to send the hat to the state crime lab. They'll examine it for DNA evidence."

She twirled, her eyes brightening. "That's great news."

He grimaced a moment. "It is. But the bad news is that it can take months to get results. We're trying to speed up the process, but our requests aren't always given heed."

The light left her eyes, but she seemed to push it aside. She handed him the water. "I see. Well, at least you're doing something. I can appreciate that." She nodded behind him. "It's hot in here. How about we go sit on the deck?"

"Sounds good."

He followed her through the house, out a ripped screen door, and onto a deck that had seen better days. Two metal chairs were there, both rusted. She pulled some cushions out of a deck box and placed them in the seats.

"I made these out of some old curtains I found," she said with a humble shrug. "I couldn't sleep last night, and I'd found my grandmother's old sewing machine."

"Seat cushions out of curtains? Kind of like Maria in *The Sound of Music*?"

That got a smile out of her. "You know your musicals. I'm impressed."

He sat down and took a long sip of his drink. He stole a glance at Charity and saw her gaze dart nervously toward the woods. What was that about?

Again, that feeling that Charity wasn't telling him everything returned. He hoped he was wrong. Because he couldn't think of one good or honorable reason why she would be deceitful.

***

Charity felt Joshua studying her and pulled in a long, deep breath. He was too observant, and she wouldn't be able to conceal her thoughts around him for long.

"Any word on the text message?" Charity finally asked, clearing her throat and pulling her gaze from the woods. Every time she glanced there, she expected to see Andrea again.

Of course, now there were only trees. No Andrea.

Joshua leaned forward on his knees and stared off into the distance. "I'm wondering if that text message you got was some kind of prank? Maybe someone knew you were back in town and wanted to scare you off."

"But no one knew about that conversation," Charity said. She shook her head, certain that wasn't the answer. There was more to it.

"A missing persons case that goes back ten years is challenging. I've heard emotions in town still run high."

Her heart panged with compassion. "I know. And I appreciate what you're doing. It's just frustrating."

"Why are you back here, Charity? Is it just to sell this house?"

His question startled her, made her straighten. "It's a long story." She hoped he would let it stop there, but she knew better.

"I've got time."

She ran her finger along a line of condensation on the glass, wondering how much to tell him. She finally settled with "I needed closure."

"Let me get this straight. You need closure, you come home, and you just happen to find Andrea's hat and get a strange text message?" He swung his head slowly. "Listen, I'm not saying I don't believe you, but for an investigator, that raises some red flags."

She swallowed hard, wanting to deny what he said but knowing she couldn't. "The truth is that I got a letter in the mail."

"What kind of letter?"

She steadied her breaths, determined not to get flustered. "It was only one sentence. It said, 'I have answers for you in Hertford, but you must come now.'"

His face remained neutral. What had she expected? Shock? Outrage? Scoffing?

"And you think Andrea sent it?" he said evenly.

Charity shook her head. "I have no idea."

He sat up and dragged in a breath, staring off into the distance for a moment. "I admit that it sounds like someone was calling you back to Hertford. I doubt it was Andrea, though. You know that, right? You know the statistics go against that notion."

She wanted to tell him about the figure she'd seen in the woods yesterday. But she knew how it would sound. He'd think she was going crazy, and she couldn't really blame him. Her story sounded crazy. "If anyone is full of doubt, it's me. I realize how insane this all seems. But I can't keep avoiding my life here forever. That's why I took leave from my job to come back. I need to tie up any loose ends to the best of my ability."

"What do you do for a living?"

"I'm an advocate for crime victims."

He seemed to perk when she said that. "Really? I was able to work with a few victim advocates while I was in Atlanta. In fact, I've been trying to talk the chief into hiring one here. I've seen the benefits they can have on a victim's life."

"I like to think that what I'm doing is making a difference."

"How'd you get into that line of work?"

Scenes from her past flashed through her mind, each one nearly like a blow to the gut. But she'd learned to withstand it. She didn't want to be a victim. No, she wanted to be a survivor.

But she couldn't tell Joshua all of that. Not now.

She opened her mouth, not sure what would come out.

That's when his phone rang. Joshua pulled his gaze from her and answered. A moment later, he rose, a frown pulling at his lips. "That was the chief. I've got to go. Maybe we can finish this discussion another time?"

Charity forced a nod. "Maybe."

And he was gone.

***

Joshua was still processing his call with the chief. In some kind of impeccable feat of timing, Buddy Griffin had just confessed to killing Andrea Whitaker and burying her body in his backyard.

As Joshua pulled away from Charity's place, he glanced at her house in the rearview mirror. Why was all of this coming to the surface now? Someone was stirring things up; the question was who.

He tried to piece everything together.

Charity returns home after receiving a mysterious letter, she gets a strange text message containing a line of conversation only her abducted friend would know, and she claims a hat that magically appeared on her porch is Andrea's.

Shortly after, a man who was once a suspect in Andrea's disappearance confesses to killing her and concealing her body on his property.

Why was this case dead for years, only to resurface in two different instances like this? Something was going on, and Joshua needed to figure out what.

He pulled up to a house about ten miles out of town. The place was more of a compound. Instead of a fence, a wall of old car parts lined the edge of the property. Atop the tires and engines was a rickety layer of barbed wire, which lent a redneck feel to the whole place.

Beyond the makeshift gate was a white clapboard house with broken shingles and window screens lying against the walls. A dog run—a large one—stretched across the property to the west, and five hyper Dalmatians snarled at the chain-link fence upon Joshua's arrival.

He spotted Chief Rollins's car parked in the driveway, lights still flashing. The chief and Buddy stood near the front door, looking like they were in the middle of a heated discussion.

Joshua slammed his door and strode up to the two. Buddy Griffin was a skinny man with pointy features, a receding hairline, and a mullet. He was probably in his fifties, and he liked to wear wifebeater tank tops with faded, ill-fitting jeans.

"Chief," Joshua said, nodding to her as he approached.

"Officer Haven, thanks for coming," Chief Rollins said. "Mr. Griffin here just confessed to killing Andrea Whitaker and burying her body in his backyard. Read him his rights."

Joshua tensed, something not seeming right. But he knew better than not to listen to his commanding officer. He slipped some handcuffs from his belt and grabbed Buddy's arm. "You have the right to remain silent . . ." he started.

"Take him to your car and leave him in the back. Then I need you here," the chief said.

What was going on? Joshua would find out soon enough.

He tucked Buddy into his cruiser. The man smelled like alcohol. Blood dribbled from the corner of his lip, and his eyes were bloodshot.

The tension and curiosity in Joshua continued to increase.

He strode back over to the chief, arriving just as she got off the phone. She shook her head as she tucked her phone back into her pocket. "A crew from Elizabeth City is on their way."

"What do you mean? What exactly is going on here?"

"Buddy apparently had too much to drink down at the local bar. He started mouthing off. In the process, he announced that he'd gotten away with abducting and killing Andrea. He said he'd buried her body here on his property."

Joshua rubbed his neck. "Really? Just out of the blue, all of this came out?"

"He had a confrontation with Ron Whitaker."

"Apparently Ron is having a lot of confrontations lately."

"What's that mean?" the chief asked.

"He confronted Charity also." Joshua slapped a mosquito that buzzed around his arm.

"Ron has had some anger issues in recent years. No one can really blame him, all things considered. First he loses his daughter, then his wife in an auto accident. The man's a walking time bomb. He was mouthing off about Charity being back in town when Buddy got involved."

"Is this his first run-in with the law?"

"Who? Buddy or Ron?"

"Ron."

"He's had some squabbles in the past—usually when he's been drunk."

"You think Buddy is telling the truth?"

"Loose lips sink ships. Maybe he just needed some

liquid courage before spilling the beans. Maybe this Charity girl being back in town stirred up something in him. We'll find out soon enough. The team should be out here soon enough to start digging up the land."

"Do you want me to talk to Buddy?"

She shook her head. "Give him some time to sober up. The important thing right now is that he gave us permission to search for evidence here. That's more than we had in the past."

CHAPTER 8

Four hours later, an excavation team had dug up a large portion of Buddy Griffin's yard. The only thing they'd managed to find was a skeleton; unfortunately, it was canine and not human.

Andrea was not here, at least not in the area of the yard Buddy had indicated. Had all of this been a wild goose chase?

Joshua looked over just as another car swerved onto the property. Joshua bristled when he saw Ron Whitaker storm from the vehicle toward the scene. Joshua put up a hand to stop him. "I'm afraid you can't go any closer."

"I have a right to know what's going on. It's my daughter we're talking about here!"

"I realize that, but there are certain protocols we have to follow. You remember that from your days on the force."

The man narrowed his eyes at Joshua and jabbed a finger in his chest. "I want to speak with the chief."

"As soon as she finishes speaking with the excavation crew, I'll see if she can talk."

Before Joshua finished the sentence, Ron Whitaker charged past him, right toward the chief.

"Wait—" Joshua grabbed his arm. As soon as he did, Ron jerked back and slammed his fist into Joshua's jaw.

Chief Rollins rushed toward the scene. "What do you think you're doing?" she asked Ron.

"It's my daughter. I need to know if you found her."

"Joshua, are you okay?" Chief Rollins asked, keeping one hand on Ron's chest to hold him back.

Joshua rubbed his jaw, casting a look of warning toward Ron. "Yeah, I'll be fine."

"You know we can arrest you for assaulting a police officer?" She turned her attention back to Ron.

"Everyone keeps playing games with me. I'm tired of it. I demand some answers!"

"Ron, as soon as we know something, you'll be the first one we tell." The chief began leading him away from the police tape and back toward his vehicle. "I'd like to get a statement from you about what happened earlier."

"I've done too much talking over the past ten years. I'm ready for action."

"Chief Whitaker, you know how this works. It's never fast. But I promise you we're exploring every possibility and taking this very seriously. You need to calm down, though. You're not doing yourself any favors right now."

Something about what she said seemed to register with Ron. Finally, he nodded. "Whatever I need to do."

"Great. Officer Haven, use my car. Get his statement. Then check on Buddy."

Joshua nodded, rubbed his jaw one more time, and walked with Ron toward the chief's cruiser. They climbed in the front, and Joshua pulled up a form on the computer there.

"I understand this is very emotional for you," Joshua started.

"Sorry about what happened back there," Ron said. The man's words slurred. He'd been drinking, too, Joshua realized. "You have no idea what it's like to live under this kind of distress for so long."

"You're right. I don't."

"Sorry about that punch to the jaw."

The spot still ached, but Joshua wasn't going to tell him that. "I'll be fine. Now, what can you tell me about what happened earlier?"

Ron drew in a long breath. "I was at my bar having a drink when Buddy came in. The two of us have avoided each other for years. Never did like him. Liked him even less when it seemed like he had something to do with Andrea's disappearance."

"Why did people think he was guilty again?"

"He abducted someone fourteen or fifteen years ago. That person just happened to be his daughter. He was in the middle of a nasty custody dispute." Ron rubbed the skin between his eyes, the numbing effects of alcohol obviously fading. "Anyway, his ex-wife got custody. But Andrea would have been around his daughter's age. That's why we thought he had something to do with it. However, we had no evidence; couldn't even get a search warrant, for that matter."

"So nothing ever came of your suspicions?"

"The man claimed he had an alibi. He was supposedly in Virginia buying a dog to use for his 'breeding business.' That's how he makes his living. Someone verified he was in a town called Suffolk at about 3:30. That wouldn't have given him enough time to get back here. But if this person's timing was even slightly off, then he may have been able, if he sped, to get back here in time."

"So what happened at the bar?"

"We'd both had too much to drink, I admit that." He moaned and rested his head back against the seat. "We had words with each other. Then the man had the nerve to smirk. He said, 'I took your daughter, I killed her, and I buried her in my yard.' That's when I punched him. He punched back. Before the chief got on the scene, he left. Now here we are."

"You think he was telling the truth?"

"Why would he lie?"

"Why would he admit this today of all days?"

"You'll have to ask him."

Joshua nodded. "If you're calmed down enough, you can go wait on this side of the police line to see what investigators find out. But if you give us any trouble, I'm going to have to take you down to the station."

Ron nodded. "Thank you."

***

Even though it was seven at night, Charity headed back toward town to talk to Sarah Reynolds, a friend from high school. Sarah was a Realtor now, and Charity needed to talk about putting the house on the market—among other things. She'd called Sarah earlier, and she'd said it was okay to stop by.

Charity pulled up to one of the newer houses in town, a nice two-story brick-and-vinyl model. She pulled in a deep breath before knocking at the door. Sarah answered a moment later.

She was chubbier now, and she had a toddler on her hip. But she was still pretty in a very natural way that Charity had always admired. Sarah had always been kind.

"Charity White," she said with a smile. "Long time no see."

"Hi, Sarah."

"Please come in." She pushed open the screen door, and it squeaked on its hinges. "It was such a surprise to hear from you."

Charity stepped inside, hating that she felt awkward.

She had to push through this, though. This was no time to be a shrinking violet. "Thanks for letting me stop by at the last minute."

"Thanks for calling. I'm sorry my place is a mess, but I have three kids. All preschoolers. So feel free to have a seat—if you can find somewhere clutter-free."

Charity moved some dolls from the couch and carefully lowered herself there. "Three kids, huh?"

Sarah beamed. "It's a lot of work, but I wouldn't trade them for anything. What about you? Are you married? Any kids?"

Charity shook her head, an unusual sadness settling in her chest at the thought. "No, not even close. But I have a nice little life in Tennessee, so I can't complain."

"Good I'm glad to hear that. You look great. Can I get you some tea or something?"

"No, I'm fine. I know you have a lot going on. I just wondered if I could have a minute of your time."

"Of course. It's been years."

Charity absently straightened the edge of her dress. "I'm thinking of putting my property up for sale, and I heard you were a real estate agent."

"You're going to sell your old property? It's been in the family for generations, hasn't it?"

Charity shrugged, her heart heavy again. "It has been. But I really just need to close this chapter of my life, you know? I live in Tennessee now. It's where I work and where I want to put down roots."

"I see. Well, of course I can help you. I can stop by early next week and do an assessment on the property. I'm not sure how long a piece of land like that would take to sell. This area isn't exactly a hotbed for home sales."

"I'd just like to get the process started."

"I'm your woman, then."

Charity shifted for a moment, wondering how to gracefully change the subject. "Sarah, I'm going to be honest. There's something else I want to ask you about. I'm also back here because of Andrea. I need answers."

"We'd all love some answers."

"Sarah, I know you've been through all of this with the police before. And I know ten years have passed. But did you ever have any suspicions about anyone who would have snatched Andrea?"

Sarah put her toddler down and lowered herself on the other end of the couch. *Dora* played on the TV, and two little girls sat on the carpet there, transfixed by the cartoon. "Wow, it's funny because I was just thinking about this. For years, I've wondered what really happened, but I never had any great ideas."

"Was there anyone who she'd had a disagreement with? Who disliked her, maybe because she was popular?"

Sarah let out a sigh, staring off into the distance. Her baby girl pulled at her shoulder-length brown hair as drool dripped from her mouth. Something about the moment captured Charity's heart. She hadn't even realized she wanted children. But some kind of maternal instinct gripped her.

"The only person I ever remember Andrea speaking poorly of was her father."

Wasn't that interesting? Sarah and Brody had said the same thing. Yet Charity had never heard this, and she'd been Andrea's best friend. "What do you mean? Do you know what was wrong?"

"Not really. She wouldn't tell me. She said she thought her life was ruined. She said her dad was no longer up on the pedestal she'd had him on for so long."

Charity let that information sink in for a minute. "Why wouldn't she tell me any of that?"

Sarah sighed again. "You know, I think it was because she looked at your home life and felt like she didn't have any room to complain. Sure, her dad wasn't perfect. But at least he didn't do drugs and bring strange men into the home."

Charity felt herself flush. "You knew about that?"

She shrugged. "Most people in town did. I know you didn't talk about it a lot. But you know how small towns are. Everyone knows everything."

Charity's cheeks heated for a moment. Did that mean that everyone knew about Will Redmere? She prayed that wasn't the case. How much more scrutiny could she endure?

"I just can't believe it. Her dad couldn't have had anything to do with her abduction . . . right?" Charity's words sounded uncertain.

"We all have skeletons in our past, Charity. Who knows what all of hers were. Since her dad was on the police force, he probably kept more secrets than the average person. I'm not saying abducting his own daughter was one of them, however. What would his motive be?"

Charity didn't know. But she did know that people did strange things in the name of supposed love. She'd seen several play out in her work as a victim's rights advocate. People killed others in the name of hurt loved ones. They tried to control people they claimed to love. They kidnapped children, thinking they could give them a better life.

She hoped that wasn't the case with Andrea and her father.

"One more thing—you said you'd been thinking about Andrea lately. Anything spark your new thoughts about her?"

"Yeah, it was the strangest thing. I was driving down Highway 17, and I thought I saw her walking beside the street. Strange, isn't it?"

CHAPTER 9

It was past midnight when Joshua got to the station. They'd dug up a majority of Buddy Griffin's yard, and they'd found no body. Now they were back here with Buddy himself. He'd sobered up and had a terrible hangover, but he seemed ready to talk.

The chief let Joshua sit in on the interrogation.

Before anyone asked any questions, Buddy started talking. "I didn't do anything."

"That's not what you said earlier," the chief said.

"I was drunk. My girlfriend broke up with me. I was feeling destructive." The man's shoulders, which were already narrow, slumped and made him look small and vulnerable. But that didn't change what he'd done.

"So you tell a man that you murdered his daughter?" Joshua asked, not quite buying his story.

"It's more complicated than that."

"Make it uncomplicated," the chief said.

He looked up at them, eyes haggard. "That man has been harassing me since his daughter disappeared."

"Ron?" the chief questioned.

Buddy nodded. "That's right. He used to stop by my house probably once a week. He's made threats. Sent letters. Let me know that if I ever slip up, he's going to nail me."

"And you never reported this?"

He shook his head. "I figured no one would believe me.

This is Ron Whitaker. People in this town think he walks on water."

"I still don't understand how that led to everything today."

"I lost any logic I had. I saw him, and I was so angry about my girlfriend leaving me. As soon as Ron started whispering with his friends about me, I lost it. I wanted him to hurt, and I wanted to see his pain firsthand so I could feel some satisfaction."

"Kind of extreme," Joshua said.

"This has been building up for years. I don't know what happened to me. I just started talking and I couldn't stop. I'd had too much to drink. I admit that. But I have no idea where all my words came from."

"You told him you buried Andrea in your yard."

"I didn't have anything to do with that girl's disappearance," he said. "Isn't it obvious? You didn't find her body."

"You're saying you had nothing to do with her abduction?" the chief clarified.

He nodded. "Nothing. It's like I told everyone back then—I was up in Virginia when everything happened. I'm innocent. I may be a screwup, but I didn't screw up that bad."

The chief sighed and glanced at Joshua. He could read her thoughts: their prime suspect had just retracted his confession. Did they even have anything to hold him on? Joshua wasn't sure.

***

Charity lay in bed that night, replaying her stay so far in

Hertford, beginning with meeting Joshua and ending with talking to Sarah today.

Brody and Sarah had both mentioned the fact that Andrea hadn't had a wonderful home life. How could Charity have been so blind?

Or maybe it was the fact that the grass always seemed greener on the other side? Maybe Andrea didn't have the perfect family, but hers had seemed better than Charity's.

Charity's childhood hadn't been a pleasant one. Her mom had strings of boyfriends come and go. Most of them were no good. After Charity hit puberty, a few of them hit on her. One took it a step further.

Meanwhile, her mom was always too preoccupied with her own problems to notice the unwanted attention or to care. Her mom had drunk away her sorrows; when that didn't work, she'd found a new man. When that didn't work, she turned again to alcohol or drugs.

Charity squeezed her eyes shut. Thinking about her childhood would do no good. What she needed to think about was everything that needed to be done before she could leave Hertford behind once and for all.

No one would want to buy this property the way it looked now. She still had grass to cut, junk to purge, walls to paint. But at least after that, she could truly leave and not look back.

Even if Andrea had appeared in the backyard and possibly sent her a text. And—

She had to stop thinking like this. Someone was obviously playing a game with her. She couldn't be naïve.

A sound outside the window caught her ear, and she froze. What was that? The wind?

She thought she'd heard a snap, like a branch or twig

had broken.

She sat up in bed, clutching the covers closer to her. Part of her wanted to charge out of bed and check out the sound. The other part of her cowered and didn't want to move.

When she heard another shuffling sound, she threw her legs out of bed. She had to do this. She had to see what was going on.

Staying light on her feet, she moved against the wall near the window. She held her breath, fear threatening to dominate her. With her heart beating out of control, she nudged the curtain aside.

Blackness stared back.

Her heart slowed.

Maybe she'd been hearing things.

Just to make sure, she traveled down the hallway and into the living room.

She blinked at what she saw there.

Something bright flickered outside her house.

With a feeling of dread, she realized what it was.

Fire.

Someone had set the house on fire.

This whole place was going to go up in flames. The flames grew with each minute. The heat already made a sweat break out all over her skin.

Charity hunched down low, trying to stay away from the smoke, which already filled the house. She was already coughing by the time she reached the hallway. Just then, a crack sounded above her.

The roof. The roof had already caught fire, also.

Fear shuddered through her. She grabbed the door leading outside and tried to twist.

It wouldn't budge.

What? Why was the door locked? She rattled it again, but it didn't budge. Was she trapped in here? She pounded on the wood.

She coughed as smoke filled her lungs. The haze was getting thicker, the heat was becoming stronger, and the flames began to lick the ceiling overhead.

The door still wouldn't budge. She had to find another way out.

Just then, a burst of fire engulfed the wall behind her.

Her time was running out. She had to think of a way to get out of here.

Before she could think any more, the ceiling collapsed.

That was the last thing she remembered.

CHAPTER 10

Joshua pulled down the lane leading to his house and felt his heart skip a beat.

Flames were coming from Charity's house.

He pressed the accelerator, and gravel kicked up beneath his tires as he sped toward his neighbor's place. Thinking quickly, he dialed Lynn and instructed her to send a fire truck out.

He pulled into the driveway and threw the truck into park. He darted toward the front door and tugged at it. It didn't budge.

What?

Looking closely, he saw nails around the doorframe. Someone had nailed the door shut?

He'd have to think about it later. Now, he hurried to the back door. He pulled his sleeve over his hand and pulled at the door handle. Heat seared his hand.

The screen door opened, but the wooden door was also nailed shut.

Someone was playing a twisted game. A little too twisted.

Wasting no more time, he went to the window. He found a chair from the deck and smashed the glass. After wiping the shards away, he climbed inside.

Smoke immediately filled his lungs and made it hard to breathe. It burned his eyes, his lungs.

That didn't stop him. He pushed his way into the house, searching for Charity.

Flames licked the walls around him. The whole place was going to go up in flames in a moment. If he wasn't careful, he and Charity would both be destroyed with the house.

Remaining low, he exited the bedroom. The hallway appeared in front of him. It looked clear.

The heat from the fire made sweat pour across his skin. Flames tried to lick his clothes. The situation was becoming more precarious by the moment. He realized his time was running out. If he didn't find Charity soon, they'd both be goners.

As he stepped around the corner into the living room, he saw someone lying on the floor.

Charity!

He rushed toward her and put a finger at her neck. There was still a heartbeat. Just as he swooped her up into his arms, something crashed behind him.

A ceiling beam.

This whole place was about to be consumed.

He couldn't go back toward the window he'd entered from. That meant he had to find another means of escaping.

Flames roared all around him.

He coughed as more smoke filled his lungs. Making a judgment call, he pushed his way into the kitchen.

The window was still clear.

He had to get Charity out through that opening. There were no other possibilities.

Working quickly, he put Charity on the ground. Then he used an old stool to knock out the window by the kitchen table. Just as he picked up Charity, the flames ripped into the kitchen.

He reached the window and saw the fire trucks had

arrived.

A firefighter helped Joshua get Charity from the house. She was safe. Thank goodness, she was safe. At least for now.

***

Joshua paused outside Charity's hospital room, taking a moment to gather his thoughts. Charity had been taken to the emergency room in the neighboring town of Elizabeth City while firefighters had finished putting out the flames. Based on the way things had looked when Joshua left, she wasn't going to have much of a house left.

The most disturbing fact he encountered had been that someone had nailed the doors shut from the outside. *Nailed* them shut. Someone had wanted Charity to be stuck inside that house.

Thank goodness he'd come home when he did. Things could have turned out much differently otherwise.

"Officer Haven," someone called.

He paused as he saw the fire chief walking toward him. "Hey, Chief."

"I thought you'd want to know that we found some footprints leading from the shed to the house, as well as some empty gasoline containers that had been thrown into the woods."

"Which only confirms this is an arson."

The chief nodded. "It could have easily been a murder. One more thing I thought you'd want to know. The footprints? They were a woman's."

"Really?"

"Really. Size eleven. It's unusual to have a woman as an

arsonist. In fact, in twenty years of my work, I've never seen it."

"They could be Charity's."

"We'll want to check her shoe size. But the way the prints are lined up makes it evident the person who left them also set the house on fire. Anyway, I'll keep you updated if I hear anything else."

Joshua stored that information away. A woman's footprints? What woman would have set the house on fire? This whole investigation was getting stranger by the moment.

He knocked at Charity's door and heard a surprisingly strong "Come in" from the other side. He stepped into the room and saw Charity sitting up in bed. He'd expected her to look broken or hurt. Instead, she appeared wide awake.

"Hello, Charity."

She smiled softly. "Joshua."

"How are you feeling?"

"I'm alive, thanks to you."

"I'm just glad I was there."

"Not as glad as I am." She pointed to his jaw. "Did you get that bruise from saving me?"

He rubbed his jaw, remembering his encounter with Ron Whitaker yesterday. The spot was still sore and slightly swollen thanks to the town's former police chief. "No, not exactly." He paused. "I need to ask you a few questions, Charity."

Charity pulled herself upright in bed. "Go ahead."

"I'd like to hear your account of what happened."

She let out a contemplative sigh and leaned her head back into the pillow. "I was trying to sleep when I heard something outside my window. I got up to investigate. That's when I saw the flames outside the house. I tried to get out, but the door was blocked. The next thing I knew, the whole house was on fire."

"I see."

She paused. "Is the house destroyed?"

"It's . . ." How did he even tell her? "It's going to be difficult to restore. My guess is that the county will condemn it."

"I see." She rubbed her lips together and stared off into the distance. "Maybe this is just a sign that I need to put this town behind me. Permanently."

Something about the thought caused Joshua's heart to pang. She was only here temporarily. It was a good idea to keep that fact in mind.

The nurse shuffled into the room. "I have discharge papers. The doctor said you're going to be fine. If you start having any problems, come back, of course."

"Great." Charity signed the papers and then rose. A moment of despair crossed her face. Of course it did. She had no car, no money, and no friends in town.

"Can I give you a ride somewhere?" Joshua asked.

"I don't think I have much choice."

"No problem." He held his arm out, directing her into the hallway. They walked silently side by side for a minute. A question kept pressing on Joshua, though, to the point where he couldn't ignore it. "Where will you go tonight, Charity?"

She shook her head, a few smudges of ash still dusted across her cheek. "I'm not sure."

"I don't want to impose, but I have a friend whom you can probably stay with, if you'd like."

"Really?"

He nodded, nearly certain Daleigh would say yes. "Yeah, she'd probably like the company."

"I couldn't possibly put anyone out like that. I can probably get a hotel in Elizabeth City somewhere—"

"Don't be silly. All your money will be gone in the first week. Let me make a call."

She cut a sharp, curious glance his way. "Why have you been so nice to me? You don't even know me."

"I know what it's like to be in a bad spot."

"I'm sorry to hear that, but thanks for your offer of help. If you don't mind, I wouldn't mind staying with your friend. At least until I can figure out insurance, get a new car, and go back to Tennessee."

Back to Tennessee. That was right. Charity was only here for a brief period.

Joshua couldn't let himself forget it, either.

CHAPTER 11

Charity stared out the window as she and Joshua drove down the street. It was still black outside, though she suspected that anytime now the sun would begin to peek over the horizon. The town seemed dead at this time of night; it looked almost peaceful at the moment.

Everything seemed surreal, like it hadn't really happened. How could someone have burned down her house? Was this connected to the fact she'd seen Andrea earlier? It had to be.

But how? Why?

Had *Andrea* caught her house on fire?

It was just too much for her to comprehend.

"You feeling okay?" Joshua asked beside her.

She nodded, not sure that she was feeling okay at all. But what else was she supposed to say? "I just need some sleep."

"That's understandable."

They pulled to a stop in front of a Victorian house right on the edge of the quaint downtown area of Hertford. "Unfortunately, you're not staying there. You're staying there." He nodded toward a smaller house behind the large one.

"It's . . . cute."

"It's nice. Right on the river. Come on. Let me introduce you to Daleigh."

As Charity climbed out of the car, she couldn't help but

think the name sounded familiar. Was it someone from her past? She didn't know. But anxiety built inside her with every step closer she came.

They climbed the steps of the small house, and before Joshua even knocked, a woman pulled the door open. She was stunning with long brown hair streaked with blonde highlights and naturally tanned skin. The woman still looked beautiful, even though she'd apparently just woken up, based on the robe she wore and her tousled hair.

"You must be Charity," she said, extending her hand.

Charity reached for it but faltered. "Daleigh McDermott?"

The woman smiled, white teeth sparkling. "That's me."

Daleigh McDermott was one of country music's rising stars. She had at least three CDs out and had headlined some major national tours. Charity had no idea Daleigh lived in Hertford.

"I have all your CDs. I . . . uh, I don't know what to say. I had no idea." She was staying with Daleigh McDermott? She felt flustered at the thought.

"Don't worry. I promise, I'm just a regular person. At the most, I'm a little strange sometimes, but nothing special." She offered a goofy smile and waved her hand. "Come on in."

"Don't let her popularity scare you," Joshua said. "She's really down to earth."

Charity stepped inside the quaint little cottage. It was small, but warm and inviting with white walls and a simple, minimalist design. Several artifact-like items decorated the space—masks from Africa and exotic-looking paintings and a colorful rug.

"It's not much, but I'm staying here until I get married. My sister lives in the big house beside us."

"Congratulations. When's the big day?"

"Only a month away. Wedding planning has been crazy. Plus, I just got back from the tour I was on. I'm still recovering." She paused in the living room. "I have a spare bedroom, but I keep my equipment and instruments in there, so you'll be rooming with some guitars, keyboards, and amplifiers. Hope that's okay."

"You're being more than generous by letting me stay here. I'll take whatever I can get."

Charity realized she had no bags to unpack. All her things were destroyed. First thing on her agenda, she'd call her bank and try to figure out a way to access her account. Then she'd figure out a way to drive into town and buy some more clothes.

The thought dragged her down. This really was more overwhelming than she'd initially anticipated. She literally had nothing right now—no identification, no money, no car, and no house.

She'd hit rock bottom before, but right now she couldn't imagine sinking any lower. She felt like she couldn't breathe. She had no choice at this point in her life except to accept the help of strangers. It was something she wasn't good at doing, not by any stretch of the imagination.

"Charity, could I talk to you a minute before I go?" Joshua asked.

She nodded, her throat constricting. "Of course."

They stepped outside. Since her clothes were burnt and smoky, the hospital had let her use some sweatpants and a faded pink "Hatteras Island" T-shirt. It wasn't the most flattering look, by any means. Not that she was trying to impress anyone, especially not Joshua. At least she'd taken the time to pull her hair back into a semi-neat ponytail and made sure all the ash and grime were gone from her face. The smell of smoke still lingered on her, though, almost as if her skin had absorbed it.

They walked over to a small pier and dock that overlooked the Perquimans. Spanish moss draped across the tree limbs, and the dark water gently lapped the shore. A full moon shone in the distance, the gentle orb reflecting into the ripples of water below.

The scene looked so serene. Too bad nothing inside Charity felt the same way.

"Charity, there's something I wanted to tell you," Joshua started, shoving his hands into his pockets. The moonlight hit his face, bathing it in a soft glow.

He was handsome, she reflected again. She'd tried to ignore it. She'd tried to ignore his kindness, even. But the fact remained that he was like someone who'd stepped out of her dreams. The thing was that she'd worked her entire life to ensure she didn't follow in her mother's footsteps. Her mom had turned to men for her every comfort. She'd gone through them like tissues. Or, should she say, they'd gone through her mom like a dog going through the trash.

"What is it?"

"When I got to your house, the doors had all been nailed shut."

"What?" Shock rushed through her. Had she heard him correctly?

As if reading her thoughts, he nodded. "It's true. There were nails around the doorframe that prevented you from getting out."

"So someone . . . someone wanted to . . ." She couldn't even finish her sentence.

"Someone wanted you either hurt or dead."

Her hand went over her mouth. "I can't believe it. I

knew people didn't like me. I had no idea someone would take it this far."

"You have any idea who might be behind it?"

Andrea came to mind. But no way would Andrea ever do something like this to her. They'd been best friends.

Unless Andrea wanted some kind of revenge on Charity for leaving her in the woods that day.

She had to stop thinking that woman had been Andrea. There had to be another explanation. That was all there was to it.

"Charity?" Joshua asked.

She shook her head. She couldn't bring herself to voice the thoughts aloud. She'd sound crazy.

"I suppose you could take your pick. As you know, Mr. Whitaker isn't very fond of me. He has a whole legion of followers he may have been able to influence to do his dirty work."

He nodded. "I'll look into it." He shifted. "What about women? Do you know of any specific women who have a grudge against you?"

The question surprised her and made a sick feeling gurgle inside. She briefly thought about mentioning Andrea, but she couldn't do it. "No, I can't say I do. Why do you ask?"

"Because the footprints leading from the shed to the house . . . they belonged to a female."

***

Joshua stared at Charity, watching her reaction carefully. She was definitely ill at ease. There was something on her mind. But he could see the walls coming up around her. She didn't trust him.

"I don't know what to say," Charity said. "Are you sure the footprints weren't mine?"

"They were for a size eleven shoe. Your feet are much smaller."

She rubbed her lips together and shook her head, as if fighting some kind of internal thought. Even in the oversized clothing she wore, she looked lovely. Her eyes had the soft hue of someone who could be trusted. But her body language said otherwise. She was uptight and jittery and jumpy.

"What are you thinking, Charity?" Joshua wished he could get inside her head long enough to figure the woman out.

"Andrea wore size eleven," she whispered, her gaze fluttering up to meet his. "She always said she hated her feet; that they were too big."

Andrea? What did she have to do with all of this? "Certainly there are other women who wear that size as well. It's just a coincidence."

She nodded but didn't look like she believed him. "Of course."

There was definitely something she wasn't saying, Joshua realized. But what? And why?

Charity White was a real mystery, one he found himself wanting to solve.

"Obviously, your friend didn't return from captivity just to burn down your house."

Her face went pale, but she nodded and cleared her throat. "Anyway, Andrea used to always tell me that I had to face my fears. Apparently that's exactly what I'll be doing here in Hertford—whether I like it or not."

He nodded resolutely, unsure what else he could say. "You've had a long night, and I should probably let you get inside. You need your rest after what happened."

"You're going to drop this, aren't you? You're like everyone else. You think I had something to do with Andrea's disappearance." A slight tremble shook her voice.

He stared at her another moment. His gut told him he could trust her. However, the last time his gut had told him to trust a woman, he'd been terribly wrong. His life had been shattered because of it.

Finally, he shook his head. "No, I'm not going to drop this. I want answers just as much as anyone in this town."

***

"Can I get you some hot tea?" Daleigh asked when Charity said good-bye to Joshua and wandered back inside.

Charity nodded. "Something warm sounds great."

Everything that had happened just seemed like a nightmare. And yet here Charity was now, being shown an unreasonable kindness. Wasn't that the way life worked? It was like Andrea had told her during their last conversation: bad things happened in fairy tales, but only as the launching pad for great things.

What if her friend had been right? But how would anything great ever come from Andrea's disappearance?

Charity only hoped she could convince Joshua that something really was going on. Without someone on her side, she'd never find any answers. Maybe she should just tell him that she'd seen Andrea standing in the woods staring at her.

He'd think she was crazy. But what if he didn't?

She'd chickened out earlier and been unable to open up. Once she put that information out there, there was no going back. There was a good chance he'd no longer be on her side, and for the moment, it felt so good to have someone who believed her.

She couldn't forget about Bradley, though. He'd seemed trustworthy at first and proven her desperately wrong.

Charity took a seat on the couch and raised the mug, taking a sip of the warm liquid.

"It sounds like you've had quite a night," Daleigh started.

"That's to say the least." Charity stared into the swirling flames and shivered. No amount of warm tea would erase the memories of almost dying in her mom's old house.

"Well, I don't know everything that's going on. But I will say that it's a good thing you have Joshua on your side. He's a good guy."

Against her better instincts, Charity found herself wanting to know more about Joshua. "How do you know him?"

"He's friends with my fiancé, Ryan, but we all go to church together, as well. It takes a lot to impress me, but Joshua has always been there for us in tough times. I think that says a lot about a person."

"I'll have to agree with that."

She leaned closer. "Look, I was in a tough spot not too long ago. Felt like everything in my life was going wrong. But somehow, with time and God and good friends, everything worked out. I don't know what's going on in your life, but I pray the same will happen with you."

A smidgen of hope burst through Charity. Maybe she shouldn't lose hope.

Even more, maybe she should start praying again.

CHAPTER 12

Charity had slept in until almost noon and then had dragged herself out of bed in order to take care of the aftermath of the fire. Daleigh let Charity borrow more clothes and had left breakfast out for her on the counter. Charity didn't know how she'd ever repay the woman for all her kindness.

Charity munched on some homemade granola before sitting down to call the insurance company. The representative gave her a list of tasks that needed to be done in order to process the claim, including making a list of everything that had been inside the house. The task was daunting.

It was at that moment she realized how dire the situation was. Maybe this was God's way of telling her she shouldn't be here.

If not God, then someone else in town was sending a message loud and clear.

Just then, someone knocked at the door. She pulled a wayward hair behind her ear as she answered.

A smile spread across her face when she saw Joshua. "Hey there."

He returned her smile. "Hey, Charity. I was going to head over to your place and put up some caution tape. I realize you don't have a car and wondered if you wanted to come with me."

"You're a lifesaver. Literally." He really was like Prince Charming, the way he continually swooped into her life at just the right moment. "I'd say let me grab my purse before we go, but I literally have nothing. It's only thanks to Daleigh that I have clothes and a toothbrush."

"This would be overwhelming for anyone." He opened the door and waited for her to step out.

"I guess this just answers my question as to whether or not I should sell the place. There's nothing to keep now."

"I didn't realize it was ever an option. You sure you don't want to move to good old Hertford? You could rebuild a nice little house on that property."

She shook her head. "There's nothing for me here."

His smile dipped. "There's always peace and quiet."

She remembered their conversation the first day. She supposed—hoped, perhaps—the old property might seem like the ideal spot for someone. It had for Joshua. "That property doesn't exactly bring back feelings of peace for me."

She climbed into his cruiser, and a moment of silence fell between them. Her mind raced. Instinctively, she felt she could trust Joshua, maybe even enough to tell him about seeing Andrea.

But she'd thought she could trust her last boyfriend too, and she'd been wrong. She had to be careful.

It only took a few minutes to reach the house. Charity flinched when she saw the place. There was nothing left, only some charred framework, puddles from the fire hoses, and the vague feeling that her childhood had been erased.

If only it was that easy.

"I know it's a lot to take in," Joshua said, parking his car in the driveway.

"That could have been my grave." She shivered as she said the words.

"Thankfully it wasn't."

"Thankfully," she repeated.

Joshua held up some caution tape. "We need to put this around the perimeter of the property, as a precaution in case anyone gets nosy. I'm sure the insurance company probably mentioned it to you."

She nodded. "They did. They also mentioned putting wood over the windows. It appears that won't be a problem." There were no windows and barely any walls.

With Joshua's help, she set out stakes and wrapped the yellow tape around the damage.

Despite all the bad memories this place had, a part of her still felt sad. This was her last tie with her childhood. She felt like a person without a family, without a home, without any safety nets. The thought did something strange to her.

"You doing okay?" Joshua asked, rolling up the rest of the tape.

Charity nodded slowly. "Everything went downhill for my family after my dad and my grandmother were killed in a boating accident. My mom went off the deep end afterward. She was never the same. She turned to drugs and men. She was just absent."

"I'm sorry, Charity."

She'd surprised herself by opening up. Now that she'd started, she might as well finish. "She couldn't hold a job. Went to jail once for driving under the influence. I almost went to foster care, but Andrea's family took me in."

"So at one time Ron Whitaker accepted you?"

"He did. The Whitakers were like the family I always wanted. I thought they were perfect."

"Even Mr. Whitaker?"

She shrugged. "I mean, sure, he was distant. But he helped fix my bicycle when it broke. He gave me advice on boys—mostly that I shouldn't trust them. He helped with a science experiment when I couldn't figure out how to make it work."

"Sounds nice."

"Then there was her mom. She was the one I talked to about boy problems—you know, when I didn't listen to Mr. Whitaker's advice. She helped me get ready for junior prom or showed me how to put on makeup. That day that Andrea disappeared, I not only lost my friend. I lost my second family."

"You've had a lot of loss, but you also have a lot of strength because of it."

"Strength? I don't always feel strong."

"You're here, aren't you?"

She nodded. "Yeah, I guess I am. For another week or so, at least. After that, I'm done. I've got to let this go."

"I want you to find the answers you need, Charity."

She smiled, a real smile. "Thank you. So do I."

***

Joshua dropped Charity off with his truck in case she needed to do any errands. Then he went back to the station to work on some paperwork. Before he started on that, he needed to talk to Chief Rollins. He started toward her office but paused when he heard her talking.

"I understand that, Ron, and I appreciate your consideration. You know I've always thought a lot of you."

Joshua bristled. Was she talking to Ron *Whitaker*?

The chief had never worked with the man, but she had to inevitably know the man from living in town. She wouldn't be feeding him information about the case, would she?

"Some things were just never meant to come to the

surface. You and I both know that. Anyone in our shoes would."

Pause.

"Of course I'll keep you updated. You can always count on me."

Something didn't sit right in his gut. He knocked at the door, and the inside of her office went quiet. A moment later, he heard a "Come in" from the other side.

Chief Rollins looked up at him, phone back on its cradle, and no evidence of her conversation visible.

"Everything okay?" he asked.

She smiled a little too brightly. "Everything's just fine. What can I do for you?"

"I'm going to head over and talk to the fire chief. Someone set that fire last night at Charity White's house. As far as I'm concerned, it was attempted murder. Her doors were nailed shut."

"That's horrible. Death by fire is a terrible way to go. Any suspects?"

"Women's footprints were found outside."

"Charity's?"

He shook his head. "Her feet are too small."

"Charity have any idea if there are any other women in town who might want to hurt her?"

"Not that she knows of."

"It sounds like we have another investigation on our hands. Things certainly have been stirred up since that woman came back into town."

He tried not to take offense at her use of "that woman." "I'm wondering if someone lured her back here for some reason. Maybe to get revenge? Maybe Charity was the real target all along? I'm not sure."

"Interesting theory. See what you can find out. I'd be

interested in having some answers to all of this, also."

But why wasn't she more interested? Some police officers would have called in the FBI by now. They would have reopened the case and put everyone in the department on it.

Chief Rollins seemed content to sit back and watch things play out.

As he stepped away, he glanced down.

He'd never noticed it before, but the chief had rather large feet. Size eleven? He wasn't sure. But it was worth keeping in mind.

***

Charity had run around town for the rest of the day, going to the bank to get a temporary debit card, stopping by the store to pick up a few items, and buying a cheap new track phone that would last at least until she left here.

When Charity got back to Daleigh's place, she found her sitting on the couch with her guitar in hand. A single string reverberated in the room as Daleigh paused. Then her earthy voice rang through the room in an almost haunting melody.

"To the girl who's fatherless, to the woman who's lost her one true love

God weeps

To the one who feels alone, to the one who longs for a warm safe hug

God weeps."

Daleigh opened her eyes and saw Charity standing there. She paused. "Charity, I didn't hear you come in."

"I'm sorry. I should have let you know I was here. Your song just captivated me."

"It's a new one I'm working on." She put her guitar back

on the stand.

"You really believe those words?"

"That God weeps for us?" Daleigh asked. "Absolutely. He loves us and hates to see us hurt."

"Most of the time I think God doesn't care."

"I know it's easy to think that. God doesn't always change our circumstances, but He can change our hearts and our perceptions. I had to learn that the hard way, Charity. Life is full of pain and disappointment. God never promises it will be otherwise. But He promises He'll be there with us for every step of the journey."

Charity smiled. "I like that." She'd have to dwell on it a little longer, though. It contradicted the impression she'd had of God for so long.

"How'd it go today, by the way?" Daleigh asked.

"I'm getting things back in order the best I can."

"That's great. Listen, I wondered if you wanted to take a walk?"

"A walk?" Charity repeated.

Daleigh grinned. "It's such a beautiful day outside. Ryan is working. I imagine Joshua is too."

"Although, that wouldn't make a difference, because we're only friends in a professional sense."

Daleigh stared a moment before nodding. "Right. Yes. I mean, of course. Anyhow, I just love strolling through town on days like today. Maybe we could get an ice cream cone at the pharmacy and then go sit by the water?"

Charity nodded. "You know what? That sounds nice. It beats what I was going to do."

"What's that?"

"Sit down and worry." Charity offered an impish frown.

"I reckon it does. We definitely need to get you out so

you don't give in to that temptation."

They headed out the door, strolling at a leisurely pace. Though it was late August, the day was balmy and a nice breeze skimmed over the water. The sky was bright blue and brilliant, and it somehow made the whole town seem more cheerful.

Charity cleared her throat. "So, why are you here in Hertford instead of Nashville, Daleigh? I just assumed—"

"—that's where all of country music's finest live?" Daleigh completed with a smile.

Charity smiled. "Yes, I suppose so."

"I've heard that before." She chuckled, but the sound quickly faded. "To be truthful, I was becoming swallowed by that world, Charity. It's nice to be here, to be a part of a small hometown and away from all the craziness. There's always a concert, a promotion, a new album, a new tour. I needed a break."

"I see."

"I realize your experience has been different than mine, but I think Hertford is a fine town," Daleigh said. "When it really matters, everyone comes together and reaches out with some of that Southern country goodness we're known for."

"That Southern sweetness can turn bitter in the blink of an eye."

"Well, I can't deny that. But I've got to believe that in the end good always wins. As far as I'm concerned, that's the story of life itself. God created man. Man messed up. Man is broken. But God redeems us. Good wins. Hope wins. Love wins."

Charity smiled. "I like that. I can't say I've felt it in my life, but I like it."

"The thing about our core beliefs is that they shouldn't be about feeling. They're a choice that we cling to."

As they neared the pharmacy, Charity slowed her steps. Something unseen made her bristle. She glanced around, looking for the source.

A man wearing a baseball cap leaned against a tree in the distance. He was staring right at them. At least, Charity felt certain he was. His sunglasses concealed his eyes.

Had she ever seen that man before? She couldn't be sure.

Of course, the man probably wasn't staring at her. He was watching Daleigh. Of course. Charity nearly let out a laugh.

Charity nudged Daleigh. "I think you've got an admirer."

Daleigh looked up and shrugged. "Never seen him before."

Despite everything Charity told herself about the man being harmless, she still felt an unusual measure of relief when she slipped inside the pharmacy.

The fact that someone had tried to kill her last night probably had something to do with her unease.

Because an even bigger question remained in her mind: Would this person try a second time to finish the task that had failed last night?

CHAPTER 13

The next morning, Joshua pulled up in his police cruiser. He'd called the night before and asked if Charity wanted to have breakfast with him and discuss the case. Charity had said yes before she had a chance to second-guess herself.

He came to the door, gave her a look of approval, and then walked her to his truck, which was already at the house, since he'd let Charity borrow it yesterday.

They didn't really speak other than chitchat until they reached the Have a Nice Day Café. The place had ruffled yellow curtains on the windows and randomly placed shelves with smiley face knickknacks. There were about twenty or so tables and booths, most with black vinyl seats. The scent of bacon and coffee saturated the air.

"This is on me, so order whatever you'd like," Joshua said, sitting down at a window booth.

"Thank you."

A waitress named Mildred appeared and automatically poured coffee for them, as well as offered a rundown on today's weather: sunny and hot. Charity ordered eggs, bacon, and toast, and Joshua got the pancake breakfast.

"This is the place you come for a true taste of Hertford," Joshua started. "Mildred is a town fixture."

"This place wasn't here when I was in high school," Charity said. "Several restaurants tried to make a go of it here, but none succeeded."

Joshua shifted, the polite chitchat fading along with the lighthearted look in his gaze. "I can't stop thinking about the fire, Charity. You said you have no idea who those footprints might belong to?"

Charity nearly dropped her coffee. She caught it before it toppled, but hot liquid still spilled over the edges. "I'm such a klutz."

He handed her a napkin. "It's no problem."

With shaky hands, she cleaned up the mess she'd made, hoping she'd avoided his question.

"What are you thinking, Charity?" He leaned closer, his gaze intense on hers.

She should have known it wouldn't be that easy. She rubbed the side of the ceramic coffee mug again, wishing her soul felt as cheery as the smiling yellow cup. "You'll think I'm crazy."

"Try me."

"Let it be known that I tried to warn you."

"Of course."

Her gaze flicked up to his. "I thought I saw Andrea the other day."

"Andrea Whitaker?" He blinked as if he hadn't heard her correctly.

She nodded. "I know how it sounds. But I don't have any explanations for it."

"Where did you see her?"

The memory flashed back in her mind, and Charity felt like she was there again. "I was on my back deck. I looked into the woods, and I saw her there. I stepped closer, but . . ."

"But what?" Joshua leaned closer.

"She ran away." She sighed and leaned back, knowing good and well how her story sounded.

"No one has seen her in ten years."

Charity nodded. "I know. But I talked to my old friend Sarah Reynolds the other day. She said she thought she saw Andrea not long ago. She was driving from Hertford to Edenton and saw a woman who looked like Andrea walking down the road."

The corner of Joshua's eye twitched. "Charity, do you really think she could still be alive?"

At least he hadn't totally written off what she said, nor had he laughed in her face. "I have no idea. I would love some answers. I don't think I can truly ever live with myself until I know what happened to her. It's been a decade, and it hasn't gotten any easier yet."

"I understand that people blamed you."

Her throat tightened. "That's correct. There had just been another case up in Virginia that was all over the news. Two girls killed their best friend, buried her body, and claimed someone else had taken her. Meanwhile, the girls had plotted to murder their friend and cover up the crime. It was horrible and senseless and . . . sad. Andrea's dad thought I'd gotten the idea from those girls and done the same thing."

She watched his expression, waiting to see judgment or fear. She saw neither. He remained focused.

"What did people think your motive was?"

Charity let out a small sigh. "Andrea was everything I wasn't. She was outgoing, popular, fearless. The police thought I was jealous. Mix my family life into that, and I seemed like a sure bet."

"You mentioned you had a rough childhood"

She pressed her lips together for a moment. "My mom was messed up. I guess people thought the apple didn't fall far from the tree."

His gaze remained on her. "That must have been hard on you."

"To say the least. But I survived."

"Living with guilt every day—unnecessary guilt—is just barely surviving."

"Well, you do what you have to do to make it through. I'm still breathing, right?"

He eased up on his intense stance and finally leaned back in his seat, letting out a breath of air. "It must have taken a lot of courage for you to come back here."

"I don't know what's worse: other people's judgments of me or my own."

Just then, their food arrived. Joshua closed his eyes in what must have been a prayer. Out of courtesy, Charity also paused, waiting until he finished before raising her fork. It must be nice to believe in a God who had everything under control, who had a plan for people's lives.

To believe like Daleigh believed.

Did God really weep? Did He really care that much?

Charity wasn't sure if that would make her experience easier or harder to accept. If God were in control, that meant He'd let all of this happen, which made Him seem cruel and heartless—loveless. But it also meant that somewhere in this mess, there was hope that good could come from bad.

"Let's assume for a minute that the person you saw, the person who left the hat, who sent the text, isn't Andrea. Who else could it be?"

Suddenly, Charity's appetite started to vanish. She forced herself to swallow the bite of toast in her mouth. "I've asked myself that before. Many times. I wish I had a great answer. Maybe it's the person who actually abducted Andrea."

"Why risk being discovered by reappearing now? This

person has gotten away with the crime for so long."

"You're a cop. You know how it is. Some people like to hurt others for the attention it gets them. They don't want to get away with it."

He raised his eyebrows. "True."

"As I told you earlier, I work as a victim advocate in Tennessee. Maybe I thought that if I helped other victims reclaim their lives, I could find a little peace in my own." She shrugged, uncertain why she'd shared that. "Anyway, I know that there's a lot of evil out there, a lot of people who destroy just for the sake of destroying."

"If not the person who abducted Andrea, is there anyone else who'd want to play mind games with you?"

She shuddered. "We've already established that there are a lot of people in this town who don't like me. I'd say maybe one of them was trying to prove a point, make me pay. But then I have to ask myself where they got Andrea's hat."

"There are no easy answers here."

"I wasn't privy to all the information on the case. Of course, Andrea's dad knew everything that had been discovered because he was the police chief at the time. But the former chief—Chief Owens—he might know something." Chief Owens had taken over the investigation when it became apparent Ron Whitaker couldn't handle it. He'd been chief before Ron and had acted as lead on the case until the FBI stepped in.

"Today's my day off. I say we go pay him a visit."

She pointed to herself, certain she hadn't heard Joshua correctly. "You want me to come?"

"I want to see how he reacts to you. Does that make you uncomfortable?"

"Everything makes me uncomfortable, Joshua. But I'll do it."

***

Joshua wasn't sure this was the best idea, but he'd already thrown it out. He wanted to pursue more of this case. Chief Rollins had left the investigation in his hands when he'd been assigned to investigate the hat left on Charity's porch. So he was just pursuing answers about whoever had left that clue. Normally, he'd never, ever take either a victim or a suspect with him. But he did honestly want to see how both the chief and Charity reacted to each other.

There had been a moment—and just a moment—this morning while Joshua and Charity were eating breakfast when he'd thought Charity was the most beautiful woman he'd ever laid eyes on. He'd seen the pictures of her in high school. She was pretty back then, but had still looked awkward. Her hair had been short and unruly, her gaze had looked uncertain, and her clothing hadn't quite fit correctly.

Today, her hair was long. Almost too long. It was still unruly, but in a way that made her seem free and uninhibited. Her gaze still remained uncertain, but now more mysterious. Her clothes were comfortable, but showed off her pleasant figure.

The fact that Joshua was attracted to her scared him. He hadn't been attracted to anyone since Justina. Even the thought of his ex-wife made his heart tight with tension.

Love made people weak. That was all there was to it. All his friends had tried to warn him, but he wouldn't listen. Justina had seemed perfectly suited for him, like everything he'd ever wanted.

How wrong he'd been. Part of him had stopped believing relationships were worth it. He'd be wise to remember his past.

He turned his thoughts back to the case as they cruised down the road.

"Did you keep up with very many people in town after you moved away?" he asked.

"No, not really. I only visited with my mom when I would come home. She died of cancer a few years ago."

She paused in thought before slowly starting again. "I suppose I did keep up with Mr. Johansson also."

"Who is Mr. Johansson?"

"Our drama teacher. I think he was the only one who believed I was innocent and encouraged me to keep my chin up."

"How often did you correspond with him?"

"Maybe once or twice a year? Hard to say. He would email to check in on me."

Something didn't sit right with Joshua about what she was saying. "Tell me more about him."

She slanted her gaze toward him. "You don't think he's guilty, do you? He was a great teacher."

"I'm just asking questions." After all, the man's name hadn't been in any of the files that Joshua had looked through.

Charity let out a long breath, as if the memories exhausted her. "Andrea and I were at drama club rehearsing for *My Fair Lady*. Neither of our parents could pick us up until later, so we decided to walk home. Anyway, Mr. Johansson was probably the last person, other than me, to see Andrea. He always liked both of us."

"Was this Mr. Johansson married?"

Charity shrugged. "You know, I'm not sure. He was younger than most of my teachers, I suppose. He didn't have kids, at least not back when I was in school. If he did, he didn't mention them or a wife."

"I don't suppose he's still in Hertford?"

"You know, I'm not sure. I haven't heard from him in probably four years."

"Any idea what changed?"

Charity shook her head. "I have no idea. Life, I assumed."

Joshua chewed on those thoughts. It seemed strange for a male teacher to keep in close contact with a student. To Joshua it did, at least. Maybe other people wouldn't think it was inappropriate. Charity certainly didn't seem to think so.

But Joshua kept that name in the back of his mind, curious to see if it would come up again.

CHAPTER 14

Charity pushed down her anxiety as they pulled to a stop in front of a stately home near downtown Edenton, one of the neighboring communities. This was where Chief Owens lived now? The house looked nice—almost a little too nice for a former small town police chief. An American flag flapped in the wind on the front porch, and a pickup truck waited in the driveway.

Joshua must have noticed her curiosity as he followed her gaze. "Apparently, his wife came into some money when her parents died a few years back. He decided to move here. He spends most of his time fishing and serves on the board for one of the local banks. That's the rumor, at least."

She nodded, still feeling uncertain. "I see."

"You ready for this?" Joshua asked.

She heard the compassion in his voice and immediately felt grateful to him. Most people wouldn't go out of their way as Joshua had done. She appreciated both his efforts and his kindness. "I guess I'm as ready as I'll ever be."

"Sometimes you just have to make yourself move forward, right?"

Just as he put his hand on the doorknob, she called to him. "Joshua, I apologize in advance."

He paused. "Why?"

"This might be ugly. You've been kind to me, and I really don't want to drag your name through the mud. I know you have a professional reputation to uphold. A personal one, too. You hanging out with me around town might not be the best thing for you."

"I'm just doing my job. No one can argue with that."

Something about his words felt like cold water had been thrown in her face. His job. Of course. What had she thought? That he was doing this for some other reason? Of course not. Not that she had any interest in that.

She nodded, grateful to know where they stood. "Okay, then. Let's do this."

They ascended the steps to the massive front porch. Before they even rang the bell, the door opened and Chief Owens stood there. The man was short and pudgy and had hair that looked like Caesar's. His skin was wrinkled with sunspots, he had bushy eyebrows, and the scent of something frying lingered behind him.

His eyes weren't on Joshua, but Charity.

"I didn't think you'd ever show your face around here again," he muttered.

She raised her chin. "I need some answers."

"You're the only one who has the answers."

"If I had the answers you claim, I would have run far and never returned." The man had always been on Ron Whitaker's side. Always.

He stared at her another moment before turning his gaze on Joshua. "You must be the new officer."

"Joshua Haven," he said, extending his hand. His voice had lost its friendly tone.

The chief quickly shook hands before returning to business. "What brings you two out this way? Not a social visit, I presume."

"Someone seems determined to bring the

disappearance of Andrea back into focus. I was hoping to ask you some questions," Joshua started.

"Did all of this start when Charity returned back to town?" He asked the question as if Charity wasn't standing right there.

"That's correct." Joshua didn't flinch; he just remained focused.

"That should be your first clue." The chief raised his chin, the same arrogance he was known for shining in his eyes.

Charity pressed her lips together. It had been a bad idea to ever come here. Why had she thought otherwise?

"Could we ask you some questions?" Joshua continued, undeterred by the man's rudeness.

"Only if you come down to the pier with me," he finally said. "The fish are biting today. I can feel it."

Charity and Joshua exchanged a quick nod.

"Great. Let me get my things. I'll meet you around back."

When he closed the door, Joshua turned to Charity. "Should be interesting."

"You can say that again."

They stepped around the house and into the backyard, where the river reached the grass, separated by a bulkhead. A nice deck sat at the end of the pier. Chief Owens was already walking down the wood planks there, fishing rod in hand. The water beyond him looked rough with whitecaps crashing every few feet.

Once they settled on the wooden bench there, the chief pulled out his fishing gear and hoisted the line into the water.

"What do you need to know?" he asked, staring into the distance.

"I've read the reports, but I want to hear your thoughts.

"Who were the suspects?" Joshua started. "Chief Rollins wasn't here when the investigation was going on."

"Chief Rollins wouldn't recognize her own hand if it slapped her in the face." He let out a deep, quick laugh.

"Who were the suspects, in your opinion? I'm not looking for an official word on the case. I want to know your thoughts, what your gut told you," Joshua continued, undeterred.

He sighed, like he didn't want to talk about it. "Buddy Griffin. But we couldn't find anything specific enough to tie him to the crime. We kept him under surveillance for months, and there was no proof that he'd done anything."

Good old Buddy. His name just kept coming up, didn't it?

"Anyone else?"

"Most people thought it could be a random stranger. That was almost the worst-case scenario, because there's so little chance of finding someone who's random. It's what everyone fears. Those cases are the hardest to solve."

"If it was a random stranger, he had impeccable timing," Charity said. "Andrea and I had never cut through those woods before. We got out of practice early, so the timing was even off. It just seems like too much coincidence."

Chief Owens looked back and nodded, as if surprised by her insight. "That's correct. Of course, he could have been keeping an eye on Andrea, waiting for just the right moment when she was vulnerable enough to grab."

"The FBI got involved, correct?" Joshua asked.

"They did. They started a task force. But they didn't get any further than we did. Those bigwigs. They think they can come in here and save the day. They were wrong. They ain't nothing but a bunch of hotshots who think they're the cream of the crop."

"You really don't think Charity is guilty, do you?" Joshua asked after a moment of thought.

His question surprised Charity. She watched Chief Owens, waiting for his response.

He let out a sigh and his shoulders slumped. "No, but I think she could have done more to help."

"She was only sixteen."

The chief nodded. "We probably weren't fair to her. Ron just never got past Charity being okay and Andrea being gone. Grief can do strange things to people. And Ron can be very persuasive."

"Were there any other suspects, Chief? Anything would help right now," Joshua said.

"There was one other person we investigated." The chief raised his shaggy eyebrows. "Austin Johansson."

"My old teacher?" Charity asked, surprise lacing her voice.

The chief looked at her, a slight smile on his face as if he were amused by her shock. "That's right, Ms. White. Your old teacher. You were pretty close to him, weren't you? Was he close to Andrea, as well?"

Her eyes widened as implications tried to sink in. She didn't want them to. "What do you mean?"

"We found some emails you two exchanged."

She pushed her shoulders up. "There was nothing inappropriate about those emails. My old teacher was just checking on me."

The chief let out a grunt that clearly indicated he didn't believe her. "Teachers need professional boundaries. He crossed them."

"Mr. Johansson knew I didn't have anyone else in my

life. My mom was . . . was absent most of the time. Maybe not physically, but definitely emotionally. He was trying to be a father figure. He went the extra mile. He'd always been kind, even when no one else was."

"Did you know he was found with Andrea's wallet?"

Charity's mouth dropped open slightly. "What?"

He nodded, way too satisfied. "It's true. He claimed that she left it at drama club."

"He would have been the last one to see us . . ." Her voice trailed as facts collided inside her head. "He would have never done anything like that."

"Then maybe you didn't realize that he also sent Andrea emails."

"What?" Her voice rose in pitch.

He nodded. "Before she disappeared. The correspondence went beyond professional, but not quite into the inappropriate."

"Why did he say he did it?" Charity's voice came out just above a whisper now. How could she not have known this? There'd been so much she hadn't known about her friend. She'd thought they'd shared everything.

"He said he wanted to go above and beyond as a teacher. He was single back then, and he was bent on making a difference. I reckon that's what every idealistic teacher wants, although most of them just want the long summer break or have no idea what else they want to do with their lives."

"Where is Mr. Johansson now?" Joshua asked.

"He's over in Nags Head. He couldn't take the heat anymore. Again, we couldn't prove anything. That's the problem with cases like this. There's no body, no proof. Makes it hard to nail down a suspect."

"Anyone else you thought could be guilty?" Joshua

asked.

"Not really." He shrugged nonchalantly.

"What about Ron Whitaker? Was it a possibility that someone abducted Andrea as revenge on her dad? He was the police chief, after all. Certainly there were a lot of bad people who disliked him," Charity said.

"You'll have to research that yourself. There was no one who stood out to us, though."

Joshua put his hand on Charity's arm. "Come on. We should go. Thank you for your help, Chief."

"Good luck. And be careful."

His ominous warning rang through the air as they walked away.

CHAPTER 15

As they walked back to his truck, Joshua gripped Charity's elbow. His heart had sped just a bit, certainly from the feeling of being watched and not from the feel of Charity's supple skin.

"What are you thinking?" he asked her.

She frowned. "I expected him to be harsh on me. But I had no idea about my old drama teacher. I can't believe he would be behind something like this."

Yes, the man's name *had* come up again.

"I want to talk to your old teacher," Joshua said. "I want to hear what he has to say."

"I want to go with you."

"The other officer, Isaac, is back in town now, so I have tomorrow and Sunday off also. Why don't we go together?" Though it was his day off, he didn't plan on easing up on his investigation.

"That would be great. You've gone out of your way. I appreciate it."

"I'd want someone to do it for me."

"Thank you."

"Now, let me get some gas—and a soda—and then we'll head back."

***

Charity headed toward the bottled drinks while Joshua paid for his gas and then went to the fountain. The plaza was large with a restaurant on the side and a convenience store in the middle. She lost sight of him for a moment.

She could mark another fear off her list: facing Chief Owens. The man had always intimidated her. He and Ron Whitaker had been close, members of the same little society of people who thought they were important.

It had felt good to have Joshua there with her, watching her back and even defending her a couple of times. If God was as loving as people claimed, then Charity would have to thank Him for sending Joshua to her. He'd been a real lifesaver ever since she arrived.

As Charity turned back around to find Joshua, someone in the distance caught her eye.

Not Joshua.

Andrea.

Her friend stood at the door, wearing a sleeveless shirt. Her hair was pulled back into a tight ponytail, and her face had thinned out over the years. But it was Andrea.

She stared right at Charity, her eyes wide and lips parted.

Charity froze. She wanted to move but couldn't. What in the world was going on? Was she losing her mind?

Charity, almost on autopilot, started toward her and refused to break her gaze. Just as she reached the end of the aisle, a flock of baseball players flooded inside and blocked her path. The crowd jostled her as they hurried inside, talking to each other and not paying attention to anything else.

Her throat tightened as she realized she was losing time. She tried to step around them, to dodge her way between them. It was no use.

When she looked up again, Andrea was gone. Like a ghost. Like she'd never been there.

***

Joshua reflected on this trip as he grabbed some coffee. He hadn't learned as much as he would have liked, but he counted the drive out to Edenton as productive. He only hated to see the burden this trip had placed on Charity.

He glanced back at Charity and saw that she'd gone pale. She stared at the door, clutching her drink like it might save her.

Moving swiftly, Joshua maneuvered through the store until he reached her. It wasn't until he squeezed her shoulder that she seemed to return to reality. She looked up at him with those big doe eyes. Her mouth opened but no words came out.

"What's wrong?" He ducked low so he could make and maintain eye contact with her.

"Andrea," she whispered.

"I know. We're trying to find answers."

She shook her head. "No. I saw Andrea."

He straightened. Had she hit her head? What was she talking about? "What do you mean?"

Charity point to the door where she'd been staring. "Andrea was just over there."

His eyebrows flew up. "You mean Andrea was here? In this store?"

Charity nodded as if in shock.

He thrust his coffee into her hands. "Stay here."

He rushed outside and surveyed the area, looking for anyone who might look like Andrea. He saw an older couple in their fifties pull away, a blonde young mom with two toddlers, a teenager on a bicycle.

But no Andrea.

Maybe there was something wrong with Charity. Could she be suffering from delusions? He hated to think that it was a possibility, but how could he not? What she was saying didn't sound rational.

How was he going to break the news to her?

When he walked back in, Charity stood there stoically, resignation on her face. "You didn't see her, did you?"

He shook his head. "I wish I had other news. For your sake. But I didn't see anyone matching her description."

"She was here, Joshua. As strange as that might sound, it's true. She looked right at me."

"I don't know what to say."

She rubbed her bottom lip a moment before something flashed in her gaze. "Can we look at surveillance video?"

It was a possibility. But, at the worst, maybe Charity could see for herself that Andrea hadn't been here. "I don't know if we have much basis to stand on. But if the owner is willing then yes."

"You have my word. I'm not lying, Joshua. My mom was a liar, and I swore I'd never follow in her footsteps. If you don't believe me when I say I just saw Andrea, then no one will."

Something about what she said got to him. Finally, he nodded. "Let me see what I can do."

CHAPTER 16

Thirty minutes later, Joshua and Charity were situated in a small office at the back of the gas station. The manager had been nonchalant and hadn't seemed to care if they looked at the video, as long as he didn't have to be bothered. Joshua hadn't told him any of the details, only mentioning that it was for an old missing persons case.

At least they only had a very narrow time period in which to search. It shouldn't take too long to show Charity that she'd been imagining things. Her proclamation that if he didn't believe her, no one would had done him in. He didn't want to let her down.

And if she had seen something, he wanted to know. At least he could put her fears at ease.

He scrolled back on the video camera. The place had a fairly nice setup, and the cameras were decent. That was a good thing. They'd be able to get a clear picture this way.

He slowed down as the time got closer, found the right camera for that door Charity had pointed to, and let the recording play.

He felt Charity tense beside him and had the strange urge to squeeze her forearm, maybe even to rub it a minute—do something to let her know that he was here and everything would be okay.

He couldn't do that, though. It was a bad idea on so many levels. For her and for him.

Her eyes were riveted to the screen. "Stop! Right there."

Joshua looked at the screen and saw a woman at the door, just as Charity had said. He paused the video and stared for a moment.

The woman did have dark hair. She was approximately the same height and had the same build as Andrea.

But was she Andrea?

He leaned closer, staring at the screen. He had to admit that the resemblance was uncanny.

Andrea would have changed in the ten years since she was last seen. Were there any age progression photos available? He wasn't sure. If not, he could find an artist who might be able to put one together for him.

"What do you think?" Charity asked. She sounded like she'd been holding her breath.

He rubbed his neck in thought. "I have to admit: that woman does look a lot like her."

"It was Andrea."

"Why are you so certain? We don't know for sure what she might look like today. Maybe she's just similar. A lot of people share features with strangers."

"She's the one who sent me that letter, who left the hat. She wanted me to come back here to Hertford. I don't know why. But I need to find her."

***

When they climbed back into Joshua's truck, silence stretched between them. It didn't surprise Charity. She'd expected the awkwardness.

Why had she expected anyone to believe her? The story

sounded crazy to her.

In Joshua's defense, he had made a copy of the video and printed out some frames of the woman. He hadn't outright said that he didn't believe her. But that was a given.

"If Andrea did survive the abduction, why would she come back now?" Joshua said. "Why would she just target you and not her father? Why not go to the police?"

Charity felt her shoulders lower some. It seemed like he was mulling everything over in his mind. She'd take that to being dismissed. "I don't know."

"I'm just trying to figure out what possible motivation she might have to do that."

"Maybe she feels like I'm the only one who can help her."

"Why, though?"

Charity stared out the window a moment, chewing on her own thoughts. "I ran into Brody Joyner the other day. Do you know him?"

"As a matter of fact, yes. We go to church together."

"He used to date Andrea. He told me that in the weeks before Andrea went missing, she and her father weren't exactly seeing eye to eye."

"Most teenagers have some sort of problem with their dads."

"I know, but Andrea told me everything. Yet she never mentioned that. Why?"

"Maybe she didn't want to burden you with it."

"I don't know. I wonder if there was more to the story. Maybe Andrea didn't feel like she could talk to anyone."

"Still, what's that have to do with this?"

"If Andrea didn't have a good relationship with her dad, in effect she didn't have a good relationship with law enforcement. He was a cop, after all."

"So she bypasses her dad and the cops and lures you here. She's going through a lot of trouble. Plus, where is she staying? Why hasn't anyone else recognized her? How is she managing to be in Hertford and Edenton? Is she following you back and forth?"

"I wish I knew the answers to those questions. It doesn't make any sense to me either."

He shook his head beside her, his jaw locked in place. "I just wish we had something more to go on, you know? It's like all the clues in this case disappeared. There are no footprints. No witnesses. Every lead dried up. It's like she just disappeared off the face of the earth."

"Until now."

"Until now," he repeated. "I'm going to see what I can find out, Charity. I promise you that."

Warmth spread through her. Maybe he was telling the truth. Maybe hope was in sight.

***

Even though Joshua didn't have to work today, he dropped Charity back off at Daleigh's place, feigning an excuse as to something important he had to do. Instead, he went to the station, found the number of an old friend of his from Atlanta, and gave her a call.

Gayle answered on the first ring. "I didn't think I'd ever hear from you again. How's Mr. Hotshot Detective doing?"

Joshua smiled. "Not so much of a hotshot anymore. In fact, I'm about as small town as you can get."

"I heard about the divorce." Her voice softened. "I'm sorry."

He really didn't want to talk about that now. "I need a favor."

"Shoot."

"I need an age progression photo done of a sixteen-year-old girl. She'd be twenty-six now."

"You have some photos?"

He glanced at the file on his desk. Several pictures of Andrea as a teen filled the folder. "I do."

"Can you scan them into your computer and send them to me?"

"Absolutely."

"I'll see what I can do for you. Is this for a case you're working on?"

"It's a cold case, but I have permission to work on it in between everything else. Does the name Andrea Whitaker ring any bells?"

"Sounds vaguely familiar."

"She's a teenager who went missing in North Carolina. There were never any solid leads. The FBI even got involved, but it's like this girl was wiped from the face of the earth."

"You know what? She sounds familiar because I think I already did an age progression on her."

"Are you sure? There's nothing in our files."

"I'm not 100 percent. Send me those photos. I'm going to look through my files. But I feel certain I've worked this case before."

Joshua hung up. Strange. Why wouldn't something like that be in the files? For that matter, there should be pages and pages of notes and reports about Andrea's abduction. Instead, there was just one box.

Unease stirred in his gut. He needed to keep his eyes open. As far as he was concerned, no one was off limits.

CHAPTER 17

After Joshua had dropped Charity off at Daleigh's place, she got busy attending to details of the house fire. As she looked up some phone numbers on Daleigh's computer, her mind raced through everything she'd learned today.

Could her former teacher Mr. Johansson really be guilty? He'd always been so kind. But behind his kindness, were there other ulterior motives? She didn't want to believe it.

She leaned back in the wicker chair by the computer, the computer screen blurring as her thoughts took over. But Mr. Johansson had been found with Andrea's wallet. Would her friend really have left something that important behind?

It was hard to say. Andrea was always so careful. But rehearsals that day had been exhausting with lots of choreography. Maybe she really had accidentally left her wallet behind.

There was so much she didn't understand. But now her life was on the line, and she had to find answers or she might not survive.

All of this was so unnerving.

She needed a break from her thoughts, so she grabbed the track phone she'd purchased and dialed Lucy's number. Her friend answered on the first ring.

"I tried to call you yesterday, but there was no answer. I was getting worried."

"My old phone is what you might call destroyed." She

explained the fire to her friend.

"Maybe you should come back here," Lucy said. "Forget everything you might believe about the importance of tying up loose ends. Just come back."

"I wish it was that easy. Lucy, I think my friend Andrea might be alive and well."

Her friend didn't say anything for a minute. "What?"

"You heard me correctly. I know how crazy it sounds. But I've seen her. I think she texted me. I think she's the one who sent me the letter in Tennessee."

"There's no logical explanation as to why that might happen, Charity. Did she waltz out of captivity, and now she's hiding out, secretly trying to correspond with you?"

Lucy had always been logical, a trait Charity usually admired. "I don't have any answers still. In fact, I'm even more confused now than I was before I left."

"It almost seems like someone planned this, Charity."

Charity trembled upon hearing her friend's words. "What do you mean?"

"I just mean be careful. I'd hate for you to find out this whole scenario was just a ploy to get you back in Hertford."

"Why would someone do that?"

"You and I have both seen a lot of evil, Charity. Take your pick."

***

After work, Joshua stopped by Daleigh's place. As Ryan opened the door, the scent of peppers and onions drifted out, making Joshua's stomach growl.

"You're just in time," Ryan said. "The ladies are fixing dinner. There's enough for you, too."

"I was just coming by to check on Charity."

"Well, it's a good thing you did, because now you get dinner, too." Ryan extended his arm behind him.

Joshua grinned. "You know I can't turn down homemade meals."

As he stepped inside, his gaze connected with Charity's. Her cheeks flushed and she smiled, almost looking shy.

Was she feeling something between them too? That was even more reason why he should stay away. He'd both failed his last relationship and been burned by it. But Charity had no one else to help her. She deserved answers, especially in light of these recent developments.

He just had to remember to keep his heart in check. He needed a lot of boundaries, lest the past repeat itself.

"Joshua Haven, have I ever told you how handsome a man in uniform looks?" Daleigh teased, stepping out to give him a hug.

"Hey, hey," Ryan said. "None of this talk. I'm standing right here."

"I'm actually pretty fond of how you look in your uniform also." Daleigh jabbed Ryan in the chest before reaching up and planting a kiss on his lips.

Joshua looked away. Those two were so in love that it was hard not to feel jealous sometimes. Something about seeing Ryan and Daleigh together stirred something in him. There was a part of him that wanted more, that didn't want to do life alone. He feared both being a failure and being hurt again. That was the way the dance usually worked, though.

"Sorry about that. Too much public display of affection. That's actually the title of one of my new songs," Daleigh said, sampling a pepper from the skillet and then closing her eyes in delight. "That's good."

"I can't wait to hear your new album," Joshua said. He'd liked her music even before he knew her.

"Well, I'm hoping to release it in a few months. After we're married, then I'll think about touring some more. For now, I'm just enjoying being in one place."

The woman was an incredible musician. She'd headlined shows for thousands of people, but decided that family was the most important thing. Her sister and nieces lived here. Then she'd met Ryan while investigating her father's death. That was the story Joshua had heard, at least.

"Give me just one minute and I'll be done," Daleigh said.

As she finished, Joshua crossed the room toward Charity. "How's it going?"

"It's going."

He nodded, wishing he could share more about the case with her. But he couldn't, especially not right now.

"Let's eat," Daleigh announced, carrying a platter of food to a small table by the window. There was just enough room for the four of them.

He glanced over at Charity as they sat down and saw her offer another shy smile. His heart sped up at the sight of it.

Uh-oh. This wasn't good. He really had to keep his emotions in check because this felt too much like a double date. It felt too much like something he could get used to. And he couldn't afford that.

Just as they started to say a prayer, a loud pop sounded outside.

"Stay here," Joshua ordered. He and Ryan rushed toward the door just in time to see smoke coming from the mailbox. A SUV squealed away, its license plate concealed by the darkness.

A rock with a piece of paper tied around it lay at the bottom of the steps. Joshua grabbed it and unwrapped the paper. It was a note.

"Get out of this town," the note read.

And he had a feeling it was directed at Charity.

CHAPTER 18

Charity wrapped her arms over her chest as she stepped onto the porch. Joshua and Ryan had stepped outside five minutes ago, but it felt like hours. Tension filled her as she tried to figure out what had that sound been.

"What happened?" Charity asked, her heart pounding in her ears as she registered the scent of smoke lingering in the air.

Joshua shook his head and shoved something into his pocket as he approached her. "It was a bottle bomb. Probably just some kids playing a prank and causing trouble."

"A bomb isn't a prank," Daleigh said, appearing behind her and shaking her head with disgust.

"Don't get too close. These things can be unpredictable," Joshua said. "It looks like it ripped your mailbox apart, Daleigh."

"I can replace a mailbox." Daleigh slipped an arm around her shoulders. "I'm sorry you have to go through this."

Charity nodded. "Me, too. And I'm sorry I'm dragging other people into it."

"That's what we're here for—to carry each other's burdens." Daleigh squeezed her shoulder again. "There's no need to apologize."

Charity wished she had even a touch of the peace that Daleigh seemed to have.

Joshua and Ryan wandered back to the mailbox. A

couple of onlookers had gathered on the sidewalk as well. Charity knew that someone was trying to send her a message.

Joshua started their way, a deep frown on his face. "I'm going to bag up the evidence and see what I can find on it. I need to go to the station and write up a report."

"You have any idea who might be responsible?" Daleigh asked, her voice warm with concern.

"I have an idea, but I don't want to incriminate anyone until I know something." Joshua's voice sounded somber. "I'll take a rain check on that dinner."

Charity forced herself to nod. She hadn't realized how much she was looking forward to his company or how disappointed she'd feel with him leaving. "I understand."

"By the way, I'm going to visit your old teacher tomorrow. Care to ride along?"

"Sure," Charity said.

"I'll see you in the morning then."

As he walked away, Charity already missed him. Which was strange. She had no reason to miss him.

He didn't seem like Bradley, she realized. Bradley was always trying to make a name for himself, trying to get ahead and impress people.

Joshua actually seemed to be looking out for Charity's best interests. But, in another way, he seemed too good to be true.

Thirty minutes later, Ryan had shooed away all the onlookers and insisted they all go inside to finish eating. They all sat back at the table, but the earlier lightheartedness was gone.

"Speaking of trouble, any word on what happened at your place, Charity?" Daleigh asked, taking a bite of her dinner.

Charity shook her head. "I haven't heard anything. I only know that someone wanted me to die in that old house."

"That's horrible," Daleigh said, squeezing her hand.

"I feel really lucky that I got out when I did. Actually, if Joshua hadn't been there, I probably wouldn't have gotten out."

"Joshua is a good guy. He's dedicated to his job, to God, and to his son."

"His son?" Charity asked, not bothering to hide her surprise.

Daleigh tilted her head. "You didn't know? Yes, he has a four-year-old boy. He's the cutest thing ever. He's on vacation with his mom and stepfather right now."

"I see." She cleared her throat, needing to get the subject off Joshua. For some reason, it hurt that he hadn't told her. But that was crazy. He had no obligation to get personal with her. He'd made it clear earlier that he was just doing his job.

The rest of dinner, they talked about the upcoming wedding, a car show, and Daleigh's new album. Charity was grateful for the lighthearted topics. It was better than thinking of the things her mind wanted to go toward.

Things like the bomb. She hoped that wasn't a warning directed toward her. And if she didn't heed this "warning," what would be next? Would someone go to even more extreme measures to get her out of this town?

***

Joshua waved to Isaac, who was busying taking a report from a woman hysterical about her neighbor's loud music.

That was good because Joshua needed a moment.

He sat at his desk and pulled the note from his pocket. The crudely written words there made him pause. *Get out of this town.*

If he had any doubt before about how much hostility there'd been directed toward Charity, he was absolutely certain now.

The note had burned in his pocket. Why hadn't he told Charity about it? He knew the answer: she would just take that note as one more sign of how much someone hated her and wanted her to go home.

Maybe there was a part of him that didn't want her to go back home. Or maybe he just wanted to protect her from the emotional hurt an incident like this might cause.

It wasn't that he didn't think Charity could handle reality. It was just a lot for anyone to swallow. She had enough on her plate as it was.

Joshua grabbed a kit and dusted the paper for fingerprints. There was nothing. It appeared whoever had written this was well versed in wearing gloves to conceal their identity.

He frowned and leaned back in his chair.

Someone was going out of his or her way to get this message across.

With a sigh, he pulled up his computer. He logged in the information for the vehicle he'd seen earlier. All he could tell was that it was a new model black Explorer.

A list of matching vehicles registered in the county popped up. He narrowed the search to Hertford. Twelve registrations were listed on the screen.

He scanned the list.

His gaze stopped by one. Lawrence Whitaker.

Could he be related to Ron Whitaker?

It was worth finding out.

***

Five minutes later, Joshua pulled up to a house not far from the police station.

There in the driveway was a black Explorer.

As Joshua walked toward the front door, he put his hand on the hood. Sure enough, the engine was still warm. Could that be because the vehicle had just been out, its owner wreaking havoc around town?

Slowly he approached the door. Situations like this could be tricky. On the surface, it didn't seem dangerous, but in reality, Joshua could be encountering someone unstable or blinded by out-of-control emotions.

He rang the bell, and a woman answered a moment later. She was in her late thirties and had a cigarette hanging out the side of her mouth. "Can I help you?"

"I'm looking for Lawrence Whitaker."

"What do you want with him?" She practically spat the words out before launching into a nicotine-drenched cough.

"I just have a few questions for him. It's official police business."

She sneered. "Well, you're in luck. He just walked in."

Joshua heard a door slam at the back of the house. Reacting on instinct, he skirted the side of the property. Sure enough, Lawrence Whitaker was running toward a garage in the back.

Joshua propelled himself forward. In four strides, Joshua had tackled Lawrence Whitaker to the ground. He pulled the man's hands behind him and took out some cuffs. The man was obviously a flight risk.

"I didn't do it," the man moaned.

Joshua pulled him to his feet, needing to look the man in the eyes before launching into his questions. He leaned him against an old picnic table. Anger sparked in the man's eyes as he glowered at Joshua.

"You've got the wrong person. I didn't do it," he repeated.

"Didn't do what?" Joshua asked.

Lawrence frowned. "Nothing. I didn't do *nothing*. Whatever you're here for."

"Innocent men don't run."

Lawrence grunted but said nothing.

"I just want to talk," Joshua continued.

The man sneered again. "You know who my dad is, right? He'll be all over this."

"He doesn't have any authority in this town anymore."

"He has more power than you think."

Joshua didn't doubt his words. "As I said earlier, I have a few questions for you."

"About what?"

"About what you didn't do."

"I was here all night."

Joshua nodded toward the man's house. "The woman who answered the door said you'd just gotten home."

The man grumbled under his breath. "What do you want from me?"

"Did you put a bottle bomb in Daleigh McDermott's mailbox?"

Something flickered in the man's gaze—a spark of satisfaction or pride. "I don't know what you're talking about."

"Then you won't mind me searching your house and garage?"

"You need a warrant."

"I'm sure I can get one." Joshua pulled the man off the table and led him toward his cruiser. "You can just wait right here while I make a call. But before I do, let me ask you this: Did your dad put you up to this?"

The man stiffened and put on brakes on the sidewalk. "Leave my dad out of this. He's been through enough."

Joshua had found the man's soft spot and knew what kind of angle he needed to work in order to get some answers. "Maybe he's been through too much. Maybe it's broken him."

"He's the strongest man I know. Stronger than you'll ever be."

"I hope he can handle seeing his son in jail, then." He opened the back of the cruiser and started to help Lawrence inside.

"Wait! I'll talk. Just leave my dad alone." Some of the stubborn pride left his gaze.

Joshua stared at the man, tired of playing his games. "Why'd you leave the bomb?"

"I just want the girl out of town. Is that too much to ask? I didn't want anyone to get hurt."

Joshua was hoping the man would see it his way. "Did you burn down her house also?"

"Burn down her house?" His voice escalated in pitch. "What? No. Are you crazy? That's, like, a serious, serious offense. What I did was more of a prank. I was just trying to send a message."

"Someone could have gotten hurt."

Lawrence shook his head, a little bit of reality seeming to hit him. Panic began to grow in his gaze. "But no one did."

"I know your family has ruled this town for a long time, but that's coming to an end, Lawrence. No one around here should be above the law."

"Spoken like a true hoity-toity city boy." The panic quickly disappeared and the man's bravado returned.

"I'm taking you into the station."

"I'll be out in an hour. Just wait."

CHAPTER 19

Charity thought she'd feel more anxiety as she and Joshua headed down the road toward the Outer Banks the next morning. But something about Joshua's steady presence made her feel calm and ready to face the day—ready to face her past, for that matter.

The Outer Banks was a stretch of land—barrier islands, really—on North Carolina's east coast. The Atlantic Ocean surrounded the area on one side and the Albemarle, Currituck, and Pamlico Sounds on the other. In the summer, it was a thriving tourist destination. In the winter, it seemed more like a graveyard of empty rental houses.

"I thought I'd give you an update on the bottle bomb," Joshua started.

Charity felt some of her familiar tension return. "Okay."

"I arrested Lawrence Whitaker last night. We found the materials in his garage, and he confessed."

"Lawrence? Andrea's brother?" She shook her head. "Wow. I shouldn't be surprised, but I am."

"The bad news is that he's already out on bail. He saw the judge this morning, and as I suspected might happen, the judge found favor with him. The amount he had to post was relatively low."

"You think that amount has to do with Ron Whitaker's influence in the town?"

"I know it does. It's also stirred up some hard feelings

between Ron and me. He seems to think I'm targeting him."

"But you said Lawrence confessed?"

"I didn't say any of this was logical. I think for so long no one messed with the Whitaker family. Ron feels like I'm intruding on his territory. I had to remind him that I'm not privy to small town politics. I err on the side of the law."

"I bet he didn't like that."

Joshua chuckled. "That would be an understatement."

"I hope you're not stirring up trouble for yourself."

"I can handle myself, Charity. Don't worry about me."

She had no doubt that Joshua could handle himself. But she hated thinking about him being in danger. She turned her thoughts back to the questions haunting her. "Do you think Lawrence is the one who burned down my house?"

"Lawrence was out of town when the fire was started. He was visiting his wife's family down in Florida."

Charity shivered. "I guess that's a relief. Except that it means someone else is out there trying to scare me."

"They're trying to do more than that, Charity," Joshua said. "Someone wanted that house to be your grave."

She shivered again. "There's something about me being in this town that's toxic."

Silence passed for a few minutes, and Charity knew she had to get her thoughts off what Joshua had just told her. Turning the new realizations over in her mind again and again was getting her nowhere; it only increased her level of stress.

"So, how long have you been here in Hertford, Joshua?" Changing the subject seemed like the best idea.

"Only six months. Not very long."

She leaned back in her seat. "You're from Atlanta, right? Why'd you decide to pick up and move at all?" Like she had any right to ask that question.

"A lot of reasons. Divorce, mainly. My wife, her new husband, and my son were stationed in Elizabeth City. Against everyone's advice, I decided to move here so I could still be close to my son."

"That's sweet." She frowned. "But I'm sorry. I shouldn't have pried." She'd expected a more outlandish reason, not something involving pain. She should have known better.

"You weren't prying. Life has a lot of ugly parts that I'd love to ignore. The ugly parts make us real, right?"

"And the nice parts redeem us?"

He shrugged. "Maybe. I kind of like that idea. Aren't we all a balance of our good and bad qualities?"

"You have bad attributes?"

"Unfortunately, I might have a few." The corner of his lip curled.

"Why did everyone advise you not to move?"

"It gives my ex a lot of control, I suppose. I mean, I can't follow her all over the country if she decides to move again. But I think I'm right where I'm supposed to be for the time being."

"That makes sense."

"How about you? Did you grow up in Hertford, or did you just live here as a teen?"

"I lived here until I graduated. Then I couldn't get out quickly enough. It was just my mom and me . . . and a string of fill-in 'dads.' As I mentioned before, my real father died when I was a toddler. He and my grandmother were in a boating accident."

"I'm sorry."

Charity held back a frown. "According to my mom, he was a good-for-nothing jerk. Of course, according to my mom, most men fit that definition, so you have to consider the source."

Charity wondered if he knew about her mom's reputation. If he did, nothing on his face indicated it. He remained unemotional, his focus on the road and his presence calm and steady.

"Where'd you go when you left here, Charity?"

"Tennessee. I went to college in the eastern part of the state and loved it so much that I stayed." Life had finally started to regain a certain sense of normalcy away from all the bad memories here. Away from her mother's influence, the future had actually seemed brighter.

Charity had tried to get her mom help, unsuccessfully. She'd realized that unless her mom wanted to change, she wasn't going to. It had been hard to swallow, but if Charity wanted to move on with her own life, she had to accept it.

"You love it there in Tennessee, but you came back here?" He stole a glance at her, but there was no judgment in his eyes. Only curiosity.

Her cheeks flushed. His question was a valid one. "It's funny the things people will do to make peace with the past. Besides, I'm only here temporarily."

Silence passed for a few minutes. Charity couldn't help but think about how surreal it was to be here now. It was hard to believe that only a month ago, she thought she'd be in Tennessee for the rest of her life. She'd had no desire to leave.

Then she'd gotten that note. She knew it would haunt her for the rest of her life if she didn't follow up. And she was tired of things haunting her. It was time to either make peace with her past and move on, or find some answers and finally have some closure.

"You think you're ready to talk to your old teacher?" Joshua asked.

She drew in a deep breath. "Are you really ever ready to

discover that someone you look up to isn't the person you thought they were?"

"Probably not. Reality can be hard to face."

"But so can living without answers," she murmured.

"Well, I hope you get some closure."

She stared at the road as the first view of the ocean came into sight. They were almost there. "Me, too," she said. "Me, too."

***

Joshua braked as tourists in swimsuits, loaded down with umbrellas and beach chairs, tried to cross the busy road that split the east and west sides of Nags Head. Beach season was in full swing, which meant the area was busy.

He turned off the main drag and a few minutes later pulled up to a small sound-side cottage. He stopped short of parking in front of the house and instead took a minute to observe their destination.

A man was outside, dragging a water hose across a crusty, sandy lawn. That was definitely Austin Johansson.

The man looked like an older version of his yearbook photos. He was tall, looked like the kind of guy who worked out, and had a head full of brown hair.

"That's Mr. Johansson," Charity said, her gaze fixated on the man. "This is weird."

"You sure you're ready for this?"

She nodded. "Definitely. No more fears."

"Fears aren't always bad, you know. Sometimes they keep us safe."

"Other times they hold us back and take control of our lives."

"I can't argue with that." Joshua could see an underlying strength in her, and he was glad she was finally realizing just how strong she was. "Let's go, then."

They climbed out of his truck and started down the sandy road toward the small house. Just as they reached the driveway, a toddler burst from the front door, a ball in his chubby hands.

Austin started toward the boy with a smile, but the action faltered when he spotted Joshua and Charity. Recognition washed across his features.

"Charity White? It's been years." He swung the boy onto his hip before approaching them, almost appearing mesmerized. "You look . . . you look great."

"Austin?" A petite blonde stepped outside onto the porch, put her hands on her hips, and stared at the unfolding scene. She looked a lot like Charity, Joshua noted.

"It's okay, Heidi. Just a minute." Austin kept his gaze on Charity. "Did something happen? Is everything okay?"

Joshua stepped forward. "I'm Officer Joshua Haven from the Hertford Police Department. I was hoping to ask you a few questions."

Austin's surprise turned to what looked like alarm. "Of course. Whatever you need. Let's go sit on the back deck. The breeze is better back there. Heidi, you have Gavin?"

The woman nodded, but her body still looked tense and uptight. Her gaze had hardly left them since she stepped outside.

They sat on a screened-in patio, and Austin pulled some water bottles from a small refrigerator in the corner. Joshua left his on the table beside him.

"We're considering reopening the case on the abduction of Andrea Whitaker," Joshua started, getting right to business. "I was hoping to ask you a few questions."

Austin straightened, and his eyes took on a new light. "Is there a new lead?"

"Potentially." Joshua shifted. "Mr. Johan—"

"Please, call me Austin."

"Austin, I understand that you were questioned in her disappearance. You were one of the last people to see her."

He nodded. "That's right. As Charity has probably told you, Andrea and Charity were two of the last stragglers to leave after play practice that day. They stayed around and helped me straighten up."

"Later you were found with Andrea's wallet?" Joshua asked, carefully watching Austin's expression.

His gaze darkened a moment. "That's correct. But it's only because she left it at school."

"Andrea didn't like carrying a purse, so she always kept her wallet in her back pocket," Charity confirmed. "She could have taken it out for practice. The scene in *My Fair Lady* we were rehearsing that day had a lot of dancing and moving. She probably didn't want it to fall out."

Austin nodded adamantly. "That's right. I found it on the piano behind the stage and took it into the office to lock it up for the night. I stuck it in a drawer because I didn't want anyone to take it."

"Do I understand correctly that you were a suspect at one time?"

The light faded from his eyes. "Not officially, even though that chief tried to intimidate me many times. I was never arrested or taken in for official questioning—that's probably why you couldn't find anything in your files. Which was a good thing because I'm innocent."

"Is the wallet the only thing that tied you to the crime?"

Joshua asked.

"It didn't even tie me to the crime!" His voice rose. "It just proved that Andrea had been at play practice. I had no reason to follow her and Charity afterward."

"But I understood there were some emails."

His cheeks reddened. "It wasn't a big deal. I just tried to encourage some of my students. There was nothing inappropriate about what I wrote."

"Why'd you stop emailing me, Mr. Johansson?" Charity asked.

"I got married, and it didn't seem appropriate anymore."

"But it did seem appropriate to email them when they were in high school?" Joshua clarified.

The flush on his cheeks deepened. "I was a little young and naïve back then. I thought I could change the world, and I thought the way to do that was by getting personal with my students."

"But there were professional boundaries in place?" Joshua asked.

"Of course! My heart was good, but my actions just needed a little refining. Looking back, I would have done things differently."

"Did you ever have any theories about what happened to Andrea?" Joshua asked, taking a sip of water.

He leaned back, obviously a little more comfortable now that the attention was off him. "At first, I thought it was just a random stranger. I mean, I couldn't imagine anyone in town doing something like that."

"But did you change your mind?"

He leaned closer as if there might be someone close by who'd eavesdrop. "Between us, I started to suspect her brother."

"Andrea's brother?" Joshua asked, surprise coursing through him.

Austin nodded. "That's right. I just thought Lawrence was behaving strangely. I always thought he behaved strange around her. Honestly, I had the impression he was jealous, like there was some Cain and Abel stuff going on."

Joshua stole a glance at Charity, and she offered a slight shrug. He'd talk to her about it more later. "Can you give some examples?"

"Andrea was her father's princess. Sure, he was hard on her. But not nearly as hard as he was on her brothers. Lawrence especially seemed bitter about it. I heard the way he talked to his sister. They argued quite a bit, but I'm not sure about what."

"And your assumptions are all based on some conversations you've overheard?"

"There were rumors around school. Lawrence was dating a teacher there at the time. He struck me as someone I didn't want to cross." Austin paused and glanced at Charity. "And my second suspect was Will Redmere."

Joshua glanced at Charity and saw her cheeks had reddened. "Who's Will?"

"He was my mom's boyfriend," Charity said softly. "One of them, at least."

"Whenever Will came to pick up Charity, his eyes stayed on Andrea just a little too long. It made me uncomfortable."

"Did you tell the police this?"

"Of course. Do you think I wanted them looking at me? They were wasting time and energy if they investigated me."

Joshua glanced at Charity, who suddenly looked very pale. What wasn't she telling him? He wanted to find out. But he had a feeling she was the one who'd need to raise the subject.

CHAPTER 20

Charity shivered when she got back into the truck. She couldn't wait to close the door and lock it. She hadn't felt that way until Mr. Johansson had mentioned Will.

She shivered whenever she heard Will's name. She wished she could permanently forget about him. She knew the questions were going to come from Joshua about the man, but Charity really didn't want to replay that time in her life.

Instead, she thought about her old teacher. Mr. Johansson seemed basically the same, only a bit older. He was still tall and thin and had some of that charisma that actors seemed to have. At times, he could be brooding. Other times, he seemed exuberant. There had been a lot of girls at the school who had a crush on the young teacher.

Was Andrea one of them? Charity tried to search her memories for something to indicate that she had been. Nothing came to mind, though.

Joshua climbed inside, and the scent of his leathery cologne filled the vehicle. For some reason, the aroma brought a measure of comfort to Charity.

He cranked the engine, and a chilly breeze flooded through the vents. The air outside was sticky hot, so Charity welcomed the AC. She glanced once more at her former teacher's house. The man's wife, Heidi, he'd called her, stood on the porch, still watching them.

"I want to hear your opinion on all of that in a minute."

Joshua pulled away from the curb. "But first, let me ask you this. While we're in the area, I'd love to eat at my favorite restaurant. Do you mind? It's my treat."

"Sounds good."

"Great. You'll love it. Best fish on the East Coast."

She figured they'd talk more about Mr. Johansson, but they waited until they got to the restaurant. The place was on the ocean with a huge deck overlooking the water. Jimmy Buffett played in the background, and the place's mascot was apparently a gigantic boogying mackerel.

"The Dancing Mackerel. Best seafood ever, huh?" Charity questioned, looking around at the gaudy decorations, which mostly consisted of cartoonish murals of sea life on the walls.

He grinned. "I promise you. Don't judge a book by its cover."

He put a hand on her back and guided her inside. As soon as he touched her, fire rushed through her blood. It had been a long time since any man had that effect on her. Maybe even never.

"I think we got here at just the right time; after lunch but before all the tourists come in for dinner."

"Excellent."

Charity inhaled the scent of fish and French fries and Old Bay seasoning. At once, the smells brought back memories to her. She and her mom had never come to the Outer Banks together, but Andrea's family had invited Charity to come with them once.

It had been a glorious weekend. Charity was probably twelve. They'd stayed in a beach house only a block away from the ocean. During the day they'd gone to the beach. At night the family had fish fries and shrimp boils and had climbed

Jockey's Ridge or flown kites and gone fishing. She smiled at the memories. She had so few good recollections of her childhood that she held on to whatever good ones she could.

The waitress seated them outside at a table by the water. Charity didn't miss how the woman openly admired Joshua. It wasn't surprising. The man was strikingly handsome.

And divorced.

Charity wondered what had happened. Had he instigated it? Had he cheated?

No, she had to stop thinking like that. It was the influence of her mom. According to her mom, every man cheated. Every man was disposable. Relationships were meant to be as temporary as a bad cold.

As she snapped back to reality, she saw Joshua studying her across the table. "You look distracted."

She shook her head. "Just a lot to think about."

"I'd love to talk about all those things. Let's order first, though. I highly recommend the boatman's stew and the flounder."

"That sounds good."

When the waitress reappeared, Joshua ordered for both of them, glancing back at Charity several times to get an approving nod before moving forward. Finally, they both settled back to talk.

"What did you think of that conversation?" Joshua started.

Charity sighed and leaned back in her seat. "I don't know. Which probably isn't very helpful. I always liked Mr. Johansson. I thought he was a good teacher. I thought he really cared about his students."

"That could all be true."

"And just because he sent me some emails, that doesn't

mean he crossed any lines. There was nothing inappropriate. Besides, there were other people at that school earlier that day. The principal was there, the janitor, the lawn guy, and maybe even a few other students."

"I had no idea there were that many people there," Joshua said.

Charity nodded. "I assumed you knew that. I assumed it was all in the reports."

He grimaced. "I think some information may be missing. I just can't figure out what might have happened to it or why."

"Maybe the FBI kept it?"

Joshua shook his head. "We should still have copies."

"The mystery deepens . . . yet again. Maybe me being here isn't the best way to find answers."

"Why would you say that?"

She shook her head. "As long as the Whitakers are in town, I'm a target."

"I'm sorry that things turned so sour between all of you. It sounds like the family meant a lot to you at one time."

"At first, I think Ron and his family were angry with me because I left Andrea in the woods to get help." She shrugged, guilt pressing in on her again. "Honestly, I was angry at myself."

Joshua reached across the table and put his hand over her wrist and gave it a little squeeze. "Nothing would have probably changed if you stayed in the woods, Charity, except that maybe you'd be either dead or missing also."

She nodded. "I know. I tell myself that, too, but the guilt just doesn't seem to go away. Anyway, I think after their initial anger at me passed, it grew into a different kind of anger because I couldn't remember enough about the man so that we could locate him."

"That's a lot of pressure to put on a sixteen-year-old."

She nodded again. "I know. Believe me, I know. But at the time, I thought I deserved any anger they had for me." She pulled her hand back and leaned toward him, her throat tightening. "Anyway, on a purely logical level, I wouldn't have had time to kill her and bury her body."

"What do you mean?"

"I called the police at five thirty. We left school around four, and a witness placed Andrea and me walking near the bridge at four fifteen. That must have been right before we decided to cut through the woods. I wouldn't have had time to kill her and bury her."

"Even if you did, there was only a limited area where you could have buried her. I know the police searched that entire stretch of woods."

Relief welled in her. He understood. "Exactly. I had dirt on me and even some blood. But that was only because we did struggle. I fell on the ground. I was the first one the man grabbed. If Andrea hadn't helped me, I wouldn't have gotten away."

"And that's where the survivor's guilt comes in."

She swallowed hard, not sure her saliva was going to go down. "Exactly."

Just then their food came. It was a relief, actually, because maybe now she wouldn't have to talk about this anymore. It had been harder than she expected it to be.

CHAPTER 21

Joshua marveled at how easily their conversation came as they ate. They turned the subject from anything heavy and instead chatted about the beach, dream vacations, and favorite foods.

Man, Charity is beautiful. Did she even realize how gorgeous she was? Her blonde hair blew in the breeze, wild and free. Her smile, when she gave it, could stop someone in his or her tracks. She was a sight to behold, for sure. The best part about it was that she didn't even realize it.

She tucked her hand under her chin and looked at him a moment. "Do I have part of my lunch stuck somewhere on my face?"

Great, he'd been staring. He looked away before she saw the truth in his eyes, and shook his head. "No, not at all. Are you ready to head back?"

She nodded. "That would be great. Thank you."

He dropped some money on the table and headed back to his truck. The name Will Redmere lingered in his mind. He wished that Charity would open up to him. But he tried to give her space, sensing that she needed it.

When Charity was tucked safely inside, he climbed in also, catching a quick whiff of fruit. Her shampoo, maybe? Whatever it was, he felt like he could inhale the scent all day and never grow tired of it.

"Thank you for lunch. It was lovely."

"You're welcome."

She stared out the window for a few minutes in silence. Finally, she cleared her throat and looked down at her hands for a moment. "So, as you know, Andrea saved my life that day in the woods when she was abducted. But there's more."

"What's that?"

"As you probably know by now, my mom went through men like dirty tissues. She always had to have someone in her life after my dad died. Some of them ignored me, some of them flirted with me. But there was one who . . . attacked me." Her voice cracked.

Joshua held his breath, waiting to hear what she said next. Part of him didn't want to know, but only because it was hard to think about what Charity might have gone through.

Her hand went to the scar at her collarbone. "A man named Will always looked at me funny, made me really uncomfortable. I tried to tell my mom, but she blew me off and said I just wanted attention. One day when I was home after school, someone knocked at the door. It was Will."

Joshua heard the emotion in her voice and wished more than anything he could fix things. But there was no way of fixing the past. Instead, he reached over and squeezed her hand. When she didn't protest, he held on, not wanting to let go.

"He forced his way inside, even though I told him my mom wasn't home. He cornered me, grabbed my hands, and pinned them. I fought him, but he pulled out a knife and held it at my throat."

"You don't have to finish if this is too hard, Charity."

"No, I want to. I want you to understand." She stared out the window a moment. "When he pulled out the knife, Andrea burst into my house. She'd heard me scream. She told Will that she'd called her dad and he was on his way and that he better get his hands off me. Her sudden arrival made his hand slip, and he left me with this nasty reminder of what happened." She touched her scar and frowned. "But thankfully that's where it ended. Things could have turned out a lot differently if Andrea hadn't shown up."

He squeezed her hand again. "This was the Will that Austin mentioned?"

She nodded. "After that point in time, Will always gave Andrea dirty looks when she was near."

"You mean your mom didn't break up with him?"

"She didn't even believe me." Charity let out a bitter laugh. "She told me I couldn't have all her attention and that I should stop making up stories. Truth was, I didn't have any of her attention."

Disgust churned in his stomach. "Did you call the police, or did Andrea call her dad? Ron Whitaker should have pressed charges—after he took you to the hospital."

Charity shook her head. "My mom talked to Ron, but nothing ever came of it. I don't know. My mom put some butterfly bandages over my cut, and she and I never spoke about it again."

"Did you ever consider that maybe Will was behind Andrea's abduction? Maybe it was some kind of twisted revenge or something."

"He had a heart attack and died about a month before she was abducted. Andrea had always been my protector. I let her down when she needed me the most, though. I should have done more."

"It was unfortunate that you fell. But none of this was your fault."

"She would have never left me . . ."

He let that information settle in. Charity had definitely

been through the wringer during her formative years. Her no-good dad died in a boating accident, along with the only woman who acted like she loved Charity—her grandmother. Her mother turned to drugs and men. The men mistreated Charity. Then Andrea was abducted.

Why hadn't Ron Whitaker done anything? He was the police chief at the time. He was obligated as an officer of the law to step in.

But that didn't help Joshua to know what to say at the moment. He finally settled with "I'm sorry, Charity. I can't imagine. It makes me mad to hear what you went through, to be honest."

"Thank you. I've had a lot of years to try and come to terms with everything."

"Have you?"

"Maybe that's another reason why I came back here. I've got to put all of this behind me. For good this time."

He knew what that meant. She had to leave Hertford; she wasn't here to stay. Joshua also knew that he couldn't move away from his son, that even if something came of this attraction he had to Charity, the likelihood a relationship would work out was slim to nothing.

He was better off to keep his distance . . . if only that wasn't proving to be so difficult.

CHAPTER 22

Andrea had always been her protector. Yet when Andrea had needed her the most, Charity had failed her. That was the resounding thought floating around in Charity's mind for the rest of the drive home.

She'd lived with guilt for so long that it felt normal, like something that wasn't supposed to go away.

She stared out the window, ideas turning over in her head. Had Andrea come back from the grave to exact revenge? Had she set her house on fire to show her grave disappointment with Charity? To make her pay for her failures?

That just didn't seem like the Andrea she remembered.

But what if Andrea was in trouble now, and she was reaching out to Charity for help? Charity couldn't turn her back on her again.

She let out a sigh, not sure what to think.

There was one thing she knew, though: having her hand in Joshua's felt good.

And that thought scared her as well. Even though she was working to overcome her fears, some of them seemed ingrained in her. Ron Whitaker was a cop and had let her down. Bradley was a cop, and he'd only used her to advance his own career. So what was in all of this for Joshua?

Maybe he was just trying to make a name for himself here in Hertford. Wouldn't everyone in town be impressed if he solved the crime that had turned the whole place upside down?

He'd probably make police chief over something like that.

Maybe a position like that would even help him get back custody of his son.

Charity shook her head. She had to stop thinking like this. There was a good chance that Joshua was just a genuinely good guy.

Maybe overcoming her trust issues would be the first step in reclaiming her life.

She squeezed Joshua's hand and offered him a smile.

***

"You mind if we stop by my house real quick?" Joshua asked. "I just need to grab something to take over to Ryan. It would save me a trip later."

"Of course."

He pulled off the highway onto the road leading toward his place.

A few minutes later, they rumbled down the driveway. He noticed Charity averted her gaze from the remains of her old house, as if she didn't want to face the memories. He couldn't blame her.

"I'm just going to get out and stretch my legs," Charity said.

"Sure thing." He stepped closer to the house and froze.

His front door was open.

Something was wrong.

"Charity, I need you to get back in the truck and lock the doors."

She looked up at him in surprise. "Okay . . ."

He tossed her his keys. "Take these, just in case you need them."

"Joshua, you're scaring me."

He pulled his gun from the ankle holster. He'd worn it today, just in case. "Just do what I ask. Please. I don't want anything to happen to you."

Finally, she nodded. With trembling hands, she climbed inside the truck door and hit the locks. Her wide, doe-like eyes stared back at him from the other side of the windshield.

With Charity safe, Joshua approached the house. Carefully, he nudged the front door open and stepped inside. He remained against the wall, keeping an eye out for any sign that something had been disturbed.

He'd locked his door when he left. He always did. Coming from the big city, it was second nature to him.

A quick scan of his living room indicated that nothing was out of place. Remaining on the perimeter of the room, he made his way to the kitchen. He checked behind the refrigerator, under the table, and in the pantry, but there was no one. That only left the bedrooms.

Slowly, he walked down the hallway. One by one, he checked each room. No one was here.

He'd just lowered his gun when he heard a noise at the other side of the house.

He darted toward the back door just in time to see someone run outside.

He followed, desperate to catch the person who'd been there. As soon as he stepped on his deck, something hit his head.

Then everything went black.

***

Charity gripped the armrest, trying to control her racing

heart. She wasn't exactly a person of prayer, but she found herself crying out to God.

Lord, please help him. Keep him safe.

Just then, Charity saw someone running through the backyard. The person darted toward the woods.

But there was no Joshua.

Where was he? Had something happened?

In a moment of decision, Charity dashed from the truck and into the house. If something happened to him because of her, she'd never forgive herself. She couldn't live with any more guilt.

She dashed through the living room and kitchen, pausing as she caught a glimpse out the back door. Joshua lay on the grass there, unmoving.

She gasped, panic rising through her. Wasting no time, she darted toward him. Kneeling on the ground, she checked for a pulse. It was there. Thank goodness, it was there. A nasty bump already welted on his forehead.

She looked up once more, in the direction that the figure had run. Whoever it was was long gone.

"Joshua, can you hear me?" she asked, her hands on his shoulders.

He moaned, and a moment later his eyes opened. "Charity?"

"Are you okay?" She almost wanted to cry, at the worst, or pull him into her arms, at best. She'd been so worried.

He squeezed his eyes shut a moment but finally nodded and started to push himself up. "Yeah, someone knocked me out."

"We should get you inside. I don't trust being out here right now." She offered one more glance around, fearing she'd see the intruder watching them from the woods again.

She put an arm around Joshua's waist to keep him steady and walked with him into the house. She didn't let go until he reached a kitchen chair and lowered himself there. She sat across from him, unable to shake her worry. "Are you sure you're okay?"

He glanced at her a moment, an unknown emotion flashing through his gaze. Finally, a slight smile feathered across his lips. He reached across the space between them and squeezed her hand. "I'm fine, Charity. Thanks for your concern."

"What happened?" Her throat felt tight as she waited for his response. That's what she told herself, at least. She knew it had something to do with the fact that his fingers touched hers. That simple motion made every cell of her skin feel alive and tingling.

"The intruder must have run outside when I came in. When I stepped onto the deck, someone clobbered me over the head."

"Any idea what he was doing here?" Charity asked, even though she knew in her mind that this had something to do with Andrea. She had no idea what, nor could she even fathom the connection at the moment. But it was there. She just had to figure out what it was.

"Only guesses. As far as I can tell, nothing was taken or destroyed. But there had to be some reason this person was in the house."

She swallowed hard. "Maybe he wanted to send a message, let you know he was out there."

Joshua's gaze locked onto hers. "There's something else, Charity. That intruder . . . she was a woman."

CHAPTER 23

Joshua watched Charity's expression as it turned from curious to shocked to fearful.

"What do you mean?"

He shook his head, which only made it ache more. "I need to see a picture of Andrea."

"All the ones I had were destroyed in the fire."

He stood, the motion again causing his head to wobble, and grabbed his laptop from a table in his living room. He didn't really need to confirm it was Andrea. But for his sanity—and Charity's—he would.

He did a quick search and pulled up a picture of Andrea. He studied it for a moment before nodding. The woman he'd seen had been a brunette. Her hair was long now, not bobbed like it was in her high school picture. The woman he'd seen had a more defined face, but that often happened as a person aged.

He had no doubt about it. The woman in his house had been Andrea.

"Maybe I'm not losing my mind," Charity whispered behind him.

As a tear trickled down her cheek, he quickly rose. Without thinking about it, he pulled her into his arms. He expected resistance, but instead she folded into his embrace.

He couldn't help but marvel at how perfectly she fit into his arms. Her head rested snugly under his chin. Her petite frame fit up against him, and something about the moment felt right, made him want it to never end.

That thought scared him.

He had no desire to be in another relationship. So what was he doing right now?

Despite the warnings in his mind, he continued to hold her. In fact, he didn't want to let go. Ever.

Finally, Charity took a step back and ran her fingers under her eyes, as if to hide any evidence of tears. Then she dropped onto the couch and stared pensively at the wall.

"I'm trying to put together what all of this means."

"Unless your friend has a twin, it looks like she is still alive and close by."

"But how could that be?" She turned those big, luminous eyes on him. There were too many questions there, too much pain. "While nothing would make me happier than to find out she's okay, there's so much that doesn't make sense."

"I'm hoping I can help you find some answers."

She stared at him a moment before a smile cracked her face. "Thank you, Joshua."

"I need to make sure nothing was disturbed." He shrugged. "I've found that sometimes it's the subtle things that you don't expect. Do you want to wait here?"

She stood, tilting off balance for a moment. But her whole world had just shifted, Joshua realized. It was going to take some time before anything appeared straight.

"That sounds good."

He started in the bedrooms. He didn't really have any jewelry or other things of much value. But there'd been a reason that woman was in his house. Was it to send a message? He had to cover all his bases.

His bedroom looked fine. There was nothing out of place.

He walked into the guest bedroom. His mom had helped him to decorate it with a vanilla bedspread and some nightstands. He searched through the room, but again, nothing.

Finally, he reached Rider's room. He stepped inside, but saw nothing out of the ordinary. He opened the closet door and paused.

There had always been a piece of wood inside the closet that had been screwed into the wall. He'd assumed that at one time there'd been a pipe burst or something, since the bathroom was on the other side, and the previous owners didn't want to spend the money to fix the wall, especially since it wasn't visible.

He squatted down and examined the space. He found it hard to believe that the wood had just come off. He touched the plaster, and it wasn't soft with moisture. No, someone had unscrewed this piece of wood and left it on the ground. But why?

"What is it?" a soft voice said behind him.

"I'm not sure," Joshua said. "Can you grab me that flashlight on the dresser?"

Charity handed it to him. He shone the light into the cubbyhole. It caught on something on the floor. What was that?

He reached into the wall and pulled out a metal box. His gut told him that this was significant.

***

Charity felt the air leave her lungs. She knelt down beside Joshua, and their gazes connected, something unspoken between them.

Without saying anything, Joshua opened the box. Inside there were three notebooks, a necklace, and some photos.

"It's almost like a time capsule," Joshua said.

"This was Andrea's," Charity whispered.

Joshua's eyes widened. "Really?"

She nodded, feeling almost numb. "This was her room. The writing on the front of that notebook is hers. And those Dalmatian stickers are definitely Andrea's. She always wanted a Dalmatian."

She picked up one of the photos. It was a professional shot taken of Andrea. Her friend wore her favorite jeans and a black top. The light hit her hair in a way that made it shine and glimmer.

Charity's breath caught when she spotted her friend's bracelet in the photo. It had been years since she'd thought about that piece of jewelry. Andrea's dad had given her the gold piece, which was lovely with its connecting hearts linked together.

"You okay with this?" Joshua asked, pausing.

Charity nodded. She wasn't sure what they'd find on those pages. But she knew there was no going back at this point. She had to know what was so important that her friend had hidden this within the wall.

Joshua sat down and leaned against his son's bed. Charity sat beside him as he pulled out the first notebook. "This one looks like the most recent. Based on the dates across the front, she kept this during the month before she was abducted."

Charity's stomach roiled with anticipation. Would there be answers here? Guilt also began to claw at her. This was also such an invasion of privacy.

Joshua began reading the first entry out loud. "Dad and Mom had another one of their fights today. I'm so tired of the fighting. Dad drinks more. Mom cries more. Then everyone gets mad at me."

Charity shook her head, fighting back pain.

"Did you know any of this?" Joshua asked.

"Not really; apparently there were things Andrea didn't think were important enough to tell her best friend."

"Maybe she had a reason." He squeezed her knee.

Charity shrugged. "Maybe. But the more important issue here is what she said. Why were they fighting?"

"Who knows? Couples fight. It doesn't mean that has anything to do with her disappearance. Why would it?"

"I have no idea. Bringing the past up . . . it can be painful."

"We can stop."

Charity shook her head. "No, I have to push through this."

Joshua continued reading. "Charity is so much stronger than she thinks she is. She has to be strong to endure what she does at home. There are times I've just wanted to march over to her house and give her mom a piece of my mind. All those men—"

Charity put her hand over Joshua's arm. "Maybe I don't want to hear the rest of this."

He stared at her another moment, compassion in his eyes. "I understand."

"My past is complicated." He had no idea, even if he thought he did.

"You don't have anything to be ashamed of, Charity. I like you for who you are right now."

Her heart warmed before quickly cooling. He said that now, but did he really mean it? "I appreciate that. But maybe I just need a break."

"I should take these down to the station, anyway. The chief will want to see them." He stared at her another moment.

"I'm sorry, Charity. I don't know everything that's in here. I hope it's nothing that causes you too much pain."

Almost instinctively his gaze seemed to go to the scar under her neck.

"Thank you."

He pulled out the necklace. "Do you know what this was?"

"Her grandmother gave it to her." Charity shook her head. "It's so strange. For years, I thought Andrea had the perfect family. Maybe no one does. We all have our issues, don't we?"

"I can't deny that. Sometimes you can try your hardest to have the perfect family and still fail."

Was he talking about his own family? About his failed marriage and having to share custody of his son? Charity didn't ask. They'd had enough somber discussion for the moment.

She glanced at the metallic box again. "There's one other thing," she started. "That woman who broke into your house. She wanted us to find these. Otherwise, she would have taken them herself."

CHAPTER 24

Charity stared at Joshua a moment as they stood on the porch of Daleigh's place. She had the urge to reach up and plant a kiss on his cheek. Her cheeks flushed at the thought.

The idea was crazy. She wasn't in a good place for a relationship. Joshua certainly didn't seem interested. Yet, despite all the warnings in her head, her heart felt differently.

As she looked up at Joshua, she wondered if he felt the spark between them, also.

He started to say something, but then stopped and took a step back. "I'll keep you updated about those journals, okay?"

She nodded her good-bye, hesitating before taking a step back toward the door. No one was in the house. Daleigh was probably with Ryan, if she had to guess. She imagined the two of them making wedding plans and getting his house ready for her to move into. Charity used to have dreams of doing that sort of thing. She hadn't thought about it in a long time.

But something about Joshua seemed to be fueling desires she hadn't known existed, even. Being around him made her long for more; it stirred up desires for family and forever and a chance at happiness.

She saw a paper on the breakfast bar and wondered if Daleigh had left her a note or maybe some instructions. She picked it up, and a scream lodged in her throat.

It wasn't a note from Daleigh.

It was a picture of Charity and Andrea. Words were

scribbled across the back: *You're the only one who can help.*

***

Joshua went back to the station, his head still throbbing from his encounter with the woman at his house.

Was she Andrea? Something just didn't settle in his gut about the whole thing. The pieces didn't fit together.

He put the box on his desk and opened the latch. Charity was right: that intruder had wanted them to find this information. But why? What was in these journals that was so important?

He opened the first one, and his eyes adjusted to Andrea's flowery handwriting.

August 29
Charity and I picked some cotton today. Then we threw it in the air and pretended it was snowing. We even tried to build a snowman. It seemed so juvenile, like something we would have done when we were eight. There are some silly things that only girlfriends can do together.

He smiled at the image that formed: the image of Charity being carefree. It was almost hard to picture. She just always seemed weighed down. But the few times he'd caught a glimpse of her genuine smile, it had delighted him. Those moments made him wonder what Charity would have been like if life hadn't taken the course it had.

Another entry read:

I found out something horrible today. It explains

why my mom and dad have been fighting so much. I can't believe it. Part of me wishes I didn't know, but another part of me is glad. Reality can be hard to face, but dealing with truth is always better than dealing with lies. I confronted my dad with the information I learned. He was angry. So angry that I thought for a minute he might hit me.

Lawrence overheard the conversation. He told me afterward that I needed to drop it and mind my own business. He said I was digging into adult matters that I needed to stay out of—if I knew what was best for me.

Has my whole family gone crazy? At one time, I thought my dad was perfect. But he's fallen off his pedestal, and I don't know what to do about it. Should I bury this information? Or come forward?

What had Andrea discovered? Had her father committed a crime? Had that crime remained hidden to this very day?

He skimmed over several other entries until his gaze stopped on one. It was dated two weeks before Andrea disappeared.

Today I asked Brody to run away with me. My dad doesn't approve of our relationship. He thinks I'm too young to date. I'm so tired of living under the strain at my house. There's so much fighting. I know I have it better than Charity and that I shouldn't complain. But if Brody would say yes, I'd be gone in a heartbeat. Well, except for leaving Charity. Of course, my dad would track me down. There are downsides of having the police chief as a dad.

Joshua leaned back. Run away with Brody? Now there was a thought. Andrea had hated living at home and wanted to get away. Would she have staged her own disappearance and abduction?

Of course, Andrea had said she didn't want to leave Charity, but if things got bad enough at home, maybe she would reconsider.

Joshua didn't feel confident in that theory, but it was worth exploring, if for nothing else than to eliminate the possibility.

Maybe it was time to pay his friend a visit and have a heart-to-heart talk.

***

"Hey, Joshua," Brody said. "What's going on?"

Joshua nodded at his friend. "Sorry to stop by without an invitation. I was hoping I could chat for a minute."

Brody's eyebrows furrowed together; the man obviously knew something was up. Brody had always seemed like a stand-up guy, and Joshua couldn't imagine him keeping a secret like this.

"Come on in." Brody opened the door to his waterfront house. The Coastie was out on the water as much as possible, so this property was perfect for him. Joshua had already discovered that in the short time they'd known each other. "Can I get you something? I've got some Gatorade and tap water. Sorry, but I wasn't expecting company."

"I'm good. I'm actually here in an official capacity."

"I'm intrigued now. Have a seat."

Stiffly, they sat across from each other. Joshua dragged in a deep breath. "Brody, I hate to ask you this, but I have to explore every possibility. Tonight, Charity and I found some journals that belonged to Andrea. They were hidden in a wall in her old closet."

"Okay."

"One of the journal entries mentioned that she wanted to run away with you, far from this town."

A sad smile crossed his friend's features. "She kept trying to talk me into it."

"Why did she want to run away so badly?"

He let out a long sigh. "It's complicated. But she just wasn't happy. She felt like there was more to life than what was here in Hertford. She'd never get out of her dad's shadow. The two of them didn't always see eye to eye."

"Do you think it's a possibility that she planned all of this herself in order to get away?"

Brody shook his head and left no room for question. "Absolutely not. She wouldn't have left Charity."

"She would have stayed around her domineering father just to remain near her best friend?"

"She always wanted to be Charity's protector. It's not that she felt sorry for her; I mean, they were best friends in every sense of the word. They were practically inseparable. She just knew that if she left, Charity would have no one."

"How about the two of you? Were you serious?" Joshua asked.

"I was probably more serious than Andrea was. I mean, she was in high school and I was in college. But there was no one else like her."

"This is going to sound strange, Brody," Joshua started, leaning forward with his elbows on his knees. "But there have been a couple of sightings around town of a woman who looks like Andrea."

Brody stiffened. "No . . ."

Joshua nodded. "I saw her myself. I have to say that the resemblance is uncanny."

"If someone took her, I always assumed they'd taken her far away. The idea that she could still be in this area, living under our noses the whole time—"

"And possibly be free," Joshua added.

Brody shook his head. "I don't know. That's unnerving. Why wouldn't she find someone, get help, run away?"

"I have no idea. Every stone I turn just seems to raise more questions."

"I'll pray that you get some answers. I'd love to have some too. I have to admit that my life has felt like it's been in a holding pattern since she disappeared. Every girl I date, I feel like I'm cheating on Andrea. Crazy, isn't it?"

"Not really."

"If there's anything I can do, let me know."

"I'll do that."

CHAPTER 25

"Please, come to church with us," Daleigh said the next morning. "I promise, no one there bites. And, if they do, I'll bite them back for you."

Charity couldn't help but smile. But the smile quickly faded. "Are you sure you want to be associated with someone like me?"

She meant the words. Being around the supposed wrong people could wreck a person's reputation.

"Oh, honey. I don't think anyone's going to think a thing. And if they do, it's their loss. I'm not afraid of criticism. I'm a musician. I get plenty of positive, but I also get my share of the negative."

Charity nodded resolutely. "Okay, then. I'll go."

"I know just the dress for you," Daleigh said. She returned a moment later with a white sundress. "This will look gorgeous with your hair."

The dress was beautiful. Simple, below the knees, sleeveless. "Are you sure?"

"More than sure. Go on and put it on. I'll meet you outside in twenty. Does that work?"

Charity nodded and hurried to get ready. It felt good to clean up, to have a reason to fix her hair and wear nice clothes. She'd never been prissy, but every once in a while a girl enjoyed feeling like a girl. Since she'd arrived here in Hertford, she'd mostly felt like both a nervous wreck and a walking mess.

Daleigh let out a whistle when she saw Charity step onto the porch. "Just like I thought. It looks great on you."

Charity smiled. "Thank you."

"Now, come on. Ryan's picking us up."

They slid into Ryan's truck and made casual chitchat on the way to church. It was less than a five-minute drive, but jitters had claimed Charity by the time they arrived. She kept breathing deeply at the thought of running into former classmates, teachers, and even people she didn't know but who knew her.

It seemed like an awkward situation in the making. She should have never agreed to this.

Once the truck was parked, she climbed out, straightened her dress, and held her head high.

Victim no more, she told herself.

She was the only person who could make herself feel this way. She was the only one who could make herself rise above it, as well.

Walking beside Daleigh and Ryan, she stepped into the church.

To her relief, no one stopped and stared. Daleigh introduced her to several people, none of whom she recognized. They all smiled politely and shook her hand.

Still, it was a relief when she was able to scoot down a pew and the church service began.

No more talking.

Halfway through "Praise the Name of Jesus," someone slid in beside her. She looked up and saw Joshua.

Her heart skipped a few beats. She attempted a smile, but wasn't sure if she succeeded or not. Joshua's bright smile in return was enough to satisfy her, though.

As they sat back down and the sermon began, she had

the hardest time staying focused. Between wondering if people were plotting ways to get her to leave and the way Joshua's leg brushed up against her, she was seriously lacking focus.

"Anyone want some barbecue?" Joshua asked when church ended.

"You know I'm always game," Daleigh said. She turned to Charity. "You have to come to. It's our Sunday tradition."

Charity shrugged, secretly delighted to spend more time with Joshua. "Sure thing."

Fifteen minutes later, they were seated at a long table with a checkered tablecloth and a plastic basket full of condiments in the middle. It appeared they'd gotten here right in time and beaten some of the after-church rush.

As Charity inhaled the scent of roasted pork and fried chicken, her stomach grumbled.

"This smells delicious," Charity started after placing her order. "Speaking of which, Joshua introduced me to the seafood at the Dancing Mackerel yesterday."

"The Dancing Mackerel?" Daleigh asked. "I've never heard of it."

"It's in Nags Head," Joshua said. "The place isn't much to look at, but it has some good food."

Charity cleared her throat, unable to keep the conversation as light as she'd like. "We saw Mr. Johansson while we were down there. Was he ever your teacher in high school, Ryan? Or did he come after you left?"

"I think he came a few years after I graduated," Ryan said. "Is he a suspect?"

Charity shrugged. "Not necessarily. He was just awfully personal with a couple of his students, and he was the last person Andrea and I spoke with before she was abducted."

"So is he a suspect?" Daleigh asked, taking a sip of tea.

"I can't officially give any statements on the case," Joshua said. "I'm just revisiting some key players from the past. You never know when someone might share something that offers a new clue. I'm a fresh set of eyes in this investigation. The original people involved weren't objective."

"You mean Ron Whitaker?" Ryan snorted. "I wouldn't think so."

Joshua leaned closer. "You've been in this town longer than I have. Do you know Buddy Griffin?"

"I think everyone does."

"What's your impression of him?"

"He's a strange one," Ryan said. "My gut tells me he's harmless. He's kind of a drama king and a recluse at the same time. But I've never seen him as being dangerous. In your line of work, I'm sure you'd tell me that anyone can be dangerous, though. Right?"

"You'd be surprised at the capacity for evil people have inside them. It's just a matter of how much you feed those negative emotions. Eventually they grow and grow until they can't be contained any longer."

Charity shivered at his words.

Whatever that evil was—whoever it was coming from—Charity sensed it was growing.

And that thought was enough to make her want to run.

***

Joshua offered to drive Charity back. The two of them being together just seemed natural. He'd even begun to forget some of his fears about trusting again as he realized that Charity wasn't anything like Justina. Charity cared about people other than herself.

Still, he had to remind himself that Charity would soon be leaving.

As they were sitting in Joshua's truck, Charity turned to him. "I found something strange in Daleigh's house last night, Joshua."

He bristled in anticipation.

She pulled something from her purse. "It was this picture."

Joshua glanced at it. The photo was of Charity and Andrea. They were covered in mud and had big goofy smiles on their faces. The chilling part was the words on the back. *You're the only one who can help.*

"This was in the house when you returned?" he clarified.

Charity nodded. "It was on the table."

"Was there any sign of forced entry?"

"There was a window open."

"You should have called me."

"What would you have done? Besides, Daleigh came home a few minutes later, so I wasn't alone. The note wasn't exactly threatening. It was just eerie."

A surge of protectiveness rose in him.

"I'm going back to the house to read Andrea's journals again. I brought them home with me so I could study them more. Would you like to come?"

Charity smiled softly. "Sure."

"I thought you should know that I paid a visit to Brody Joyner last night."

Her head swung toward him. "Why?"

"One of Andrea's journal entries mentioned that she was trying to talk Brody into running away with her."

"Andrea would have never run away. Besides, why

would she have wanted to?"

"People have mentioned she was disappointed with her dad. Maybe she found out something that was a major blow to her image of her father."

She crossed her arms, and her voice turned sad. "She never mentioned anything to me. Why didn't she do it?"

"I suppose she considered everything she was leaving behind."

Charity was silent a moment. "What did Brody say?"

"He confirmed that Andrea had brought up the subject."

"You don't think he's involved in this somehow, do you?"

"No, I don't. I'm just trying to examine every possibility."

"So far, there's been Ron Whitaker, Ron's sons, Austin Johansson, and Buddy Griffin. Somehow, I can't quite believe any of them would be a part of this. Did they all make mistakes? Yes. Are they all imperfect? Absolutely. But I can't see them taking it this far."

"I used to work in the missing persons unit back in Atlanta, Charity. I've seen people commit horrendous crimes for reasons that seemed asinine and unfathomable. The extent of what people will do when they believe a lie is astounding."

"When they believe a lie?"

He nodded. "It starts with just a seed of an idea. Maybe they think their life would be perfect if only they had a certain person in it, or if they obtained a particular amount of money, or if someone who wronged them suffered. At first, the idea might seem outrageous. But over time, it starts to make more sense. Too many things begin to hinge on them achieving their ideal. It then becomes a truth."

"Kind of like sin. Isn't that what the pastor talked about this morning?"

"Exactly. He compared it to cooking a frog. At first the water just feels warm, like a hot tub. Before long, that water is boiling and those frogs are dead."

They pulled up to his house. As they started toward the door, he reached over and grabbed Charity's hand. It felt good to hold her hand in his. He sensed that Charity needed to take it slow. That was good because he also needed to take baby steps. Rushing into relationships seemed to always end in disaster, and there were so many uncertainties between them.

She sat on the couch, looking lovely in the white dress she wore. Instead of grabbing a journal, she picked up a picture of him with Rider. "Tell me about your son."

Joshua sat beside her and stared at the picture. "He's the best thing that ever happened to me. He's four, he loves trucks, and he talks nonstop."

"Do you get to see him very often?"

"I have custody every other weekend. More in the summer and on holidays. He's on vacation with his mom and stepdad right now."

"You miss him?"

"Every day. Life wasn't supposed to turn out like this for him."

"What happened?"

He squeezed his lips together a moment. "I was working. A lot. I'd applied for the FBI and been accepted to their academy. But in the process, I lost my family. I suppose I should have seen the warning signs, but I didn't. I came home one day, and my wife and son were gone. She'd moved in with her new boyfriend."

"That had to be hard."

"More than you could imagine. If I could go back and do it over again, I would. But life doesn't work that way."

"Do you still love her?"

He thought about it a moment before shaking his head. "No, she's remarried. We actually only knew each other two months before we tied the knot. It was truly a whirlwind relationship. Three months after we were married, we found out she was pregnant. Everything happened quickly."

"I don't see you as the type to jump into a commitment like that."

"I'm not usually. I haven't always been the person I am today, though."

"I have a hard time seeing that."

"When Justina left me, I turned my life around. I started going to church and got my priorities straight. I actually decided not to follow through with the FBI Academy and decided to do everything I could to be a good father to Rider. I begged Justina to give me a second chance, but it was too late. She got remarried. A year later, I found out Justina and her new husband were moving to this area. Now here I am."

"Isn't that the important thing? That we see our mistakes and turn our lives around?"

"I suppose it is. For all of us." He leveled his gaze at her, hoping she'd apply her own advice.

Charity swallowed deeply and rubbed her throat. She got the message loud and clear. "Maybe we should start looking at those journals."

CHAPTER 26

As Charity sat beside Joshua on the couch, she couldn't stop thinking about what Joshua had told her. She just couldn't imagine Joshua not being the man he was today. The person she knew was honorable, committed, and trustworthy. Those attributes were what she liked about him.

He wasn't putting on a front for her, was he?

Bradley had been so career oriented. At first, Charity admired him for it. But then it became apparent that his career was more important than their relationship. In fact, he saw their relationship as a means of getting ahead in his career. Every conversation revolved around her past and ignited some kind of hunger in his gaze.

She should have known. He hadn't become interested in her until she opened up about her past. Then he almost seemed obsessed.

When he started prying into her background without mentioning it to her, that had been the final straw. She didn't want to be a case study; she wanted to be his girlfriend. She'd ended things.

Charity blinked several times, determined to focus her thoughts. She needed to concentrate right now on Andrea's journals. Her entries showed a different side of Andrea than she remembered. Apparently her friend had always tried to be strong for Charity, while at home she'd been unhappy.

A lot of teenagers rebelled against their parents during their teen years and thought their lives were terrible. Charity had seen it enough times in her line of work. But Charity wondered if Andrea's angst went beyond that.

"What are you thinking?" Joshua asked, pulling her from her thoughts.

Charity looked up at him and frowned. "I guess I'm thinking that sometimes you think you know someone, only to find out you don't. I thought Andrea and I shared everything, but it's becoming exceedingly obvious that we didn't."

"She was probably trying to look out for you."

"Maybe. What could her father have done to disappoint her so much? Everything is so vague."

"I've been surprised at how much she mentions her mom and dad fighting," Joshua said. "Originally, I was thinking maybe Ron had covered up a crime. But what's the number one reason couples fight?"

"Unfaithfulness," Charity muttered.

Joshua nodded. "What if Ron wasn't a very faithful husband?"

"Do you think that has anything to do with her disappearance?"

"I don't know what to think anymore. But I just might give Chief Owens a call again. Maybe he knows something and doesn't even realize it."

***

First thing in the morning, as soon as he got to the station, Joshua called the town's former police chief. The man answered on the first ring.

"Chief Owens, it's Officer Haven from the Hertford—"

"I remember you. What do you want?"

"I'm looking into Ron Whitaker's background, and I had a question for you."

"You really think he has something to do with his daughter's abduction?" Chief Owens asked.

Joshua slowly pushed out a breath as he contemplated his words. "I'm just exploring every possibility. I found some information that seems to indicate Ron Whitaker wasn't faithful to his wife. Do you know anything about that?"

"I stay out of my friends' affairs—and that's just an expression, not a concession."

"I'm not asking you as Ron's friend. I'm asking you as the former police chief."

The man remained silent a moment. "You didn't hear any of this from me. Understand?"

"Of course."

"Ron had a special fondness for what he liked to call Badge Bunnies."

Joshua bit back his disgust. Badge Bunnies were women who were practically groupies for cops. They learned the places cops frequented, and they frequented those places also, all in an effort to play out their romantic aspirations.

"Anyone in particular?"

"Lucinda Ballantine. There were a few others here and there. She was the one who lasted the longest."

"Did Roberta Whitaker know?"

"Most people in town did. I'm sure word got back to her eventually."

"One more question."

"Go ahead. I'm going to start charging you as a consultant, though."

"How many files were there on this case?"

"Boxes and boxes. Why?"

"There's only one box here at the station."

"That can't be right," Chief Owens said. "We had people calling in from all over the country. There were all kinds of sightings, though none of them panned out. We kept records of all of them, though."

That's what Joshua had thought. So what *had* happened to all that information? "Thanks for your help, Chief."

"I hope you do find out what happened to Andrea," Chief Owens said. "I'm a little older and wiser now. I wish there had been things done differently, looking back. Everyone deserves justice. Everyone."

Fifteen minutes later, Joshua was on his way to see Lucinda Ballantine. She actually didn't live in Hertford, but over in Elizabeth City, a town that was only about ten minutes away and considerably larger than Hertford.

He pulled up to an old house in the historical part of town. The outside was plain with no flower beds, but the exterior still remained neat. An old sedan rested in the driveway.

Joshua walked up the faded steps and knocked on the door. A moment later, a woman in her fifties appeared, a cool glass of tea in her hands. The woman was blonde and trim and wore snug clothing that drew attention to her cleavage.

"I'm looking for Lucinda Ballantine," he said.

"What can I do for you?" she said, her voice almost having a purr-like quality.

"I'm Officer Joshua Haven with the Hertford Police Department. I'm hoping to ask you a few questions."

"Pertaining to?"

"The disappearance of Andrea Whitaker."

The light left her gaze. "Andrea. I see. Yes, yes. By all

means, come in." She pushed the door open.

Joshua followed her past the foyer and into her living room.

"Can I get you some sweet tea? Everyone always says I make the best." She raised her eyebrows as she waited for his answer.

"I'm fine. Thank you, though."

With a nervous swipe of hair behind her ear, she lowered herself into a chair across from him. "How can I help you, then?"

"We're considering reopening the investigation into Andrea Whitaker. Your name came up today."

Her head twitched ever so slightly. "Did it?"

"Ma'am, do you mind if I ask you if you knew Andrea's father, Ron Whitaker?"

She nodded stiffly. "I did know him. We met at the Red Horse Inn. I was working as a waitress there, and several police officers used to frequent the place."

"What was the nature of your relationship?"

She lowered her lashes in mock modesty. "Women of character don't speak of such things."

"It's important to the investigation, Mrs. Ballantine. I realize it might be uncomfortable. I apologize for that."

Her coy expression vanished, and she leaned back against the couch, some of her pretense disappearing. "We fooled around. I knew he was married. I knew it was wrong. But I did it anyway."

"What happened?"

"We weren't serious. He wasn't leaving his wife. And that was that. I'm not sure how this pertains to Andrea's disappearance. The man loved his daughter. He'd never do anything to hurt her."

"What did you think happened?"

She shrugged. "I didn't know. I didn't even have any good ideas. Honestly, the whole thing just broke him. That's how I know he couldn't be behind it. But there is something I need to confess, just to get it off my chest after all these years."

Joshua's neck tightened. "What's that?"

"When the FBI stepped in, I told them I was with Ron when the crime occurred. I didn't admit to having an affair with him; I just said he'd been at the Red Horse. The place was empty at the time, so there was no one else there to verify the story."

"Why'd you lie for him?"

"He asked me to. Said the police always looked at the person closest to the victim. He didn't want them to waste time examining him when the real kidnapper was out there."

"Interesting. When did the two of you break things off?"

She frowned and stared into the distance. "About a month later. He began crumbling. He wasn't himself at all."

"Do the two of you still speak?"

"We haven't in two years."

"Two years?"

She nodded. "He showed up at my door one day. Said it was a mistake to ever let me go." Her frown deepened. "The truth eventually came out. His wife was going to leave him for someone else. He just showed up here as some kind of revenge."

"His wife was leaving him?" That was the first Joshua had heard of that. Was it relevant to the case? Probably not. But sometimes the most unexpected tidbits could lead to answers.

She nodded. "That's what he said. Who knows what happened? She died five days later in that auto accident."

CHAPTER 27

Charity still had an hour before she was supposed to meet Joshua for lunch. He'd called her last night and asked if he could see her, and, of course, she'd said yes. She'd finished with today's task earlier than she'd anticipated, though, and now had time to kill.

This morning she'd met with an insurance adjuster to go over the claim. She was surprised when he'd told her the amount she'd most likely receive because of the fire. It was more than she'd ever imagined. Not that she'd anticipated the money, but it would be nice if she was able to get ahead.

She paced over to the small pier behind Daleigh's home. The small wooden structure stretched into the Perqulmans River. In the distance, she could see the town's "famous" S bridge, as well as the large memorial bridge that was a part of the Ocean Highway.

The area felt like a little oasis. Cypress trees dotted the water, making the water look almost tealike in appearance. Spanish moss draped the limbs, almost making it feel spooky, even in broad daylight. With the insurance money Charity might get back, she might be able to afford her own little oasis somewhere.

But not here in Hertford, she reminded herself. It would never work for her here, even though she'd been trying to convince herself to believe that it could recently. Even if she could put closure to the tragedy surrounding Andrea, there were too many bad memories.

Her mind turned to those journals and the intruder at Joshua's house. What if it had been Andrea? What if she'd *wanted* them to find those journals? Why? What was inside those pages that someone would want discovered?

The longer Charity stayed here in Hertford, the more unsettled she became.

She shook off the thoughts.

Behind her, she heard a mower starting. She glanced over and saw a man with long hair in Daleigh's sister's yard. Her sister, Hannah was her name, was also on vacation this week. School started next week, so more than one family in the area had that idea, apparently.

The man looked slightly familiar, and he waved to her as he began pushing the mower. At least he hadn't shunned her the way some people in town had.

So much for her peace and quiet, though. Maybe she should take a walk to pass some time. It beat turning over her thoughts again and again.

As she started past Hannah's house, the lawn mower died. She looked over and saw the man looking at her. Immediately, her muscles tensed.

"Sorry, I don't mean to stare," the man started. "It's good to see you back here."

She paused. "Do I know you?"

He shook his head. "No, but everyone around here knows who you are. I always thought it was wrong that those people drove you out of town. I'm glad you're finally showing people what you're made of."

Charity felt her cheeks heat with gratitude. "Thank you. I appreciate that."

He nodded and then got back to work.

As she walked down the street, she had a new spring to her step. Funny how one little affirmation could do that.

She stopped at a couple of shops, realizing that she was taking some kind of step toward overcoming her past by doing these simple acts by herself. Even better, no one confronted her or demanded to know why she was back in town.

As she was about to leave a hardware store, she paused at a figure she spotted in the window.

Lawrence Whitaker.

He was staring right at her.

When he saw her, he burst into a run.

***

Joshua noticed that Charity looked paler than usual when he picked her up for lunch in his cruiser. Before he could ask her about it, he had her sign a waiver so she could ride with him. He didn't want to be accused of favoritism.

"Am I an official ride-along participant?" Charity asked.

He smiled. "Just keeping things official in case anyone says anything. You're a witness in a cold case that's being reopened. There's nothing wrong with you being with me while I'm at work. I just have to cross every *t* and dot every *i*."

"I can appreciate that."

He shoved the clipboard under his seat before taking off. "Everything okay?"

She sighed. "I just caught Lawrence Whitaker watching me when I went into the hardware store."

Joshua's muscles tightened. "Did he say anything? Do anything?"

Charity shook her head. "No, it was just eerie. He ran when he saw me. I don't know why he'd be watching me."

"Because that whole family is up to no good. If you see him again, call me. He may not be responsible for the arson at your house, but I still don't trust him."

"How did it go for you today?" She leaned back in the seat.

He filled her in on his conversation with Lucinda.

"So Ron Whitaker was cheating on his wife? No wonder Andrea was mad. As a child, she idolized her father."

"He didn't just do it once, either. It was a habit. Anyway, before I left, Lucinda told me that there was a rumor going around town that Roberta had enough of Ron's philandering ways. She'd met someone and was going to leave Ron."

Charity's eyes widened. "Did she give you a name?"

Joshua nodded. "Sam Childs. I plan on going to see him after lunch."

Joshua wanted to speak with him, just to rule out any information that could help the investigation. He felt like it was probably a wild goose chase, but he didn't want to leave any stone unturned.

"I can't wait to hear what he has to say."

"Speaking of lunch, any preference?"

"You mean between the Have a Nice Day Café, the pharmacy, and the barbecue restaurant?" She smiled, a teasing tone in her voice.

"Hey now, there are a couple of other places on the outskirts of town. And we do have a few traffic lights here, so we're not that small of a town."

"You pick. I'm just along for the ride."

Just then his radio crackled. It was the chief. "Our good friend Buddy Griffin is threatening to kill himself. Would you mind swinging by his place to talk him down from the ledge, so to speak?"

"Of course. I'll be right there." He hung up and looked apologetically at Charity. "I'm going to need a rain check on that lunch."

"Don't worry about taking me home. How about if I wait in the car while you handle the call? I know time is of the essence."

"You wouldn't mind?"

"Not at all."

Joshua turned on his lights and accelerated toward Buddy's house. When Joshua pulled up, he spotted the man pacing near his dogs with a gun in his hands. "Whatever you do, stay in the car," Joshua told Charity.

She stared at Buddy in the distance. "No problem."

Joshua made sure his own gun was easily accessible as he climbed from the car. He slowly, carefully approached Buddy, noting the rotten scent of swamp mixed with the stench of manure that filled the air. Buddy's house could easily be condemned; the conditions were practically squalid.

"Why don't you put your gun down?" Joshua called

"Don't worry—I won't use it on you." Buddy spit on the ground and continued pacing.

"I don't want you using it on anyone."

Buddy shook his head and continued pacing. "I'm not gonna use it on anyone. I'm just so tired. I can't catch a break, from my lousy ex-wife, who turned my daughter against me, to my good-for-nothing girlfriend. I have nothing to live for anymore."

The man must want a reason to hope. Otherwise, why would he have called the police to report what he was about to do? People did strange things in moments of desperation. Joshua had seen it again and again.

Joshua's gaze fell on the dogs. "You have your animals.

They depend on you."

The dogs were wound up, barking as if they knew something bad might happen. They each raced along the fence, teeth bared and hair raised.

A smile cracked Buddy's face, but his eyes still looked sad. "You think they love me. You know what they really love? They love the fact that I feed them and give them water."

"Love is still love."

Buddy paused and chuckled—the sound lingering a little too long, to the point of feeling uncomfortable. "You know, I used to want to be an animal trainer, back when I was a teenager. I even went to school out in California for a while. I bet you wouldn't guess that, would you?"

"I had no idea."

"People make animal training sound so normal, so decent. But you know what it really is? You know how to get animals to do what you want them to do? You deprive them of food until they become obedient. That doesn't sound very humane, does it?"

"No, it doesn't."

"Then, when they're at their weakest, they'll do what you want. Then you reward them. They learn obedience must happen in order for their needs to be met. I've never thought that was the way to earn love, though."

"Now that you mention it, it does sound kind of harsh."

"My dogs are all I have. I never kept anything from them. But if they got desperate, I'd be the first thing they ate. Hunger and desperation can make all of us—even dogs—do terrible things." He squeezed the skin between his eyes.

"Did you do something terrible, Buddy?"

"No, I've tried to do all the right things. I have nothing to show for it. People think I'm terrible, and I haven't done a thing to harm anyone. That's what I'm tired of. I'm ready to end all of this."

"There are better ways, Buddy. You're giving other people too much power in your life."

"I'm out of options."

"Have you been drinking again, Buddy?"

"It's the only thing that makes me feel better."

"Put the gun down, Buddy." Just then, Joshua's phone beeped. He ignored it, not wanting to break up the conversation. Answering now would set back any progress they'd made.

"I don't want to." The man started pacing again.

"Don't do something you regret."

"I won't be able to regret anything if I'm dead." He raised his gun in the air as if going into battle.

"I don't know about that. There are people you can talk to, though. I can help you find support."

He paused and instantly seemed to sober. "I didn't have anything to do with that girl, Officer."

"I know."

His eyes brightened. "You believe me?"

"I have no reason not to."

Joshua's phone rang again. He saw it was the police chief.

"Please, put the gun down," he said again.

Buddy stared at him and finally handed Joshua his gun. His shoulders slumped and sadness crossed his gaze. "Maybe today's not my day to go."

With a sigh of relief, Joshua helped Buddy get settled back inside his house. He called Buddy's brother who lived about thirty minutes away, and the man promised to come right over. As soon as Joshua had the chance, he stepped outside and called the chief back.

"Guess who just called? The state lab."

"And?"

"The DNA on the hat that Charity found outside her house? It belongs to Andrea Whitaker. This investigation is officially open again."

CHAPTER 28

Charity sat in the police cruiser, the window cracked to allow some air to come in. She shivered as Joshua's conversation with Buddy floated into the car.

She'd never thought about the way animals were trained, but hearing the explanation that came from Buddy's lips made it sound awful and inhumane. Food deprivation until the animals did whatever you wanted? It seemed barbaric.

She stared at the dogs in the kennels across the property. Dalmatians. Was it a coincidence that Buddy raised the same kind of dog that Andrea had loved?

Fanning her face with her hand, she scooted farther down in the seat. Instead of dwelling on those dogs, she tried to process what Joshua had told her earlier.

Ron Whitaker had multiple affairs.

Mrs. Whitaker was possibly leaving her husband for someone else.

It was true: nothing was as perfect as it seemed. Nothing.

People used their delusions to justify remaining in bad situations. People used their false perceptions to feed untruths, which led them to do horrible things to other people. It made murder seem okay, made hurting people seem acceptable, or made stealing seem like the right thing.

Charity preferred to live without any misconceptions. But was that possible? Maybe that concept was a delusion in itself.

For so long, she'd felt like God was a delusion. But then Joshua had talked about how deepening his faith had turned his life around. Daleigh had talked about living with a hope outside of this world. She'd sung about a compassionate God who loved His creations.

Though Charity, in theory, believed in God, she knew she wasn't living as one of His followers. Maybe something inside her was starting to change. She desired to change her life, to see beyond her earthly circumstances.

Just then, Joshua climbed into the car, bringing with him that scent that was becoming all too familiar—leathery aftershave. She could soak in that soothing aroma all day.

"Sorry you had to sit through that," he started.

"It was no problem. How's Buddy?"

"I think Buddy is okay," he started. "The chief doesn't think I need to take him to the psych ward over in Elizabeth City. His brother is coming over instead."

"I could talk to him. I've talked people down from the ledge before. I just don't want to intrude."

Joshua shrugged. "I don't think he had any intention of ending his life. I think he just wanted someone to talk to."

"Most people do."

He started the cruiser. "Listen, I know we didn't get that lunch in. How would you feel about me grabbing some sandwiches and going back to Daleigh's place? There's something I want to talk to you about. Then I'm going to have to write up a report on Buddy, unfortunately. Visiting Sam Childs will have to wait until later."

"Sure thing." The look in his eyes had Charity curious.

He had news.

She wasn't sure she'd like what Joshua had to say,

either.

Joshua pulled up to the pharmacy and ran inside. He returned ten minutes later with two bags saturated with the scent of toasty bread and gooey cheese. They didn't say much until they reached Daleigh's. They walked out to the pier and sat in the chairs there, but neither of them touched the food.

Anticipation made Charity's heart beat in her ears, made her throat ache. A million worst-case scenarios raced through Charity's mind.

"I didn't want to tell you this in public. I thought privacy would be better." Joshua drew in a long breath. "In light of everything that's happened recently, the chief was able to push through the DNA testing on that hat from your porch. We got the results back today."

Charity's shoulders tensed. She couldn't decide what news she wanted to hear: that the DNA did or didn't match Andrea's. Both would have different consequences on her psyche.

"Okay," she managed to croak out.

Joshua's eyes bored into her, something unspoken there. He rubbed the back of his neck and let out a small gasp of air. "Charity, the DNA matches Andrea's."

She let out a slight gasp.

"I know this is probably hard to hear," he murmured.

She shook her head, the implications of what he'd said still racing through her head. "Then . . . then Andrea really could still be alive. Maybe I'm not going crazy."

***

Joshua hated to leave Charity, but the extent of her involvement in this official investigation couldn't go but so far without crossing professional boundaries.

Right now he needed to talk to the chief.

Lynn waved from the filing cabinet when he walked in, and Joshua knew that Isaac was out on another call. He walked toward the chief's office and started to knock when he heard her voice ringing out on the other side.

"I understand that, but it's not best for this town if she's here. Look at all the trouble that's been stirred up."

Silence stretched as Joshua imagined the person on the other end responded.

"It won't matter soon anyway. Everything's going to change. I hope Joshua understands."

He bristled. What was the chief talking about? This was the second suspicious conversation he'd overheard. The chief was definitely hiding something.

His first instinct was to burst into the office and demand answers. But he had to be careful how he played his hand. In a split-second decision, he decided to hold on to this information and see what else he could find out before tipping off the chief.

He tapped at the door with his knuckles.

Silence stretched another moment—or was she whispering?—and finally Chief Rollins called for him to come in.

"Officer Haven." Her face was unusually absent of emotion, almost as if she was trying too hard to look innocent. "What can I do for you?"

"I wanted to talk to you about that DNA."

She shook her head slowly, as if in awe. "I couldn't believe the news either. Sure enough, that hat belonged to Andrea."

"So what's the state of this investigation?"

She straightened. "It's back open. I don't want it on the back burner anymore. Do what you need to to find some answers. This takes priority now. I'm about to call Ron Whitaker and inform him of the news."

Just then, her phone rang again. She put her hand over the mouthpiece after she answered and whispered to Joshua, "If you'll excuse me a moment."

Joshua nodded, trying to gather his thoughts. Something was going on with the chief, and he'd really like to know what.

In the meantime, he retreated to his office and pulled up his computer. As it booted, the questions played in his mind: Could the chief have it in for Charity also? Maybe Ron had brainwashed her with his lies as well. Joshua would need to keep his eyes wide open.

When his email popped on the screen, Joshua was surprised to see an email from his forensic artist friend Gayle Trent. He clicked on it, his eyes scanning the words there.

She had an age progression photo ready. She also made a note that she *had* worked on this photo several years ago.

So why wasn't it in the files? Joshua wondered. Something was starting to smell fishier all the time.

Joshua held his breath as he clicked on the attachment. A moment later, a picture appeared on his screen.

He froze when he saw the image there.

It perfectly matched the woman he'd seen in the gas station.

The woman who'd been in his house.

It perfectly matched Andrea.

CHAPTER 29

Someone cleared her throat behind Joshua. Quickly, he closed the picture file and turned. The woman who'd stopped by earlier in the week stood awkwardly in the doorway. Something about her looked different, he realized. Perhaps it was the fact that her gaze looked haggard, maybe even desperate.

"I was hoping I might have a moment of your time, Officer Haven." Her voice was so soft he could barely understand her.

"Of course." He directed her to a seat across from his desk. She sat across from him. The woman didn't appear nervous as she looked at him, but sorrow lined her eyes. "How can I help you?"

"There's someone I know. I'm afraid she might be in trouble." Her voice quivered.

The woman had Joshua's full attention now. "Trouble how?"

"I'm afraid someone is going to hurt her."

Joshua shifted, wishing she wouldn't talk in riddles. Yet he knew the intricacies of domestic abuse situations. Fear usually tarnished the victim's every emotion, every decision, every word. "Can you be more specific?"

She closed her eyes, as if gathering her courage. When she pulled her eyelids open, she avoided Joshua's gaze and instead looked down. "No, not really."

"I really want to help, but it's going to be difficult without more details. Would you like to file a report? Get a restraining order?"

The woman's fingers twisted together in her lap. "I'm not sure I can give more details."

"What can I do to help, then?"

"I'm not really sure. He's growing more unstable, though. He's acting irrationally . . . again. I fear what might happen."

"Who's growing more unstable?" He could only assume it was her husband or boyfriend.

The woman suddenly stood, as if she'd been spooked. "I should go now."

"Ma'am?" Joshua called after her. This was why the police force here needed someone on staff like Charity. Victims needed someone to be on their side, and not all of them trusted police officers, for one reason or another.

She had taken two steps away but paused, hesitantly turning her head toward him. "Yes?"

"Could I have your name at least?"

She rubbed her lips together. "You can just call me Jasmine."

With that, she left.

***

Charity tossed in bed that night, unable to find rest. She had too much on her mind, and every time she drifted to sleep, images of Andrea haunted her.

More and more, the evidence seemed to point to the fact that Andrea was alive. Not only that, Charity felt like her friend was here in Hertford and that she was reaching out to her.

But so much still didn't make sense.

Why was her friend still hiding? Why not just come to Charity or the police or her father, even? Wouldn't that make more sense?

There was obviously more to this story than Charity understood.

Her time here was ticking away, and soon she'd have to make some decisions. Could she really go back to Tennessee if she didn't have any answers? But what about her job? Would she be able to hold on to her position if she stayed in Hertford longer?

Just then, a strange sound caught her ear. She froze. What was that?

Maybe Daleigh was awake and getting some water. That was probably it.

Yet the sound—a subtle creak—seemed like it came from somewhere closer.

Her room?

Charity's skin crawled at the thought.

No, that was silly. The sound couldn't have come from so close.

Then why wouldn't she pull her eyes open? Why did fear grip her?

Charity held her breath, listening for something else—anything else.

Silence crackled.

She must have been imagining things. Maybe the house was settling. Or maybe a branch from outside had scraped the roof. There was no need for her to overreact.

All the eerie things that had happened recently messed with her head.

With that thought in mind, Charity tugged the covers up a little closer around her neck and squeezed her eyes shut. She just needed to get some sleep. A good night's rest could make everything seem clearer.

She still had so much to do. She had to finish filing the proper paperwork for the house fire, figure out what to do with the property, and try to rid herself of the spell Joshua seemed to have on her.

After all, she couldn't ever stay here. And with his son close by, Joshua couldn't ever leave. Their relationship was doomed before it even started. Circumstances had thrown them together, but now her emotions were playing with her head.

Her body went stiff again.

There was that sound again—a subtle creak.

Where had it come from?

Be brave, Charity reminded herself. Fear was only effective in dangerous circumstances, not when it was irrational.

Right now, her fear was irrational. It was a by-product of her circumstances.

Lord, I know it's been a while. But I need You now. More than ever.

She counted to three and drew in a deep breath.

Then she opened her eyes.

Before she had time to scream, a figure wearing a black mask pinned her down. A needle pricked her skin, and then everything went black.

***

First thing the next morning, Joshua went to talk to Sam Childs. Sam was the man—although it was just rumor, as

Lucinda had said several times—that Roberta Whitaker was going to leave her husband for. He still lived in the area, and Joshua couldn't help but think he might know something. It was a possibility worth exploring.

He pulled up to a newer home in a subdivision built especially for seniors. The area was well kept and on the water—one of the newer additions to Hertford. He found unit number 372B and rang the doorbell. A man who hardly looked old enough to be retired answered.

He was medium height with a middle-age pooch at his midsection and salt-and-pepper hair, both atop his head and across his chin, cheeks, and upper lip.

"Sam Childs?"

The man stared at him cautiously. "Yes?"

"I'm Joshua Haven with the Hertford police. I was hoping you might have a moment to chat."

He stared a moment before nodding crisply. "Come in. I was hoping you might come by. It took you long enough."

Joshua's curiosity sparked. What did that mean?

The man didn't offer him a drink or even a place to sit, really. But when Sam lowered himself into a small beige recliner, Joshua took that as a cue and lowered himself into the wooden chair across from him.

"You've been expecting me?" Joshua asked.

Sam rubbed his beard. "That's right. You're here about Roberta, correct?"

Joshua nodded, more intrigued than ever. "Correct."

"I've always believed there was something more to her accident. I couldn't get anyone to believe me, though."

Anticipation buzzed through Joshua's blood at the man's implication. "Why did you think that the accident wasn't so accidental?"

Sam let out another sigh, rubbed his beard one last time, and leaned back. He'd been carrying this burden a long time, Joshua realized.

"She started looking into Andrea's disappearance," Sam said. "She called me and told me she needed to talk to me about something she discovered."

"Did she say what she discovered?"

"No, I just know she was going to meet someone. She was supposed to tell me the other details later. The accident happened before she could do that." He swung his head back and forth, a certain melancholy washing over him. "I guess I'll never know."

"Mr. Childs, what was the nature of your relationship with Roberta Whitaker?"

"We wanted to get married. She was going to leave her husband." His voice caught and he looked away.

Joshua could see that Sam was struggling, and he softened his voice. "How did the two of you meet?"

A faint smile feathered the man's lips. "Believe it or not, we met on a dating website."

"You knew she was married?"

His smile disappeared in an instant and was replaced with a scowl. "She was miserable."

"Why?"

"Ron was never the same after his daughter disappeared. All his negative qualities were amplified. He drank more, worked more, and cheated more. She couldn't take it anymore. She should have left him years earlier. Maybe this would have never happened if she had."

While Joshua let that thought settle, another question came to mind. "Did Ron know that Roberta was leaving him?"

Sam rubbed his hands against his legs. This was

obviously hard for him to talk about. "She'd just told him three days before. He wasn't happy. He said she couldn't leave him. They had too much history together, and she was his rock."

"Did that sway her?"

Sam shook his head. "No, she was done and ready to announce to the world that she loved me. She wasn't afraid to go public with everything she'd been hiding for so many years. On the outside, everyone thought they were a perfect family. But they weren't. They were as dysfunctional as families come."

"How so?"

"Cheating. With the cheating came fights, distrust, arguments. They tried to protect Andrea from all of that. When she was gone, there was nothing to hold them back. In fact, they blamed each other. Ron blamed Roberta for being at a meeting and unable to pick Andrea up. Roberta blamed Ron for not being able to find her. It was a mess."

"What did you mean when you said you could never get anyone to believe you about the accident?"

"I reported what I knew to the police chief."

"Chief Rollins?"

Bitterness stained his eyes. "That's right. She brushed it off. Said my story was the most ridiculous thing she'd ever heard. She didn't exactly use those words, but I got the message loud and clear."

"Did you have any evidence?"

Sam locked gazes with Joshua. "Roberta told me her husband threatened her. Isn't that enough?"

Joshua didn't bother to tell him no, that wasn't always enough. The man wasn't in the right mental state to hear that revelation.

"But there was more to it. I think the reason Chief Rollins never followed up on my suspicions was because of Ron.

She thinks a lot of him. Ron has a lot of people under his belt."

"What purpose would it serve to stage a car accident?"

"Maybe it was the whole 'If I can't have you, no one can' mentality."

Joshua had seen it happen before and knew that could be a real possibility. "That does happen."

Sam leaned toward him, his gaze still intense. A new emotion appeared in his eyes. Outrage, maybe? Suspicion? Hatred. "The only other possibility was that Roberta discovered something about Andrea's disappearance that someone didn't want her to know. Maybe someone killed her for it."

CHAPTER 30

Charity sensed something was wrong, even before she was fully conscious.

She tried to open her eyes, but they were still so heavy. But something had changed—in her gut she sensed it. The air smelled and even felt different around her. Her mattress didn't feel soft, but instead lumpy and sharp. And she was unusually hot.

Pay attention, Charity.

What else felt different? Something tickled her leg, she realized. What was that?

And why did it feel like there was a fan blowing on her, gently swaying her hair away from her face?

Wake up, Charity.

With a start, she jerked her eyes open. She sucked in a deep breath at what she saw.

Trees surrounded her. Mosquitoes buzzed around her face. Birds chirped.

Something tickled her leg again. She glanced at her bare calf and saw a hairy spider creeping across her skin.

She flung it away, subduing her scream as she scrambled to her feet, desperate to get off the ground. But she nearly fell over as she drew herself to full height. Her head spun; her thoughts were fuzzy.

What was going on?

How did she get here?

Where was *here*?

As her breaths came faster, shallower, she backed up until she hit a tree. She attempted to suck in a deep breath, but her unease prevented her.

Get a grip, Charity. Assess the situation.

She tried to take some controlled breaths in order to steady her heartbeat. She had to think clearly here. Her life depended on it.

When her heart rate slowed—even just slightly—she tried to gather her bearings. She scanned the area.

Trees stared back at her from every direction. There were no other markers to identify which set of woods she might be in.

How had she gotten in the middle of nowhere?

Then, like a punch to the gut, she remembered.

She remembered the creaks in her bedroom. She remembered sensing movement. Then someone was on top of her, covering her mouth. She'd felt a prick.

She'd been sedated, she realized, rubbing her arm where the needle had poked her.

Then she'd been dumped here?

At once she realized exactly where she was.

She was in the very spot where Andrea had been abducted.

She shivered, despite the heat outside.

Quickly, she glanced down, assessing herself. She didn't appear to be injured. Her clothing was intact, and there were no obvious signs of struggle. At least she could be thankful for that.

She had to get out of here. But which way should she go?

Calm down, Charity. Think. Breathe.

She closed her eyes a moment. The river ran north to

south. Her house was to the south of the woods.

Glancing above her, she spotted the sun hanging in the sky to her right. She'd use that for her guide right now, and determine which direction was south.

She took her first step and winced. All she'd worn to bed was an old tank top and some flannel shorts, so her bare feet weren't protected from the rocky, gnarled soil beneath her.

Despite her discomfort, she kept moving forward. With each step, she listened for the sound of anyone nearby. What if the person who'd done this to her was still close? What if he watched her now?

The thought caused nausea to churn in her gut.

Just keep moving, Charity. Keep moving.

She reached the area where the woods turned swampy. Her gut roiled again as she inhaled the rotten, putrid scent of the wetlands. There was no way she'd get through this part without sinking her feet into the stagnant water.

She could do this. She had no choice.

Holding her breath, she tried to step across the first puddle. Her feet sank into the mud on the other side. She squirmed as imaginary critters raced across her skin.

The swamp was no place to be barefoot.

But that was the least of her worries right now.

Who had left her here? Why? What message was this person trying to get across?

It couldn't have been Andrea. She wouldn't have been able to lift Charity and carry her here. But who? Lawrence Whitaker, maybe?

Just then, something slithered in front of her.

A water moccasin.

Charity drew back just as the snake coiled and prepared to strike.

GONE BY DARK

***

Joshua slowed as he passed Kicking Cotton Bar after leaving Sam Childs's house. The chief and Ron Whitaker exited the building, talking like old friends.

What exactly was the chief doing at the bar at this time of the day? He glanced at his clock. It was only 10:00 a.m., so the bar wasn't even open.

He started to pull in to get some answers once and for all when his phone rang. He saw Daleigh's number and took the call.

"Joshua, have you seen Charity?" Panic laced Daleigh's voice.

Tension pulled between his shoulders. "No. Why?"

"She's gone."

His heart skipped a beat. "What do you mean gone?"

"I thought she was sleeping in, and I didn't want to disturb her. But a few minutes ago I decided to check on her, to make sure she was okay. Her bed was empty."

"Could she have gone on a walk?"

"Joshua, I've been awake since seven. No one has come or gone since then. Besides, her window is open and all her things are still here, including her phone."

Fire rushed through his blood. Something was wrong. Majorly wrong. He should have seen this coming, but he'd have to address that later. "I'm on my way to your place right now."

He turned on his lights and sped down the road. Quickly, he dialed the chief, putting aside for the moment the fact that he'd seen her with Ron.

"Charity White is missing," he told her, his heart hammering with each word. "I'm on my way to the scene now."

"Missing? I'll meet you there. I'm just leaving a meeting now."

Joshua's mind raced. Charity. What had happened to her? A sick feeling gurgled in his gut. If someone had hurt her . . .

He shook his head. He couldn't think like that. He had to remain in control of his emotions.

His knuckles whitened as he tightened his grip on the steering wheel.

Lord, watch over her. Protect her. Open my eyes and help me see how to find her.

He reached Daleigh's place in under five minutes, hastily threw his car into park, and then hurried toward the house. Daleigh stood on the porch, her arms pulled tightly across her chest. Ryan was with her. The tension etched across his friend's features deepened his own apprehension.

"We didn't touch anything because we didn't want to mess with the scene," Ryan said.

"Show me her room."

Daleigh led him down the hallway of the small house. He paused at the doorway and observed the space.

The bedsheets were tangled. The window was open—all the way open—and the screen was only partly on the window, probably shoved back in place in someone's haste to leave.

"You didn't hear anything?" he asked Daleigh.

She shook her head. "I sleep with music playing, though. I should have thought ahead and realized—"

Joshua shook his head, cutting off her thought before she had time to develop it. "Don't blame yourself. You couldn't have known."

But he should have.

"We did have the windows open earlier. The breeze

coming in from outside was so nice. She may have kept her window cracked as she slept. She said something about loving fresh air."

He walked to the other side of the bed, looking for a clue about what could have happened. As he leaned down on the floor, something under the bed caught his eye.

It was a syringe.

Had someone drugged Charity and then abducted her?

He had to find her.

As soon as possible.

He knew with certainty that her life depended on it.

CHAPTER 31

As Charity stared at the snake, goose bumps covered her arms.

The snake stared back.

Her blood went cold as the standoff continued. Slowly, Charity took a step back.

The snake looked poised to strike at any minute. She wouldn't stand a chance out here if the moccasin's venom seeped into her blood. These woods would be her death. Her nightmare had started here. Would it end here also?

Trying to keep her nerves at bay, she scooted back ever so slightly. Her foot hit something wet.

She didn't care. Not at the moment.

The snake remained unmoving.

She took another step and water covered her ankles, the mud below it suctioning to her feet and causing willies to race across her skin.

When she reached the other side of the dirty muck, the snake lowered its head and finally slithered away.

She let out the breath she held.

That had been close. Too close.

She had to get out of these woods. If the elements didn't kill her, anxiety would.

Charity burst into a run, moving as fast as she could across the uneven ground. Thorny underbrush, unseen roots, and nearly invisible spiderwebs met her at every step. Her feet were bleeding and sore, but she didn't care. She just had to get out now.

Her lungs burned under the strain of her run. Sweat poured down her neck and forehead. Her hair clung to any available skin.

All she could think of was getting to safety.

If she were honest with herself, all she could think about was finding Joshua. Somewhere along the line, she'd begun to think of him as her shelter.

Don't be like your mom, an internal voice said.

Her mom had always turned to men as the answer. Charity didn't want to be that woman, didn't want to follow in her mother's footsteps.

But at some point the lines blurred. At some point, people had to depend on others, not out of weakness but out of wisdom.

Finally, rays of light broke through the foliage ahead.

She pictured the field behind her house and prayed that her instincts were correct.

In her haste to get to safety, her foot came down on something sharp. She jerked her leg up and saw a broken stick, one of its ends raised in the air and now covered with blood.

She checked, and sure enough, the bottom of her foot had a large gash.

She clenched her eyes shut. The wood had gone deeper than she'd thought. She picked some splinters from the wound, biting back the pain, resisting the urge to squirm.

Using a nearby tree, she pulled herself up. She tried to put pressure on her foot, but pain rushed through her. She wanted to cry but couldn't allow herself that luxury.

It was going to take some time, but Charity was going to move. She was going to get out of these woods if it was the last thing she did.

And it very well might be.

***

The chief and Isaac were both on the scene at Daleigh's house. Isaac took photos and dusted for fingerprints while Chief Rollins took plaster impressions of the shoe prints outside the window.

Joshua had interviewed some neighbors, searched Charity's phone records, and begun to put together a rough timeline. But similar to Andrea's abduction, there was little evidence to go on. He couldn't stop pacing as his mind ran through possibilities.

Ryan put a hand on his shoulder. "What can I do for you?"

"I wish I knew. I have no idea where someone might have taken her, but I feel like I'm not doing anything right now. The further we get away from the time she disappeared, the more likely it is that she'll never be found."

Just like Andrea, he thought. He didn't voice the thought aloud.

"You can't think like that," Daleigh said.

"I know, but this is what I did for a living for five years. I know the statistics."

"Statistics are wrong all the time. I used to work the stock market, so I should know," Ryan said.

An idea began to form in his head. Chief Rollins said yesterday that she was going to tell Ron Whitaker about the hat. What if Ron blamed Charity again? What if he thought she'd planted that hat when she came back into town? The man wasn't rational. Could he have recreated Andrea's abduction in order to teach Charity some kind of morbid lesson?

He started to tell the chief his theory, but then changed his mind.

He didn't trust the chief right now. Until then, he needed to stay quiet.

"I'm going to pay a visit to someone," he told his friends.

"Don't do something you'll regret," Ryan said. "You want me to come with you?"

"No, stay here, just in case you hear something. I'll keep you updated."

***

Charity reached the edge of the woods and spotted Joshua's house in the distance. If she could make it there, maybe she could get inside and call for help. In the very least, she could wait for Joshua to get home. It beat being lost in the woods.

Besides, she wasn't going to make it much farther on her own. Her body ached. Her head swam. Fear kept trying to creep in.

She stepped onto the field, the grass rough and coarse beneath her. She limped along, trying to reach the house. His truck was out front, but she knew that was only because Joshua was in his police cruiser today.

Her own house stood in the distance—at least the remains of it did. What was left of it almost seemed like a tombstone or a sad memorial to her past. She desperately wanted to be victorious, to change the course that seemed to have been set in motion for her as a child.

When she finally reached the back door of Joshua's

house, she nearly fell against it. Her foot was still bleeding, and it ached worse than ever. Her legs were covered with sludge and welts from mosquitoes and biting flies.

She turned the knob, but it didn't budge. Of course Joshua's house was locked up. He was smart enough to do that. But back when she and Andrea were children, the window to Andrea's room had never locked properly. The girls had been able to sneak in and out. As adolescents, it had seemed harmless. Looking back, it was anything but.

That window was the only chance she had of getting into Joshua's house, other than busting out one of the glass panes on the back door.

She pulled a wicker deck chair over to the area where Andrea's room was. Climbing up, she carefully pushed on the panes. To her relief, the window slid up. All these years, and no one had either checked it or bothered to fix it.

She pushed it up high enough that she could climb inside. Using the last of her energy, she heaved herself into the opening and fell onto the floor on the other side.

She was safe. For a moment, at least.

***

Joshua pounded at the door to Kicking Cotton. He kept knocking until finally someone answered.

"We're closed," Ron Whitaker started. When he spotted Joshua, he did a double take. "Officer Haven."

Joshua stepped forward, making sure his foot blocked the door. "Did you do something to her?"

"Do something to who?" The man narrowed his eyes, his voice rising.

"Charity."

Ron's hands went to his hips, and a knot formed between his brows. "Why would I do something to her?"

"To run her out of town. To make her pay for mistakes she made a decade ago. Because you think revenge will make you feel better."

"Slow down, now. I don't like the girl, but I wouldn't hurt her. What's going on?"

Joshua tried to subdue the anger simmering inside him and remain a professional. Being a hothead wouldn't get him anywhere. In fact, it would make him take steps backward. But he knew time was of the essence right now, and he didn't want to play games.

"Charity is missing, and I'm not convinced that you don't have something to do with it," he said, his voice even.

Ron raised his eyebrows. "That's a big accusation."

"I know the chief told you about Andrea's hat."

"You think that I think Charity planted it?"

Joshua waited for his response. "Do you?"

"The thought crossed my mind. None of this stuff started happening again until she came into town. You know the saying 'The apple doesn't fall far from the tree'? Well, Charity's mom was neurotic. Maybe Charity has some of that in her also."

Joshua raised a finger, fighting the impulse to do something stupid—like punch Ron Whitaker in the face. "If you laid a hand on her, it will be my one and only goal to make sure you see justice."

Ron stared at him a moment before raising his hands. "I've done some stupid things. But nothing that stupid."

"Were you stupid enough to kill your own wife?" Joshua put the question out there, knowing it could be dangerous to bring up. But he wanted to see the man's reaction.

Surprise flashed in his eyes, and then anger. "What are you talking about?"

"The fact that her accident may not have been an accident. That you found out she was cheating and leaving you, and you couldn't stand it."

"You best keep your mouth shut, boy." The man's hands clenched into fists, and he looked ready to snap at any minute. "You have no idea what you're talking about."

"I think I do."

"How dare you come on my property with these accusations? You have a lot of nerve." The man's nostrils flared.

He wished he had enough to bring the man in, but he knew he didn't. Not yet at least. But Ron Whitaker remained at the top of his suspect list.

Joshua started to reply when his phone rang. He squinted at the number on his caller ID. It was . . . his own?

As tension crept between his shoulders, he stepped back and answered. "Hello?"

"Joshua. It's me. Charity. I'm at your house. Please help me."

CHAPTER 32

Charity splashed water on her face again. She'd managed to drag herself into the bathroom and bandage her foot. She'd also pulled her hair back and borrowed a sweatshirt from Joshua's drawer to cover her tank top.

While she was in his room, she'd taken a moment to stare at a picture of Joshua and his son atop the dresser. Joshua looked so happy with his arms wrapped around the boy and the beach in the background. Joshua should be close by for his son; it was the right thing.

As she dried her face with a towel, her legs collapsed beneath her. Her adrenaline had worn off, taking any energy she had with it. She sank to the floor.

She pressed her face into the bathroom cabinet, relishing its coolness. Thanking God she'd made it this far. Pushing away her questions, knowing she'd have time to dwell on them later.

Victorious. The word repeated in her head again. She was determined to live it out in her life.

The front door opened, and Joshua's voice cut through the air. "Charity?"

"Back here," she called, her voice weaker than she would have liked.

Footsteps hurried through the house until Joshua appeared in the doorway. The next instant he was in front of her. His hands grasped her face, his thumb stroking her cheek.

"Oh, Charity. Are you okay?"

She nodded. "Now I am."

He quickly assessed her with his gaze. "What happened? I need to get you to the hospital."

"No, I'm fine. Really. I just need a shower and some clean clothes."

He pulled her into his arms. Her head fit perfectly beneath his chin, like they were made for each other. He didn't let her go; she didn't pull away.

And, in that moment she felt certain that Joshua was the kind of guy who'd give up his life for someone he loved. Maybe he'd even give up his life for her. Her heart twisted at the thought.

He kept an arm around her and reached into his pocket. "I've got to call the police chief, okay?"

She nodded.

"How about if I get you off this bathroom floor first?"

Before she could say anything, he stood and swooped her into his arms. He carried her to the couch and laid her there. The soft cushions had never felt so good.

He stayed beside her, almost as if afraid to let go as he dialed a number on his phone. He mumbled a few things to the police chief, and when he hung up, his eyes were warm with concern.

She squeezed his hand. "Sorry about breaking into your home."

"How—?" He shook his head. "Never mind. Let me get you some water."

She nodded. Her heart felt full as she watched him walk away. She'd be a fool to ever let someone like Joshua slip by. She'd never really felt that way in her life about anyone.

He appeared a moment later with some water and

some crackers. She pushed herself up and took his offerings. The water had never tasted so good.

As she gulped some down, he sat on the end of the couch and looked at her foot. "What happened?"

"I stepped on a stick. I think I cleaned it out."

"You mind if I take a look?"

"I suppose not."

He started to unwrap the bandage. She squirmed even thinking about the injury. But all of this could have been worse. Much worse.

"Are you . . . are you hurt in any other way?"

"No," she said before adding more firmly, "No. I'm just scared and bruised. But I'm okay."

"So what happened?"

She ran through the story, all the way up to climbing in through Andrea's old window. Talking helped distract her from the sting of ointment that Joshua applied to her foot.

"You think it was the same person who snatched Andrea?" Joshua asked, resting his hand on her leg.

"It all matches. The mask, the sedation. But why leave me in the woods? That's what doesn't make sense."

"I don't know either, Charity. But I'm going to find some answers for you. I promise."

***

Despite Charity's protest, Joshua took her to the hospital. She needed a blood test to see what she'd been injected with. He also wanted to have her foot looked at. With an all clear from the doctor, he dropped her off with Daleigh two hours later.

Joshua wished he could spend the rest of the day with

Charity. But he left her with Daleigh and Ryan and went into the office. He had to find some answers, and with every second that ticked past, his chances diminished.

As soon as he walked into the station, the chief came toward him. "Who do you think you are?"

"Excuse me?"

"You questioned Ron Whitaker?"

"Someone had to."

"What's that mean?" The chief's hands went to her hips.

"It means Ron Whitaker should be our prime suspect in this case, and you seem to be protecting him."

"That's not true." She raised her chin.

"I saw you with him this morning at Kicking Cotton."

Something flickered in her gaze. Surprise, maybe? Finally she nodded slowly. "If you must know, I have been working with Ron Whitaker on a new initiative."

"What kind of initiative would that be?" Doubt edged his voice.

"I can't speak about it right now."

He leaned closer and lowered his voice. "Are you covering up something?"

Her eyes narrowed. "I thought you knew me better than that. And do I need to remind you that I'm your superior?"

Joshua didn't back down. "Ron Whitaker has a hold on this town. He shouldn't be treated any differently than anyone else."

"I promise you, I'm not giving him any special privileges."

"Then let me bring him in for questioning."

"On what grounds?"

"I have journal entries written by Andrea Whitaker as a

teen that mention him, I have a woman who said she gave Ron a false alibi during the time of the abduction, and I have a man with anger and control issues."

She stared at him a moment, puckering her lips in thought. Finally, she said, "We'd be opening a can of worms like you've never seen."

"It would be a disservice to the people of this town if we didn't properly question him."

"Just because someone drinks, has a temper, and is a sorry excuse for a person doesn't mean they abducted their own daughter."

"I'm not saying he did. I'm just saying he should be questioned. I'd also like to look at the accident report for Roberta and see if there was anything suspicious."

"His wife?"

He nodded. "She was investigating her daughter's death before she died."

Her eyes widened with surprise. "Interesting. There's one other thing I want you to seriously examine: Charity White's involvement in all of this."

"Why would Charity be behind this?"

"She's the link that connects all of this. This trouble only started when she got back into town."

"You think she set her own house on fire and nailed her doors shut?"

The chief maintained her gaze. "She could have climbed in and out of a window."

"Why?"

"I heard she might receive a hefty insurance settlement."

Joshua still wasn't buying it. "And she staged her own abduction?"

She pressed her lips together for a moment. "I'm just saying to keep your eyes open."

"I will. And I'm keeping them on Ron Whitaker."

***

Ron Whitaker didn't appear happy when Isaac led him into the station. He stared at Joshua with open hostility as he was ushered into the interrogation room.

Joshua sat across the table from Ron, noting Mr. Whitaker's stiff posture and cold, aloof gaze.

"You don't know what you're stirring up," Ron grumbled.

"I'm not afraid of you, Ron."

The man glared. "You should be."

"If you're so innocent, you won't mind answering a few questions. Are you behind the attempts on Charity's life?"

"Haven't we been over this?"

"Just answer the question," Joshua told him.

"Of course I wasn't behind the house fire. I'm not stupid."

"Your oldest son did place a homemade explosive device in Daleigh's mailbox when Charity was there. Your family is the most likely ones who'd want to run her out of town."

Ron's face went pale. "You've got nothing to prove it. I know my boys. They'd never take it that far."

Joshua leaned toward him. "I've also discovered that some of the files in the case have mysteriously disappeared. There's no way there's only one box of reports on Andrea's disappearance. There aren't even any records of leads that have been called in in recent years. Something about that doesn't ring true. Anything you want to tell me?"

Ron raised his chin. "I don't know what you're talking about."

"I think you do."

He held his gaze with Ron until the man looked away. Joshua didn't speak; silence pressured people to say things they might keep quiet about otherwise.

"I may have taken a few things home with me," Ron finally admitted, his jaw clenched.

Bingo! Just as he'd thought.

"I need to see them. And you could face charges for stealing police property. I'm sure you already know that, though."

"I was just trying to find out what happened to my daughter. Everyone else moved on and forgot. But I haven't. I can't."

"I need to see them," Joshua repeated.

Ron seemed to sober and nodded begrudgingly. "I'll bring them in. And I promise, I didn't hurt Charity."

"Like you didn't hurt her by not reporting when one of her mom's boyfriends attacked her?"

His eyes widened. "You know about that?"

Joshua nodded. "I do."

Ron rubbed his eyes a moment. "That was a hard day. I still regret that."

"So why didn't you do it?"

"It's complicated."

"I have time."

He frowned. Looked at the ceiling. Tapped his foot. "Because I'm not a faithful man."

"So I heard."

"I'd fooled around with Charity's mom once," Ron continued. "She threatened that if I took action against Will, she'd tell my wife that I'd been unfaithful. I didn't want to lose Roberta. Despite everything I put her through, I loved her."

Outrage flashed through Joshua. "So you let a teenage girl suffer?"

He closed his eyes, his shoulders slumping. "I know it wasn't right. But, at the time, we were fighting all the time. I was trying to look out for my own little girl and salvage what was left of her childhood."

Ron's words made him sick to his stomach. How could the man live with himself?

Someone tapped on the two-way window behind him. He pushed away from the table, giving Ron one last dirty look. Then he stepped outside. It was the chief.

"The hospital's on the phone. You're going to want to hear what they have to say."

CHAPTER 33

Charity had to fight the tremors that quaked from her soul the rest of the day. Every time she closed her eyes—sometimes even when she didn't—she remembered the terror of waking up to find someone in her room. Of waking up again and not knowing where she was. Of trying to fight her way out of the woods in order to find help.

Daleigh wouldn't let her do anything except sit on the couch with a book in one hand and the TV remote in the other. It was just as well with Charity; her foot still ached, and whatever she'd been injected with caused lingering lethargy.

Daleigh came and sat across from her, a cup of hot tea in hand. She patted Charity's leg before leaning back with a sigh. "So, just for the record, I'd like to say that I've never seen Joshua so worried about someone. He was beside himself this morning."

"It's his job to worry," Charity said. He was a police officer; she couldn't let herself forget that.

"I don't know about that." Daleigh shrugged. "I mean, sure, he's a cop. But I think he's going above and beyond for you. I think he really cares about you, Charity."

Charity's cheeks heated, yet she couldn't deny that the idea made her insides feel warm. She had to keep reality in the back of her mind, even though her heart kept taking her in a different direction. "Joshua makes it easy to want to trust. I've been let down every time I put faith in someone, though. I can't say I'm in a hurry to do it again."

"I know it's hard. Believe me, I know. But Joshua is a good guy. I promise. If there's anyone you can put faith in, it's him. Back in June, he helped to coach a local Little League team. He's always the first to volunteer when something needs to be done at church. You can't fake that kind of sincerity."

Though the images warmed Charity's heart, she reminded herself again that she couldn't let her emotions run wild. "He is a good guy. But, even if I didn't have trust issues, our lives could never merge together. I live in Tennessee. That's where my life is. I couldn't ask him to move away from his son. That relationship is too sacred."

Daleigh raised her eyebrows. "But you could move here."

Charity shook her head, nearly scoffing aloud at the thought. "My life isn't here in Hertford. It never will be. This place is like a haunted house—wherever I go, there are bad memories popping out and traumatizing me."

"I never thought I could have a life here, either. So much of country music is centered around life in Nashville. But it's funny how things work out for the best when we take leaps of faith. I don't miss my old life at all. I feel so much more grounded here, yet at the same time I've grown. Being here is more than I could have ever imagined."

"I wish I had the kind of faith you do," Charity said. "But I've learned I can only rely on myself. I don't want to be my mom. Men were like drugs to her."

"You may share your mom's DNA, Charity, but you're the one who determines who you are. Don't ever forget that. Besides, no one can only rely on themselves. No one."

Charity let her words sink in, her first instinct to deny

what she'd said. But, in her heart, Charity knew that her friend had spoken the truth.

That, however, didn't change the decisions she had to make.

Life was too short to live in a place that reminded her of all the pain she'd endured. No amount of good done here would ever change that.

***

The police department had been granted a warrant to search Buddy Griffin's property after the hospital confirmed that the substance injected into Charity was a tranquilizer, one that was usually reserved for animals.

Maybe Buddy, who'd bred dogs and used to work for animal control, would have a drug like that on hand. The judge seemed to agree, which was the only reason they were here.

Chief Rollins, Isaac, and Joshua had all been at Buddy's for three hours, searching anything small enough to hold tranquilizer or syringes. Joshua had taken the inside of the house, which was just as junky as the outside. The man probably hadn't cleaned the place in years.

Buddy ranted in the background, mumbling things to himself as he paced on his porch. Joshua ignored him and kept searching through kitchen drawers, cabinets, canisters, and the pantry. If there was something here, they were going to find it. They had to in order to put an end to this nightmare.

"Chief, over here!" Isaac called from outside.

Joshua stepped onto the porch and followed the chief over toward the junk car parts that lined the front of Buddy Griffin's property.

Isaac held out a bag. As they approached, he opened it

with his gloved hands. Inside, there was a black mask and a syringe.

Joshua's heart skipped a beat as he tried to reconcile this evidence with his own instincts. Something wasn't adding up in his mind.

Buddy Griffin? Could he really be behind all of this? Even Andrea's abduction? It just seemed too easy.

"I think we've found our man." The chief gave a pointed look toward Joshua, one that clearly indicated he'd been off base by suspecting Ron Whitaker. "Let's arrest Buddy. I think we finally have some answers in this case. Ron Whitaker, as well as the rest of this town, will be very happy to get some closure."

What if Buddy didn't hide those items on his property, though? What if he'd been set up? Joshua knew they'd be wise to examine that possibility.

***

At ten that night, someone rang the doorbell at Daleigh's place.

Ryan, who had insisted on sleeping on the couch, answered. "Hey, Joshua. Come on in."

Charity sat up straighter, her heart lifting when Joshua came into view. Something about seeing him also made her feel better.

"Hey, there," she murmured.

He still wore his police uniform. And he looked tired. The fact that she hadn't heard from him since this afternoon probably meant he'd been busy. But with what?

"I hate to stop by so late, but I hoped I might talk to Charity for a moment."

She stood, wincing as she put pressure on her leg. "Sure

thing."

In the blink of an eye, Joshua was by her side. He slipped an arm around her waist and helped her take some pressure off her injury. "You think you can make it outside?" he asked.

She nodded, despite her gritted teeth. "Of course. The fresh air will be nice."

"Sorry to steal her away from you," he called over his shoulder.

"I suppose we can spare a few minutes away from her." Daleigh winked.

Joshua helped Charity onto the porch steps. She lowered herself there, stretching out her leg. He sat down beside her—right beside her. Close enough that their legs brushed and she could feel the body heat coming off him.

Something about that realization made her cheeks warm. Joshua Haven definitely had an effect on her, whether she liked it or not. The attraction between them was real and fluid and electrifying.

The night around them seemed perfect—too perfect, almost. Crickets chirped and frogs sang their nighttime song. A gentle breeze brushed over the water, making the temperature comfortable and keeping away any nocturnal critters. The smell of approaching rain tinged the air with a sweet scent.

And being beside Joshua made it even more perfect.

"How's your foot?" he asked, his voice soft.

"It will be okay. It hurts right now. But it could have been worse. That's what I keep telling myself." She paused, sensing he was delaying his real purpose for being here. "Why do I have a feeling you have something heavy on your mind?"

His smile faltered, and he rubbed his neck a moment. Finally, he turned toward her. "I wanted to let you know that we've arrested Buddy Griffin. The chief believes he's the one who abducted you and the one who abducted Andrea."

"What?" Her voice was just above a whisper.

He nodded slowly. "The substance you were injected with was an animal tranquilizer. Buddy had vials of the drug on his property, apparently from his work with animals. However, while searching, we also found a black mask."

"I can't believe it."

He pressed his lips together silently, but a storm raged in his eyes. What wasn't he saying?

"You don't believe it either, do you?" she asked.

He let out a long breath. "It seems too easy, too convenient. I'm not convinced yet. The chief is. She's already claiming this is a victory."

"I guess time will tell." But Joshua was right. The clues seemed to have appeared easily—too easily, perhaps?

"Plus there's the fact that a woman's footprints were found at the arson. Even if Buddy is guilty, either he's working with someone or we have a separate crime committed by a separate perpetrator."

His words chilled her. He was right. This whole investigation was more intricate than Charity would like. The end still might not be in sight.

"There's more," Joshua continued. "I thought you should know that I talked to Ron Whitaker about Will Redmere. Ron told me the reason he never opened an investigation into Will was because, at some point, Ron had an affair with your mom."

"What?" Charity gasped.

Joshua nodded, his eyes soft with compassion. "It's true. Your mom threatened that if Ron made a big deal over what Will had done, she'd air all of Ron's dirty secrets."

"She chose her comfort over my safety." She shook her head, an overwhelming ache squeezing her heart. "She doesn't even deserve the title of mom."

"But look at you. You turned out well, despite everything."

"Thanks. But I can't believe my mom would stoop that low. She didn't ever care, did she?"

He squeezed her knee again. "I didn't know your mom, Charity. But I know drug addiction can change nice people into monsters. You okay?"

Charity nodded. "I wanted to know, even though it was hard to hear. I just want to put that part of my life behind me."

"I knew you were strong enough to handle it," Joshua said. "In the meantime, we still have to be careful. I'm glad Ryan's staying here tonight. I'm going to be working late—maybe all night, even—to process all the evidence from today."

"I understand."

He let out another long sigh. He looked tired, and Charity wished she could offer something to help. But short of making him a cup of coffee, there was little she could do.

"I should be getting back, Charity," he said, his voice low and almost apologetic.

"Thanks for stopping by." She didn't want Joshua to leave, yet she knew he had to go.

Joshua helped her to her feet. Heat rushed through her as his fingers grasped her elbow. This wasn't good. Maybe Charity was beyond the point of caution, despite her better instincts. Her feelings seemed to be fueled and ready for takeoff.

They stood in front of each other on the porch for a moment, nature singing its symphony around them. A pattering of rain had started on the roof overhead, and thunder gently rumbled in the distance.

Charity wasn't sure exactly what to say. She licked her lips and tried to formulate a proper thank-you.

"You should know that I'm meeting Sarah Reynolds tomorrow," she blurted. "It's about selling the property."

An unknown emotion flashed in his eyes. As quickly as it appeared, it was gone. "I see. You should let me go with you, just to be safe."

"You have a lot of work to do. I'm sure I can handle this. Besides, Sarah will be there."

"I can meet you there. Like I said, I just want to be cautious, especially until we know something for sure."

She nodded. "Okay. I'll wait for you there. Ten thirty."

His gaze caught hers and made her heart do somersaults that were Olympic worthy. In the next instant, his arms reached around her waist and he pulled her closer.

Time seemed to slow down for a moment. He leaned toward her, drew her in, and lowered his lips toward hers. The kiss only lasted a minute before he pulled her into a hug, burying his head in her hair, her neck.

"I was so worried about you," he murmured. "I don't want anything to happen to you, Charity."

She clung to him a moment, unable to deny her feelings, unable to deny their connection. "I always feel safe around you, Joshua. There are very few people I can say that about. Maybe only you, for that matter."

He pulled away, a tortured look in his eyes. He brushed his lips against hers another moment. "I have to go."

"Good night, Joshua."

That's when she realized that leaving Hertford—leaving Joshua—would be one of the hardest things of all.

CHAPTER 34

Joshua got two hours of sleep the night before, but he was back in the office by 6:00 a.m., ready to work. He had too much on his mind to rest.

Charity remained at the forefront of his thoughts. He'd thought about her all night, wondering how she was. Remembering his fear when he'd heard she was gone. Replaying how his heart skipped a beat when he found her on his bathroom floor. Relishing the tender, honest look in her eyes as they'd shared their lives over the past several days.

One thing was certain: Charity wasn't Justina. It wasn't that Justina had been a bad person; it was mostly that Justina veered on the side of being superficial and selfish. The moment things hadn't gone her way, she'd looked for greener pastures. If only they could have talked things out, if she'd made him aware of the way she was feeling before it was too late.

But all of that was water under the bridge now. Justina was remarried, and he'd gotten over her.

Charity, though, seemed so much deeper and more natural. She was beautiful without all the hair and makeup and fancy clothes. Her difficult past had molded her into a person with character and substance, to the extent where she spent her life helping people, a way of using her own experiences and hardships.

But she had no intention of staying here. He had to remind himself about how hard it was for Charity to be here. Of course she wanted to get as far away as possible. There were too many bad memories for her in Hertford.

When his thoughts weren't on Charity, they were on Buddy Griffin. The more Joshua reviewed the facts of the case, the more he couldn't believe that Buddy Griffin was guilty. His gut told him something was off.

He'd talked to the chief last night and convinced her that the man might have an accomplice. She'd agreed to let him investigate more, but gave Joshua a stern warning that he needed to run things by her—especially matters involving Ron Whitaker.

Joshua still didn't know what exactly was going on between Ron and Chief Rollins. He tried not to jump to conclusions, but secrets made it difficult to know who to trust. Ron definitely seemed to have the chief in his pocket. Who else was covering for him?

"There are some boxes on your desk," Lynn said when Joshua walked in.

"Boxes?" He paused.

She shrugged. "They were there when I came in this morning. I didn't look inside."

"Interesting." He went to his office area, and sure enough, at least ten cardboard boxes were piled there. He pulled the top off the first one.

These were the files on Andrea's case that Ron Whitaker had taken with him. The chief must have let Ron inside at some point so he could leave these. At least the man had followed through.

There was also a cell phone lying on his desk calendar. Joshua picked it up and flipped it open. The date and time popped onto the screen, so the device was charged. But who did this belong to?

He picked up a piece of paper underneath it. "This was my wife's," it read. "Just in case there's anything that might help you here, take a look. You have my full cooperation. Ron Whitaker."

Joshua had to wonder what the man's tone was when he wrote the words. Most likely: sarcastic. Joshua had a hard time believing cooperation was even in the man's vocabulary.

He sat down at his desk and opened the most recently dated file. Sure enough, there were hundreds of Andrea sightings throughout the years, some from here in North Carolina, others in California, and one even in the Philippines.

This was going to take some time.

Which Joshua might not have, especially if the chief considered this case closed.

Two hours later, Joshua had sketched some notes. There had been several witnesses interviewed that Joshua had never heard about, including the school's principal, janitors, landscape crew, and even the superintendent for the county school system. Though he didn't see anything revealing in the notes, Joshua wanted to follow up with everyone possible.

Maybe someone would remember something. Maybe there'd be some new piece of evidence that would blow this case wide open.

Because Joshua couldn't live with knowing the wrong person was behind bars or that there was an accomplice out there who'd gotten away with this crime.

***

Bright and early in the morning, Charity heard Daleigh's phone ring. And ring. And ring.

The sound pulled Charity out of bed, and she stumbled

sleepily into the kitchen. Daleigh stood at the kitchen counter, a cup of coffee in one hand and her phone in the other. She rolled her eyes as she hit END.

"That's unbelievable," Daleigh muttered.

"What's going on?" Charity asked, pressing her hands into the cool granite countertop as she braced herself for whatever Daleigh was about to say.

"The media somehow caught wind of what's going on here in Hertford. They've been calling all morning and trying to get in touch with you for an official quote on the arrest of Buddy Griffin."

As Charity's knees began to buckle, she quickly lowered herself onto a bar stool. "Really?"

Daleigh nodded. "Really. I called Joshua after the first three phone calls. He says there are news crews parked outside the police station as well. He doesn't know how they found out, but he did say they're like vultures. They showed up about an hour ago."

"I guess you know a thing or two about the media."

Daleigh let out a snort. "They can be your best friend or worst enemy. For the time being, I'd suggest you just ignore them. I'm assuming you probably don't have anything to say about Buddy's arrest."

"Only that I'm not quite confident he should have been arrested."

"I'd suggest lying low until things pan out some more, then."

"Good idea. I guess it's a good thing I woke up." Charity glanced at the clock on the wall. "I'm supposed to meet Sarah Reynolds in an hour."

"Sarah? I didn't realize you knew each other."

"We went to school together. She's supposed to help

me put my property on the market. Of course, who's going to want to buy it with a huge fire pit that used to be a house in the middle of the land?"

"Maybe someone will see the potential." Daleigh paused. "How's it feel to take this step?"

"A little scary. But it's what I should do. I should have done it a couple of years ago, truth be told. I'm not sure why I've been holding on."

"Sometimes when we let go, we fear we'll free-fall. What we don't realize is there's someone who gives us a soft place to land."

Jesus. Charity knew exactly who Daleigh was talking about. The mental image her words evoked made Charity smile.

She got dressed, and when she stepped outside, she nearly withdrew when she saw the reporters on the street. *No*, Charity told herself. She'd be strong. She'd be victorious.

Keeping her head high, she ignored the probing questions that were thrown her way as she walked toward Daleigh's car.

"What do you think about the recent arrest of Buddy Griffin?"

"Do you finally feel like you have closure?"

"How has this arrest changed your life?"

Charity slammed the door, started the car, and took off down the road. Their questions still rang in her head, though.

How would Buddy's arrest change her life?

Not that much, not until she knew for certain the right man was behind bars. But she wouldn't dare share that with reporters. Anything she said would be used against her; she felt certain.

Charity shuddered again when she pulled up to her property; repetition didn't seem to lessen the gut-wrenching experience of seeing the shambles of her childhood home.

Sarah arrived right on time. Though Joshua wasn't here yet, Charity knew it wouldn't do any harm to meet Sarah. Certainly he would be here any minute. As the drops of rain started to plunk down from the sky, she reached under the seat and found an umbrella.

"My mom has the kids today, and I actually feel halfway human," Sarah said with a laugh. She straightened her shirt. She'd even gotten dressed up in a business suit to meet Charity. It was a shame that the rain dampened both her suit and her straightened hair. Charity tried to shelter them both with the umbrella.

"I'm glad you could make it out," Charity said.

Sarah's gaze fell on the ruins of the house, the caution tape around it, and the overgrown grass. Sarah didn't have to say anything for Charity to read her friend's thoughts.

"I know. It's going to be tough to sell this place," Charity muttered.

"We just have to find the right buyer," Sarah said, offering an overly optimistic smile. "Someone who's looking to build and put down roots, who will love raising a family here."

"I'm going to have to have the building demolished, aren't I?" Charity frowned as she remembered her dwindling checking account. If the insurance money came through, maybe she could use that money.

"It wouldn't hurt, but I know that's an extra cost to you. I can run some numbers." She scanned the area. "As far as the property itself, I think we could get a decent amount. It's a nice piece of land with the woods in the back, the cotton fields on the side, and a handsome single cop as the only neighbor. Some people might see that as a plus. It's far enough away from the highway to feel secluded, but close enough to town that you don't feel overwhelmed. You sure you want to sell this place?"

A lump formed in Charity's throat. "Yes. I mean, it's not like I can move back here to Hertford. Or that I'd want to." Even as she said the words, her gut twisted.

"I know you probably have some not-so-fond memories. But it's really not such a bad place. Every area has a few bad apples, but it's a shame when those people ruin it for everyone else. There are also a lot of really good people here."

Joshua's image filled her mind, and she smiled. "There are definitely good aspects of staying here."

"Besides, I heard Buddy was arrested. It's the talk of the town. No one can believe it. I mean, we all knew he was strange. But no one thought he was dangerous."

Charity's throat burned. "You just never know about people, do you?"

"You sure don't." She paused before snapping back to the matters at hand. "Well, let me take some photos. As soon as the insurance company okays it, we can put a sign out and I'll list it. Sound good?"

"Sounds great."

Sarah didn't move, though. She licked her lips instead and shifted uncomfortably.

Charity gripped her umbrella more tightly and waited, sensing that Sarah had something else on her mind.

"Charity, I know I probably shouldn't say this," she started. "I'm probably wasting my words, especially now that Buddy has been arrested. But on Sunday at the barbecue restaurant, I was actually sitting behind you—you didn't see me, but I overheard part of your conversation."

"Okay . . ." Charity tried to imagine where this was going.

"I heard you and Joshua talking about going to see Mr.

Johansson. I wasn't trying to eavesdrop. I promise." She drew in a deep breath. "You know my dad was friends with Ron Whitaker, right?"

"They were on the force together for a while, if I remember correctly."

"That's right. Anyway, you're going to think I have a bad habit of eavesdropping, but I remember my dad was talking about a disagreement Ron Whitaker had with Austin Johansson. I never really thought much about it. I figured it was adult stuff. But now I wonder what it was all about."

"You heard this recently?"

She shook her head. "No, I actually heard it ten years ago."

Charity processed what she said. Could that have anything to do with this investigation? Why would Ron and Mr. Johansson be arguing? She hadn't even realized the two men knew each other. Unease sloshed in her gut.

"It's probably nothing," Sarah continued. "But now, with everything getting stirred up again, I just have to wonder . . ."

CHAPTER 35

As Charity watched Sarah pull away, she began to climb into her own vehicle, wondering why Joshua hadn't shown up. It was unlike him.

She paused midway into the vehicle when a movement in the distance caught her eye. Her breath caught.

The motion had been so slight, it was almost like she'd imagined it.

But she hadn't.

Something had been in the woods.

Against her better instincts, Charity stepped away from the car. The rain hit her now, drenching her hair. She didn't even bother with the umbrella this time.

Sure enough, Andrea stood in the distance. She hovered behind a tree, her gaze focused on Charity.

Charity took a step toward her but stopped.

She couldn't go into the woods, not knowing that the footsteps leading to her house on the night of the fire had belonged to a woman. Not after being abducted. Not when someone seemed determined to kill her.

Something wasn't right.

Yet Charity couldn't pull her eyes away either. Her emotions clashed inside—she wanted answers, yet she valued her safety.

"Charity," Andrea said.

Her throat clenched. Andrea was calling to her, trying to

draw her out.

As if to shoo away any doubts, Andrea looped her hand in a circle, urging Charity to come closer.

Charity started to take another step forward but stopped herself. She had to give heed to the warning bells sounding in her head. There was too much that didn't add up, too much that didn't make sense.

Besides, why wouldn't Andrea come to her? Why hide in the woods and call to her?

"Please, Charity," Andrea said, her hand moving in faster circles.

Even from where Charity stood, she could see the desperation that began in her friend's eyes. She'd always had expressive eyes that easily conveyed her thoughts.

This was Andrea. Charity felt certain of it. The DNA on that hat had proved it, right?

Before Charity could ponder her choices, a car rumbled down the road. It was Joshua. He stopped beside her and climbed out. "I'm so sorry I'm late. The chief had a press conference and—"

Charity glanced toward the woods again. Andrea was gone. She frowned.

"What's wrong, Charity?" Joshua asked.

She pointed in the distance and shook her head, perplexed by the way Andrea came and went. "Andrea . . ."

"She was here?" Joshua asked.

"Just until you pulled up. Now she's gone again."

"I've got to see if I can catch her. Stay here. In the car." He burst into a run toward the woods.

Charity closed her eyes and lifted up a prayer.

Would he catch her? If he did, maybe Charity would finally have some answers.

Was that too much for a girl to ask?

***

Joshua reached the edge of the woods and paused to scan his surroundings.

He saw no one.

But Charity had said Andrea was just here. She couldn't have gotten but so far away. He needed some answers; this craziness had gone on for too long.

He slowly stepped into the forest, listening for the sound of anyone moving. All he heard was the *tappity-tap-tap* of rain hitting the leaves. Everything else seemed eerily still.

He glanced at the ground.

Footsteps led away from the area. Size elevens? He wasn't sure. But someone had been here.

He followed the impressions until they ended at a puddle of water. He searched the ground on the other side, looking for where the footsteps picked back up.

He saw nothing.

Strange. The person couldn't have just disappeared. So why weren't there any footsteps?

He continued to search the area, looking for something—anything—that would give him a clue. But all signs that the woman had been here disappeared. Finally, he turned around.

By the time he got back to Charity, his uniform was soaked and his shoes were muddy. Neither of those things compared to the disappointment he felt at losing the trail.

Charity climbed out of the car when she spotted him and met him halfway in the field. The rain made her hair cling to her face and neck, made her cotton dress hug her skin. His thoughts went where they shouldn't, and he had to look away.

"Well?" Charity asked. Her eyes were full of hope.

His gut twisted. He'd been so close. So close. "I didn't find her. But I did find footprints. They disappeared where the ground got swampy."

She closed her eyes, disappointment evident in her slumped shoulders and downturned mouth.

"She puddle jumped," Charity muttered.

"What?"

"We read a book about it as kids. We thought the idea was brilliant as a way for someone to cover their tracks. The protagonist in the story jumped from puddle to puddle, knowing it would be almost impossible for someone to track her if her footprints were hidden by the water."

"Well, that makes sense."

Charity stared toward the woods again and shook her head. "I just want some answers, Joshua. I feel like this woman is playing games with me, and I don't understand why."

He pulled her into a hug. He didn't care about the rain; he didn't care about anything else. He only cared about the woman in his arms.

When Charity stepped away, he took her hand and tugged her forward. "Let's go inside a moment and get out of this rain."

He led her into his house, drawing on every ounce of his self-control not to pull her into a long kiss. He sensed she needed emotional support right now more than she needed romance. Besides, he had to remember that he was on the job.

"Help yourself to some coffee. There are single-serve cups beside the maker. I've got to go get something," he said.

When he returned with a map, she had two cups of coffee on the dining room table. He handed her a sweatshirt.

With the AC blasting in his house, Charity would be shivering soon. "I thought you might need this."

"Thank you." She slipped it on and pulled her hair back.

His throat was dry as he tried to focus on the case. Being around Charity right now made it very difficult. He put a map on the table and cleared his throat.

"What's this?" Charity asked.

"When I saw those footprints disappear, it made me think. What if Andrea was put on a boat after she was abducted?"

"It's a possibility. We weren't far from the river."

"Exactly. There would be little evidence left if she was." He pointed to where the Perquimans met the Albemarle Sound and then led to the ocean. "If she was taken this way, she could be anywhere. But I have a different idea."

"What's that?"

"What if she was taken the opposite direction? The Perquimans ends up north, but several smaller streams spawn from it. This one, Goodwin Creek, leads all the way into Chowan County. If someone had taken her that way, she could have been held somewhere in this area." He circled the north end of the river with a red marker.

She nodded. "It's a possibility."

"Roberta Whitaker was in a car accident on her way to check out a lead in the case. Her accident occurred right here." He marked the place on the map.

"That would fit with your theory about the river. It's close to the same area."

He nodded. "Plus, think about it. You've seen Andrea here at your house, but we also saw her in Edenton. The area where I've marked is right in between the two counties."

"I think you could be onto something, Joshua. But isn't

that where Buddy Griffin lives? Does this just prove that he's guilty?"

Joshua shook his head. "He claims he's not. Plus, his property is far from the river and much closer to Hertford."

"Are there any suspects who live in the vicinity?"

"That's what I need to find out. I have almost a dozen boxes of case files that Ron Whitaker thought were his own personal property. I'm in the process of weeding through everything."

"There's one more thing. This might not mean anything, but Sarah Reynolds told me that she overheard her father—a former police officer—saying something about an argument between Ron Whitaker and Austin Johansson ten years ago."

"I'll look into it." He reached across the table and squeezed her hand. "I wish I could stay here with you longer, but the case is too hot right now."

"I understand. I appreciate everything you're doing, Joshua."

Hearing the gratitude in her voice was enough motivation to keep him going for a long time.

CHAPTER 36

Back at the station, Joshua extended his hand as he stood from his desk. "Thank you again for coming in, Principal Watkins. I appreciate your time."

"Maybe we'll finally have some answers in this investigation," Principal Watkins said. "It's been too long coming."

"You can say that again," Joshua said.

He walked the principal to the door. Joshua knew the man from church. Unfortunately, he hadn't learned any new information through speaking with him.

Joshua had also talked to three other people this afternoon, and he had two more people lined up to come in. Everyone seemed overly willing to help out. Maybe they wanted to be a part of this story or get a sense of what was going on with the investigation. Either way, he didn't complain.

Before he got back to his office, he heard the door open behind him. He turned and saw a man with hair to his shoulders standing there.

"You must be Larry Davis," Joshua said. Larry was Joshua's 5:30 appointment.

The fifty-something man nodded stiffly. "I am."

"Come on back to my office." They settled there before Joshua started. "As you've heard, we're questioning people about the abduction of Andrea Whitaker. I appreciate you coming in."

"Happy to help, but I thought it was odd. Didn't you make an arrest?"

Joshua nodded, noting that the man smelled like grass and dirt. He seemed like the outdoorsy type. "We're just trying to eliminate the possibility that Buddy was working with someone."

"I see. Well, what can I do?"

"You worked on the facilities team for the school system, correct? And you were at the school on the day Andrea disappeared?"

The man nodded again. "Correct, and correct. I worked for the school system for about six years. Mostly worked outside. But I was at the high school that day. I'll never forget it."

"The report I read said you actually saw Andrea and Charity walking away from the school."

He nodded again, his stoic personality not showing much emotion. "I did. It was unusual to see them walking home. The school is a bit off the beaten path, so most kids catch the bus."

"And you also said you saw a car pull away not long after they did. A 1998 Toyota Camry?"

The man shifted, seeming like the type who preferred working alone rather than being social. "Yes. Nothing ever came of that lead, however. I assumed it hadn't checked out."

Joshua glanced at the file. "Apparently no one at the school had a vehicle that matched that description. Do you remember seeing anyone strange at the school that day?"

The man shifted again. "Anyone strange? Can't say I did. Just the normal after-school folks—the principal, the football team, the custodian. And Mr. Johansson, of course."

Interesting that the man had called out the teacher

specifically. "Did you know Mr. Johansson very well?"

"Can't say I did. He didn't give much attention to someone like me. I wasn't pretty enough."

The statement stopped Joshua's thoughts. "Are you saying he gave attention to girls in the school?"

He nodded. "Especially Andrea and Charity. They seemed to be his favorites. It was really surprising considering the man had a girlfriend."

"I wasn't aware of that. Do you remember her name?" This could be his most revealing meeting yet.

Larry shook his head. "I don't. All I remember is that for such a small woman, she had big feet."

Joshua straightened. "Tell me more."

"I don't know how much more there is to say. She stopped by school sometimes. I can't remember her name. But she was tiny and blonde. And she always looked at her boyfriend like she didn't quite trust him."

His description sounded an awful lot like Austin's current wife. "Can you elaborate on that any?"

"I walked into the auditorium once to fix a lightbulb. Andrea and Mr. Johansson were talking about something—whispering, actually. As I was leaving, I ran into Mr. Johansson's girlfriend. She looked like she was crying. She'd just come from another exit from the auditorium. I think she saw the two of them talking also."

"Does the name Heidi ring a bell?"

The man's eyes brightened. "As a matter of fact, yes. That's her."

***

If Buddy was behind all of this, who might his

accomplice be?

    That was the question swarming in Charity's head as she hung out at Daleigh's place. Though she was, in theory, helping Daleigh put together some packets for the car show this weekend, Charity's mind was far from the task at hand.

    As hard as she thought about it, no one came to mind—except Andrea. And she couldn't bear to face the possibility that Andrea was somehow involved in trying to harm Charity.

    Charity shook her head, knowing she'd go crazy if she dwelled on this much longer. But she was practically a prisoner in the house right now. The media were still outside, so she didn't want to go anywhere else for fear of being hounded. Daleigh was on the couch, working on some new songs. When Charity's phone rang, she saw it was Lucy and answered.

    "I'm just checking in," her friend said. "I saw the news this morning. They mentioned your friend Andrea Whitaker."

    "Everything here has kind of exploded," Charity said, moving the curtain and staring at the news crew outside.

    "I thought you'd want to know that Bradley actually stopped by the office today looking for you."

    "Oh, did he?"

    "I told him you weren't in town. I think he wanted to talk to you about the case. You were right—that man is married to his career. In fact, I heard he was seeing someone else. She's a crime victim, also. His obsession is kind of creepy."

    "Maybe he just has a superhero complex." Her thoughts went to Joshua. Thank goodness he didn't have that same vice. His reason for helping wasn't superficial and didn't revolve around advancing his own career. He genuinely cared about people.

    "Anyway, I can't wait to see you on Monday," Lucy said.

    "Monday?" Charity repeated, dropping the curtain.

"That's when you have to be back at work. You didn't forget, did you?"

Charity's heart sank. She actually *had* forgotten. She'd known she had to go back, but she hadn't realized how soon her stay here would be ending. "I guess I just lost track of time."

"You *are* coming back here, aren't you?"

"Tennessee is where my job is. My apartment. And you, of course." Charity couldn't stay here forever. She had no money or career to support herself. She had no place to live, and she couldn't expect to stay with Daleigh indefinitely. To think otherwise, she'd be fooling herself.

But the thought of leaving Joshua in three days twisted her insides.

"Hope you're able to wrap things up there, Charity, and truly move on."

Her throat felt dry and achy. "Yeah, me too," she managed to croak. "Thanks for calling."

Just as Charity hung up, her phone rang again. Without even looking at the caller ID, she answered, "Yes, Lucy?"

Silence stretched for a moment. And then someone whispered, "Run."

CHAPTER 37

After another long day of working nonstop, Joshua knocked at Daleigh's door that evening. Daleigh and Ryan scampered outside as soon as he stepped into the living room.

"We have a few things to do for the car show. We'll be back at a reasonable hour. We promise." Daleigh flashed him a mischievous smile.

Joshua watched them leave and shook his head. They'd been in a hurry to get away. Or, knowing Daleigh, she just wanted to give him and Charity some time together.

Charity offered a shy smile and patted the space on the sofa beside her. He'd run home to change into jeans and a T-shirt before coming over. He was going to sleep on the couch here tonight and give Ryan a break. Until he was certain Buddy was truly guilty, he couldn't take a chance that someone might invade the house again.

It felt good to see Charity, though. To see her smile. To smell the scent of fresh strawberries that always seemed to accompany her. To look into her luminous blue eyes.

He stole a quick kiss before taking her hand into his. "I have some updates."

Her eyes flickered with curiosity. "Okay."

"I did some research, and it turns out that Austin Johansson, when he worked in Hertford as a teacher, rented some property between here and Edenton."

Charity's eyes widened. "No . . ."

"There's more. The property backed up to the water, though a person would have to cut through some woods to get there. Add to that the fact that ten years ago your teacher was dating the woman who is now Heidi Johansson."

"What does she have to do with any of this? I mean, sure, I thought they didn't get married until a few years ago, but I'm not connecting the dots."

"There are implications that Heidi may have been jealous of Austin's relationship with Andrea. Even when we were at their house last week, I saw Heidi giving you strange looks. I didn't question it too much at the time. But one of the landscaping crew said he saw a Toyota Camry pulling away from the school around the time both of you left. It just so happens that Heidi owned a Toyota Camry ten years ago."

Charity shivered. "Wow. That's . . . both creepy and disturbing."

"She also apparently has large feet. We're not sure if they're a size eleven or not, but it's a possibility worth exploring."

"You think she's involved? That she worked with someone?" Charity said.

Joshua shrugged. "I can't say for sure. But it's a distinct possibility."

"That would mean that Buddy is the wrong man. Were Heidi and Mr. Johansson working together?"

"That would make sense, but we're still tracking down clues."

"You just never know who you can trust, do you?" Charity leaned her head back against the couch and stared into the distance.

Joshua couldn't pinpoint exactly what it was, but Charity seemed especially burdened at the moment. He caught her gaze before asking, "What are you thinking?"

She rubbed her lips together a moment. "I got a phone call today, Joshua. The person only said one thing. Run."

He furrowed his brows together. "Run?"

She nodded. "It was a woman. She whispered it, so I couldn't identify the voice."

"How did someone get your cell number?"

"I had my old one transferred. The number is the same one that I got the text message from. The one that said, 'Do you want to walk through the woods?'"

This investigation just kept getting stranger and stranger. "You think Andrea is trying to warn you?"

"I have no idea what's going on, Joshua. No idea."

He pulled her into his arms and didn't let go.

She can't stay here forever, Joshua reminded himself. But, at the moment, he didn't care. All he wanted was to somehow help take away Charity's pain, despite the impact her departure would have on his heart.

***

Charity opened her eyes with a start. Just like the previous morning when she'd awoken in the woods, she knew something wasn't right, wasn't familiar.

She blinked as the living room came into focus. Her hand was flung across . . . Joshua's chest?

They'd fallen asleep together on the couch!

She quickly sat up, at once feeling foolish.

Joshua shifted and ran a hand over his face, looking far more awake than she did. "You fell asleep last night," he murmured. "I couldn't bear to wake you up. I just didn't expect to fall asleep also."

"The two of you were resting so peacefully, I decided not to bother either of you," Daleigh said from the breakfast bar. She smiled mischievously before taking a sip of her coffee. How long had she been there?

Despite how self-conscious Charity felt at the moment, she had to admit that she'd slept better last night than she had in a long time. She hadn't had her normal nightmares or night sweats or paranoia.

She stood up, already missing Joshua's warmth. "I should get ready for today."

"You have plans?" Joshua asked.

She let out a feeble laugh. "Not really. Of course, I didn't have plans to fall asleep in your arms last night, either."

He pushed himself to his feet and stretched. "I need to get into work. I've got a long day ahead of me. I'll try to check in when I can, okay?"

Charity felt her cheeks flush. His voice sounded husky, personal; its tone made it clear they were more than friends.

She was setting herself up for heartbreak, wasn't she?

"Be safe today, okay?" she said.

He nodded and kissed her forehead. "I will. You too."

He waved to Daleigh before leaving.

As soon as he was gone, Charity pulled her gaze up to Daleigh. Her friend's eyes danced with delight. "I was going to ask how things were going between the two of you. I take it they're going well."

She crossed her arms and leaned against the wall. "I'm not sure why either of us are exploring something that won't work. But when I'm around Joshua, it just feels right."

Daleigh smiled again, almost as if she knew something Charity didn't. "I pray that you'll find some of those answers, Charity. And soon. But I have to say that I know the real thing when I see it. What you and Joshua have—there's no denying the two of you are great together."

Charity couldn't bring herself to nod. Instead, she pressed her lips together in contemplation.

No job, no house, no money.

Not to mention Joshua lived in a town where most of the residents hated her. Why would Charity ever want to come back to a place that had treated her so badly? That had made so many judgments of her?

She knew the answer: she wouldn't. Ever.

***

After going home to shower and change, Joshua took off to Nags Head to talk to Heidi Johansson. He knew Austin was already back in school, since teachers went back earlier than students. But Joshua needed some answers from Heidi anyway, and he didn't want to give her too much warning.

He pulled up to her place at 10:00 a.m. and knocked at the door. She answered a moment later, a toddler on her hip and clothed in sweatpants and a T-shirt. She obviously hadn't been expecting company.

"Can I help you?" she asked, staring suspiciously.

"I'm Officer Haven from the Hertford PD. We met last week when I was here talking to your husband."

Her gaze flashed with recognition before turning cold again. "Well, Austin's not here right now, so I'm sorry you wasted a trip out this way."

"I actually wanted to talk to you."

She stared, her gaze pensive and her muscles tight. "I'm not sure I have anything to say."

"It's just a few questions about Andrea Whitaker's

disappearance."

Her eyes narrowed. "Her abductor has been captured. I saw it on the news."

"Could we talk?"

She finally pushed the door open. He stepped into her house—a small place littered with toys. She didn't offer him a seat or the opportunity to go any farther than the entryway. "What can I do for you?"

"Mrs. Johansson, how long have you been married to Austin?"

"Four years. Why?"

"How long did you date?"

"On and off for six years before that."

Joshua nodded. What she said confirmed his initial thoughts. "I understand you didn't care for Andrea Whitaker. Is that true?"

"Go play, Gavin." Once the boy scrambled away, she crossed her arms. "Now why would you say that?"

"Rumor has it you were intimidated by your husband's relationship with his student."

She broke eye contact and looked away for several seconds, as if gathering her thoughts. "Yes, that's true. At first, it really bothered me. I thought he might have an inappropriate relationship with Andrea. But he explained everything to me later."

"Explained what?"

She sighed and crossed her arms. "Andrea had discovered her dad had a girlfriend. She didn't know who to talk to about it. Not her mom or brothers. She feared her whole family was going to fall apart. So she talked to my husband and got his advice."

"What did he tell her?"

"To stay out of it. It was an adult matter, and she wouldn't be helping anything by getting involved. Apparently, Ron found out about their conversation, and the two of them nearly got into a fistfight. Ron told Austin to mind his own business and to stay away from his daughter."

So that was the fight Sarah Reynolds had mentioned to Charity.

"I also have a feeling that was one of the reasons Austin was never formally a suspect," Heidi continued. "Ron knew if he pressed charges or made too big a deal of things, Austin could bring up the affair."

That was why someone shouldn't have a broken moral compass and be an officer of the law: there were too many ways people could leverage their indiscretions against them. Ron Whitaker was a case in point.

"Just one more question."

"What's that?"

"What size shoe do you wear?"

"Ten and a half. Why?"

"Just wondering."

She stared at him. "I didn't have anything to do with this. There's something else you should know, though. Despite the fact that my husband and I haven't been on the best terms lately, I have been worried about him."

"Why's that?"

"He acted strangely after you and Charity stopped by. Kind of moody. But two days ago, he decided he needed to take off for a while. Right before he left, he was kind of freaking out. I haven't heard from him since."

CHAPTER 38

"Joshua, I need to see you in my office," Chief Rollins said as soon as he arrived back.

"Yes, ma'am." He followed her through the door, closing it behind him, and sat across from her. "What's going on?"

She laced her fingers together on her desk and locked gazes with Joshua. "There are a couple of things I need to tell you. The first is about Ron Whitaker."

"What about him?"

"I know you think something suspicious has been going on between us, and I can finally set the record straight. I've been speaking to Ron because he's friends with the former police chief down in Wilmington."

"That's where your son lives, right? Is he okay?"

"Jason is fine. He's more than fine, actually. He and his wife are having a baby."

Joshua's eyes widened. "That's great. Congratulations."

"Although I'm way too young to be a grandmother, I'm very excited. So excited that I'm taking a new position down in Wilmington so I can be closer."

"What?" Certainly Joshua hadn't heard correctly.

The chief nodded. "I'm leaving. Ron helped me meet with the right people, and he put in a good word for me. That's what all the secrecy has been about lately. I couldn't say anything until I knew for sure."

"I don't know what to say. Congratulations."

"Thank you." She nodded. "I want you to know that I put in a good word for you with the mayor. I think you'd make an excellent chief. You're more than qualified. You don't back down to people, and I think you'd actually be good for this town."

"Thank you, Chief. That means a lot."

Her smile fell. "But there's something else we need to discuss. Charity White."

His muscles tensed. "What about Charity?"

"We actually got word back from the North Carolina Bureau of Investigation. We sent them the shoe prints from the fire at Ms. White's house. Lab analysis indicates that the person outside Charity's window was wearing shoes that were too large for them."

"I don't understand."

"I'm saying that someone was trying to throw us off her trail. The shoe impression wasn't even, indicating the tips of the shoes were empty. All the weight was in the center, for lack of a better scientific term."

"I see. But what does this have to do with Charity?"

She frowned, the lines on her face deepening. "I had Isaac go through her trash can today."

A moment of outrage flashed through him. "You got a warrant?"

She shook her head. "It's trash day, so the can was on the street. It's fair game. Anyway, we found these inside." She reached under her desk and pulled out a pair of tennis shoes.

When she turned them over, Joshua saw that the markings on the bottom matched the prints found at the scene. He also saw the "Size 11" on the sole.

But why were they in Charity's trash can?

There was no way she was involved in this . . . was there?

"Let me talk to her."

"Are you sure you can be objective?"

"Yes. You have my word."

The chief nodded. "I expect nothing less."

***

Charity felt that familiar delight when she saw Joshua at her door. But when she stepped out to greet him, she immediately noticed he seemed stiff, professional.

"Can I come in a moment?"

Any joy she'd felt disappeared. Something was wrong. "Of course. Come on in. Daleigh's practicing some songs in the back."

He sat on the couch, but not beside her. He purposely waited until she sat down, and he sat across from her. More unease sloshed inside her.

"Charity, I have to ask you something. It's going to be uncomfortable."

"You can ask me anything, Joshua. I'm not keeping anything from you." Despite that, a touch of perspiration trickled down her back.

He shifted, obviously uncomfortable. "Charity, the chief found some shoes in your trash can today. They were size eleven, and they match the ones from the arson."

"Okay . . ." She shook her head, trying to shake out the fact and shake away the confusion. "I don't wear a size eleven." She held up her feet.

He swallowed hard. "No, but we have evidence that proves whoever wore the shoes outside your house didn't fit into these shoes. She wore them to mask the true size of her feet."

"What? Why would someone do that—?" Her face fell as reality hit her. "Oh. Someone wanted to make it look like Andrea."

"That's correct."

"But who—?" Realization hit a second time. "You think I did that?"

Joshua shook his head and reached for her hand. "No, Charity. I didn't say—"

She pulled away from his touch. "You didn't have to say it. I think it's pretty clear."

"Charity, listen. It's my job to follow every lead. I didn't want someone else to come here and tell you this."

She stood, all her emotions rising to the surface in one volcano-like explosion. "To tell me that I'm guilty?"

"I don't think you're guilty." He said the words a little too calmly, almost like he wanted to placate her.

"Why was someone looking in my trash in the first place?" Her hands went to her hips. She knew it would be an understatement to say she was feeling defensive.

"Charity, please, sit down."

"I don't want to sit down."

He let out a quick breath. "The chief found out you're receiving a nice insurance payout from the fire. She thinks you had the most to gain from the arson."

"But you saw Andrea. What does she think—that I hired someone who looks like my friend and asked her to show up at random times?"

Joshua didn't say anything.

Charity sank back to the couch and buried her face in her hands. "I can't believe this."

Joshua moved closer. "Charity—"

She shook her head. "Save it. I thought you were different."

"I don't think you're guilty, Charity."

"I don't know who to believe anymore. This town thought I was guilty ten years ago, and now they're still trying to think of reasons I might be guilty." She looked at him, her gaze hot. "Are you taking me into the station?"

Joshua shook his head. "No."

"Then I think I'm going to lie down."

Before Joshua could say anything else, she hurried back to her bedroom. Suddenly Monday seemed like a really long time away.

CHAPTER 39

Despite the craziness this week, Joshua felt like he had an obligation to help with the fund-raiser the next day. His heart felt heavy as he replayed his conversation with Charity yesterday. He couldn't stop thinking about it. The hurt in her eyes had been enough to give him nightmares.

How could Charity think he wasn't on her side? Hadn't he proven that? Things had been going so well between them. Couldn't she see he was trying to look out for her?

Of *course* he didn't think she was guilty. She'd been set up. Maybe Buddy had been set up also. By who? Austin Johansson?

There was an APB out for the man, but he hadn't been spotted yet. Joshua needed to question him; the man had disappeared for a reason. Did it have to do with this case?

Joshua manned the grounds at the car show as Daleigh warmed up onstage. The weather was looking perfect for the day—warm, but not too humid or hot. A good number of people had shown up for the event, so he hoped it would be a good fund-raiser for Ryan's nephew. That's what this was all about.

As he patrolled the area, he stopped to greet several people. He glanced over at the ticket booth and saw Charity there, smiling at a family at the entrance.

His heart warmed quickly before cooling. His gut twisted when he thought about her leaving, when he thought about their fight.

He'd known from the start that Hertford was only a temporary stop for her; Charity's life was back in Tennessee. Yet a part of him had begun to hope.

If he were honest, he'd admit that he couldn't stop thinking about her. She'd surprised him. The emotions Joshua felt when he was with her surprised him. He didn't think he'd ever feel this way again, not after Justina broke his heart. Yet here he was. Despite the pain in his past, he hoped for love again. At least, he had until yesterday.

Charity caught him watching her and narrowed her eyes at him. She was still upset. Would she ever forgive him?

He sighed and paced around the perimeter of the property, making sure everyone was behaving in an orderly manner. Isaac was here somewhere also, but both had their radios on, just in case something popped up somewhere else in town.

Joshua paused and scanned the area.

Why did a bad feeling churn in his gut? Everything appeared to be going smoothly.

Yet he couldn't help but think that maybe this would be the perfect place for whoever was behind the recent crimes in town to strike again. He wanted to keep an eye on Charity, just in case trouble stirred.

Daleigh began crooning from the stage, her smooth voice quieting the crowds. People began migrating toward the stage area with every strum of her guitar. So far, so good.

"How's it going?" Ryan asked.

"Everything is running smoothly." Almost too perfect. He kept that part to himself.

"Good. That's how I wanted everything to play out." His friend paused and looked at him. "What are you thinking?"

"What do you mean?" He hadn't wanted anything to ruin his friend's day, especially since he was so excited about helping out his nephew.

"I know we've only been friends for a few months, but I can already tell something's bothering you," Ryan said.

He glanced over at Charity again. She still stood there at the ticket booth, smiling warmly and looking surprisingly at ease. "I hope no one will use this venue to advance their own agenda. You know what I mean?"

Ryan nodded slowly. "Unfortunately, I do. With everything that's happened, you never know when danger will strike again. I'll help keep an eye on Charity for you. Does that work?"

"I'd appreciate it."

"I heard the two of you had your first fight yesterday."

"You did?"

Ryan shrugged. "I guess Charity was pretty upset. Despite that, I know she cares about you. Just give her some time."

"Thanks, man."

Ryan's gaze zeroed in on someone in the distance. "I was kind of hoping he wouldn't show his face around here."

Joshua followed his gaze. Ron Whitaker. "Yeah, I was thinking the same thing. But too many people in this town think the man walks on water. He's too prideful to hide away from the world."

As if Ron sensed Joshua was talking about him, he stormed over to them. "I take it your got my files."

"I did."

He leaned closer, lowering his voice. "I want to be in the loop."

Joshua understood his implications, but knew better

than to show his outrage. "Of course we'll share any information that we can."

Ron leaned even closer. "If you don't, I can ensure you won't make chief. Don't forget that."

Joshua tilted his head, certainly he hadn't heard the man correctly. "Are you threatening me?"

Ron glared. "I'm just stating the facts."

Before Joshua could respond, his radio crackled. It was the chief. Maybe that was a good thing, but Ron Whitaker was about to get an earful.

"Excuse me." He stepped away.

"I just got a call from the Edenton Police Department," Chief Rollins said. "They found a body. I need you to go and check it out. Now."

"I'm helping with the car show, and that's out of our jurisdiction."

"It's important. You'll see when you get there."

***

Charity looked up from collecting tickets and saw Joshua walking toward his car. Why was he leaving? Had something else happened?

Yesterday crashed into her mind. She'd trusted Joshua, and he'd let her down. As if that wasn't bad enough, that evening she'd overheard Ryan telling Daleigh that Joshua was up for chief. Maybe he was just like Bradley and all about his career. How could she have been so blind?

"Hey, Charity."

She looked over. Ryan and Brody had approached. She'd been so distracted she hadn't noticed them there.

When she saw the looks of concern on their faces, she

frowned. "What's wrong?"

"Joshua got called away on a case," Ryan said. "We just wanted to check on you."

Her eyebrow twitched with annoyance. "Did Joshua put you up to this?"

"He's worried about you, Charity," Ryan said.

"I don't know what to say. I really don't want to talk about it, either." She took tickets from another family. "This is a bad time."

"Well, if you need anything, just let us know," Brody said. "Okay?"

"I appreciate it. Thank you."

Despite her hard feelings toward Joshua, knowing he wasn't here anymore made her feel more exposed. She didn't have much time to think about it, though. More families were coming through.

She let out an inward sigh. She had more important things to worry about than Joshua anyway—things like untangling the mystery of what had happened to Andrea. She felt like she was close—so close. But the answers kept slipping away, right before she could grab ahold.

As the crowds started to die down, Sarah turned to her. They were working the ticket booth together. "I'd say this event was a smashing success," Sarah said.

"I'm so glad. I know Joshua, Ryan, and Daleigh put a lot into this."

"Why don't you go take a break?" Sarah said. "Grab something to eat, listen to the concert for a minute, maybe even sit down."

"I don't want to leave you."

Sarah waved her off. "Oh, don't worry about me. I'll be fine. This is really a one-person job at this point. Most people who wanted to come are already here, since the concert has started."

"I think I will take a little break, then," Charity said. "I'd love to listen to Daleigh for a minute."

"Go and enjoy yourself. Daleigh is worth listening to."

Charity stepped away. As she started toward the stage, she glanced over at the woods surrounding the property. A movement there caught her eye. She paused and shook her head.

No, she was seeing things.

Her throat tightened. Not this again. It couldn't be.

But a figure slowly emerged from the woods.

Andrea.

Her friend stopped at the tree line and stared at Charity. How long had she been there? Had she come just to watch Charity?

A chill raced down her spine.

It was time to put an end to this, once and for all.

She needed to talk to the woman who kept appearing. She didn't have time to tell anyone where she was going; if she did, her friend might be gone. Charity would only go to the edge of the woods and would maintain a safe distance.

She took off in a jog and bypassed antique and classic cars. As she moved, she kept her eyes on Andrea, afraid she might disappear. But she didn't; her friend remained right where she was.

Charity pushed herself harder, afraid the opportunity to get some answers would vanish. She wanted to see her friend close up and confirm she was still alive. Surprisingly, Andrea still didn't move.

Charity glanced back, just for a moment. Everyone was talking amongst themselves; there was no one to see where she was going, what she was doing. She hoped she didn't regret this.

She reached the woods, and sucked in a deep breath as she got her first close-up look at her friend's features.

"Andrea?" she whispered. "It is you!"

CHAPTER 40

Joshua blanched when he pulled up to the scene in Edenton. He knew he'd seen this address somewhere before.

This was the property Austin Johansson had rented when he taught in Hertford.

A swarm of police cars surrounded a wooded area of the lot now.

Joshua walked toward the police line, flashed his badge, and then ducked under. He found the officer in charge and explained who he was. Officer Wagner was in his fifties and had a thick mustache and serious eyes.

"We thought this might concern your police department, so we wanted someone here to check it out," Officer Wagner said. "At noon today, we received an anonymous call saying that there was a body on this property. An officer came to check it out. At first he didn't find anything."

The two of them started walking toward the woods. Joshua could see a sheet draped over something in the distance. Something that looked an awful lot like a body.

"Two more officers came out, just to make sure the lead wasn't bogus. After a more extensive search, a woman's body was discovered."

As they reached the edge of the woods, the officer pulled back the sheet.

The face Joshua saw there made him suck in a deep breath.

It was Andrea Whitaker. Dead.

***

"Andrea . . . what happened? Why are you here? Where have you been?" Charity asked. She started to reach for her, unsure if she could believe her eyes. But Andrea withdrew.

Her friend looked both directions, as if fearful of being seen. Then she motioned for Charity to step deeper into the woods, deeper out of sight.

"Just a little farther," she whispered. "Please."

She seemed scared. Why would Andrea be scared?

Answers seemed so close. After years of wondering what had happened . . . Charity could stop guessing. Maybe she could regain some of her peace.

Just a step farther wouldn't hurt anything . . . would it? Charity hesitantly walked into the woods. She looked behind her, noticing that she was out of sight now of most of the people at the car show. A shudder raced through her.

"Let's go to the police, Andrea. You can explain everything there. Your family will be so happy to see you." She needed to reason with her friend before this went any further.

"I can't," Andrea whispered. "Can't you see?"

"I don't understand," Charity said.

"It's so complicated, Charity. But I've thought about you nearly every day for years. I've been waiting for this moment." Her friend's face twisted in a bittersweet smile.

"You know I don't like the woods, Andrea. Can we go somewhere else? To Daleigh's house, maybe."

Something flashed through Andrea's eyes. That's when Charity paused.

This woman's eyes were brown. Andrea had blue eyes.

Charity sucked in a deep breath at the realization. Something wasn't right. Something was majorly wrong, in fact.

"I'm sorry, Charity," Andrea whispered.

"For what?" Instinctively, she took a step back, an internal voice urging her to run.

"For this." Andrea pulled her hand from behind her back.

Charity hardly had time to see what she held. Before she could put everything together, a wave of electricity shot from the device. The next instant, Charity was on the ground. She couldn't move. Couldn't scream. Couldn't escape.

She was at the mercy of . . . a stranger.

***

After Joshua called the chief, he called Ryan.

"Do you see Charity?" he asked, pacing outside his police cruiser at the scene.

"Not right now. Is everything okay?"

Nothing was okay, but he didn't have time to go into details. "I need you to find her for me. It's urgent."

"I'll look around."

"When you find her, don't let her leave your sight. And call me right away, okay?"

"Yeah, man. I'll do that. I don't know what's going on, but it doesn't sound good."

Joshua looked at the body in the distance. "It's not."

He slid his phone back into his pocket and joined the other officers. He squatted near the body and stared at the woman in front of him. This woman definitely looked like Andrea Whitaker. But how could that be? The body wasn't decaying at all, yet Joshua didn't think she'd died recently either. Something was off.

Her clothes were damp, her hair looked sticky, and her skin had a blue tinge. There was no odor like he might expect from a body that had been left somewhere for an extended period of time. Rigor mortis hadn't set in, either.

If Joshua had to guess, this body had been frozen. It was the only way to explain all the facts in front of him.

So who was that other woman, the one he'd seen in the gas station?

Unease churned in his gut.

Something was majorly wrong.

"Any idea who called in the tip?" Joshua asked Officer Wagner.

"We ran the number. It belongs to someone named Ron Whitaker."

Joshua shook his head. "I just saw Ron. He wouldn't have been that sloppy. He's a former police chief."

Officer Wagner stared at him a moment. "You think he's being set up?"

"I think a lot of people are."

His phone rang, and Joshua saw Ryan's number. He answered before the first ring ended. "Ryan. What's going on?"

His friend's voice cracked. "Joshua, it's Charity. She's gone."

CHAPTER 41

Charity's head pounded. Her tongue felt dry. Her muscles trembled.

Everything rushed back to her, and she jerked her eyes open. Fear instantly gripped her.

As her body worked faster than her mind, she scrambled to her feet. Something pinched her ankle. She glanced down and saw a metal cuff attached to a chain. The chain was anchored to a pole.

A shudder rippled through her. She glanced around, feeling like none of this could be real. She was surrounded by a cage. Outside. A water bowl was on the ground. A bag of bread was in another bowl.

She looked up. A canopy of trees stretched above her. She was in the middle of the woods, she realized. In some kind of enclosure.

A small shed, one that looked like it had been pieced together with scrap wood, was in the corner. But otherwise, there was nothing as far as she could see.

She remembered seeing Andrea. She remembered feeling a shock.

She'd been Tasered, she realized. Andrea had Tasered her.

But it wasn't really Andrea, was it? The woman had looked like Andrea, but there was something different.

This had all been a trap. Had it been a ruse to lead her

here? To this point?

Her throat felt so dry. She stared at the bowl of water. It looked like something that would be left for dogs. Was that for her to drink?

She took a step toward it, hoping to maybe splash some on her face at least. But she jerked to a halt. The chain on her leg didn't reach that far. The bowl was just barely out of reach.

Her energy was waning already, probably an effect of the electrical charge her body had experienced. She slid down the pole, praying her head would stop wobbling.

Lord, how am I going to get out of this?

She pulled at the chain attached to her ankle. It was thick and heavy. There was no way she could break through.

Despair tried to creep into her thoughts. She couldn't let it. She had to stay positive if she was going to get out of this.

And she really didn't want to die out here, all alone.

***

Joshua wove through the crowds at the car show. He, Chief Rollins, and Isaac were questioning everyone to see if anyone had seen Charity.

"Officer Haven, can I speak with you a moment?" Ron Whitaker said. The man's eyes looked bloodshot. But instead of looking angry, as he usually did, he seemed somber. Chief Rollins must have broken the news to him about Andrea. Compassion pulsed inside him.

Joshua nodded. "Of course."

"I saw Charity walking toward the woods about an hour ago." He nodded in the distance.

"When was this?"

"About two o'clock."

"Did you see anyone else?"

"I didn't." He shook his head.

Joshua stared at him. "How do I know you're not making this up to distract us from something else?"

"You don't. But I am telling the truth. I meant it when I said I wanted to help you and that I didn't want to see anything bad happen to Charity."

"Where's your phone?"

Wrinkles formed in the corner of the man's eyes. "My phone? What's that have to do with anything?"

"Just answer the question."

"I lost it this morning. It disappeared while I was at Kicking Cotton."

Joshua nodded, not having time to go into all of this now. There'd be time later to question Ron more thoroughly. "Is there anything else you can remember about Charity?"

"She almost seemed like she was in a daze or something. She was definitely on a mission."

"Did you think about following her?"

"I did go after her, but by the time I got to the woods, she was nowhere to be seen."

"And you didn't think to call the police?"

"She didn't seem to be in danger, and I tried to go after her. Look, I'm sorry. I'm a lousy drunk. I always have been. Alcohol has messed up my life in more ways than I can express. I had a few drinks before I came, and I'm not as quick as I would like."

"You want me to feel sorry for you?"

He shook his head. "I've spent too much time feeling sorry for myself."

He called Ryan and Isaac over. "We need to search these woods."

"Let me help," Ron said.

"I'm not sure I can trust you to do the right thing."

"I promise. You can."

Finally, Joshua nodded. "One wrong move and I may have to take justice into my own hands, though."

Joshua searched the edge of the tree line, around the area that Ron had indicated he'd seen her. He really hoped the man wasn't trying to lead him astray. But something in his gaze had looked broken. Joshua only hoped he wasn't making a mistake.

"Joshua, over here!" Ryan called.

He ran across the grass toward him.

"Look. There are some footprints here. Maybe some drag marks," Ryan said.

He studied the ground. Sure enough, there were two sets of prints. Both were on the smaller side. Two women, maybe?

His chest tightened.

Sure enough, beyond the footprints were drag marks, and based on the distance between the lines, the imprints could have been left by a person being dragged through the woods.

As he followed the tracks a considerable distance, an image formed in his mind of what had happened, and he didn't like it. Charity had been sedated again. Then someone—most likely a woman who was imitating Andrea—pulled her through the woods.

The marks ended at a dirt road that cut through the woods. There were fresh tire tracks there.

Charity had been put into a truck. That meant she could be anywhere by now.

His gut twisted. This wasn't good. It wasn't good at all.

***

Charity straightened as she heard footsteps. Was someone coming? She wasn't sure if she felt relieved or more horrified. There was no telling what this person might do to her once he or she arrived. Just what was their plan for her? Maybe she didn't want to know.

A moment later, the woman who looked like Andrea appeared. She walked to the fence, linked her fingers on the metal, and stared at Charity.

When she didn't speak, Charity finally did. "What do you want with me?"

"You're going to like it here. I promise." She smiled, her gaze full of hope.

"I'm chained up like a dog." Charity tugged on her restraint, knowing it would do no good.

"It's for your own good."

Charity jerked at the chain again. "I fail to see how."

"We're going to be such good friends," the woman said, a puzzling smile on her face. Her gaze didn't quite register reality. "You'll see eventually."

"Who are you?"

She tilted her head. "You don't know."

Charity shook her head. "No, I don't."

"We're going to be like sisters, Charity. Just like you and Andrea were. Every girl deserves to have a friend like you."

"I don't understand." Charity tried to put the pieces together, but nothing made sense.

"Andrea was my sister."

Charity shook her head. "Andrea didn't have any sisters."

The girl laughed a little too long. "But she did. Ron

Whitaker is my father. That makes Andrea my half sister."

The man had a history of being unfaithful. But he'd fathered another child. That would explain the uncanny resemblance.

Charity licked her lips. "Who snatched Andrea?"

It wasn't possible that this woman had done it. A man had taken Andrea. A large man. But somehow this was all connected.

"No, my father did."

"Ron Whitaker?"

"Ron Whitaker only gave me his DNA. My real father is a decent man who loves me."

The sickening truth began to settle in Charity's mind. "Did you keep Andrea locked up here, too?"

The woman smiled that empty grin. "She fought it at first, too. But eventually she came around. She started to like it here. Didn't even try to run away. You'll like it, too."

Charity took a step closer. "You've got to let me go. There are a lot of people who are worried about me."

"Dad's going to take care of them. You should just forget about the people from your past."

Something lodged in Charity's throat. "What do you mean?"

"Well, I'm really just talking about that police officer you're always with. Father thinks he could be trouble, so he's going to take care of him. So don't worry. Life is so much simpler out here. You'll see."

A small cry escaped from Charity. No. Not Joshua. Please, no.

The woman started to walk away.

"Wait!" Charity called, panic edging in.

The woman paused. "Yes?"

What was Charity supposed to say? She had so many more questions; there was so much she didn't know. Instead, she blurted, "What's your name?"

"Claudia."

"Claudia, I'm thirsty." She glanced at the water bowl, the one just out of her reach.

A look of what almost appeared to be satisfaction—maybe smugness—flashed in Claudia's gaze. "As soon as you learn obedience, you can have food and water. It seems harsh, but it's the only way. You'll see soon." She turned again.

"No, Claudia. Wait, please! Don't leave me!"

The woman kept walking. As she disappeared from sight, reality smacked Charity in the face.

This was what had happened to Andrea.

And Andrea hadn't been seen since then.

Would that be Charity's fate also?

CHAPTER 42

Charity's stomach grumbled and her head swam. She needed food and water. She needed shelter, something other than this shack where she huddled at night.

The darkness surrounded her now. Every once in a while, she heard the sound of something moving through the forest. The sound was slight—the crackle of dry leaves or snapping branches. Maybe it was a squirrel or a raccoon or a possum. She had no idea.

She had to figure out how to get out of this place. But with the chain attached to her ankle, she had no idea how.

The words of Daleigh's song floated through her head. *God weeps.*

Was God weeping right now?

Somehow, instinctively she knew that He was. He wasn't a God who relished suffering but a loving God, a father.

Please, Lord, help me now. I don't know what to do.

She leaned her head into the pole where the chain was attached. Sleep wouldn't find her, despite her body's exhaustion. Finally, the sun peeked over the horizon in the distance, patches of orange and pink appearing through the trees.

What would today hold? Did she want to know?

As the sun rose higher, a figure appeared in the distance.

Claudia.

A dog walked beside her . . . a Dalmatian? This was all too strange.

"Father requests you put this on. It's your first test of obedience." She held out a shapeless dress that had small flowers dotting the beige surface.

"I don't want to put that on," Charity said.

Claudia frowned. "It's your first test. You should do as he asks."

"Why can't I wear this?" She pointed to her denim shorts and T-shirt.

"Please, just do as you're asked. Things will be easier."

As Charity stared at the woman, her initial thought was reaffirmed: something wasn't quite right with Claudia. It was more than this situation; there was a little bit of crazy in her gaze.

"Is this what Andrea had to do also?" Charity asked.

Claudia rubbed her dog's head. "She resisted at first. But eventually she came around and lived a good life here with us."

Charity's heart panged at the thought of her friend living like this. She must have been terrified.

"When do I get to meet your father?"

"You're not ready yet," Claudia said. "But you will when the time is right."

Who was the father? Buddy Griffin?

"If you're obedient now, you'll be able to drink some water."

Charity stared at her, weighing her options. She could wear that stupid dress. She supposed it wouldn't hurt anything. At least she'd get some water, and water would help her to stay alive.

"Fine," she finally said. "But I can't with the chain on

me."

"You're already wearing shorts. You'll be fine. Slip this on over your other clothes for now." Claudia stuffed the outfit through the fence.

Charity glanced away. Her gaze zeroed on a camera perched on a tree in the distance. Someone was watching her. Her cheeks heated. How had she not seen that earlier?

"One minute," she muttered. She stepped inside the shed and pulled the new dress on over her clothes.

As she looked at her new outfit, she realized that with every minute that passed, her pride was being stripped away.

That was probably the purpose of all of this, wasn't it?

The new dress looked like a pillowcase, almost. It was sleeveless and came to her knees. It had no shape, and the material felt scratchy, cheap.

"Now I'll get you some water," Claudia said. She unlocked the padlock at the gate and then slipped into Charity's pen. She grabbed a cup and dipped it into the water that had been left out all night.

Normally, the thought would turn Charity's stomach. Right now, she didn't care.

"You've been watching me," Charity said. "Why?"

"I've always wanted a sister." She handed her the cup.

Charity took a long gulp before saying, "So you lured me here?"

"That's correct. Andrea always talked about you. I've been keeping up with you for years."

"What happened to Andrea?" Charity finished the water and handed the cup back to Claudia, hoping for more. Instead, the woman dropped the cup on the ground.

Claudia's smile dipped. "She had a good life here."

"What happened to her?"

"She got sick. She . . . she didn't make it." Tears glistened in her eyes.

Charity's heart lurched. "She got sick how?"

Claudia shrugged and shook her head sadly. "I'm not sure. But she was so weak and pale."

"Did you take her to a doctor?"

"We treated her ourselves. Lots of herbs and water and oils. But it wasn't enough."

Oh, Andrea. "When was that?"

"Two years ago."

A small gasp escaped from Charity. Andrea had been held here for eight years. Eight years. She could hardly stomach the thought of her friend living like this.

"Did you catch my house on fire?"

Claudia didn't answer. She clicked the padlock in place and stepped away. "Until tomorrow."

"Tomorrow?" Charity said. "Please don't leave me here that long."

"You'll get used to it."

Tears pushed their way to Charity's eyes.

Living here might be worse than dying.

***

Charity had been gone for twenty-four hours. Joshua knew the statistics, but he didn't want to think about them at the moment. He had to remain focused and positive.

"Joshua, come look at this," the chief said.

He joined her by her desk.

"We ran the numbers on Roberta Whitaker's phone through the system as you suggested. This is the list we received. I did a search on some of the numbers. Do any of these look familiar?"

He scanned the list and frowned. His gaze stopped by one name.

"When did she call this number?" He pointed to one on the list.

The chief looked over his shoulder. "The day she died."

"I think I know where Charity is. I need some aerial views of the county."

"You want to tell me what's going on?"

"This name right here? He was one of the witnesses who saw Andrea as she left school before being abducted. He owns a landscaping business. According to these records, Roberta Whitaker also talked with him right before she died. That can't be a coincidence."

"We're going to need to call in some police teams from the surrounding cities. We can't handle this alone."

"We don't have time." Joshua straightened, a plan already forming in his head.

"We can't get sloppy. When we're sloppy, people end up dying. Just wait an hour and we'll assemble a team, get the proper warrants, and make sure everything is in place. Okay?"

Hesitantly, Joshua nodded.

Just then, the door opened, and the same woman who'd been in twice before came inside. The woman with the braid. Jasmine.

His heart sank. He just didn't have time to handle this right now.

"I was hoping we could talk," she stated, wringing her hands together nervously. As she stepped out of the shadows, he saw she had a black eye and a busted lip.

"I would love to talk sometime. But I need to let you talk to our dispatcher, Lynn, right now. We have an urgent matter we have to attend to." He hated having to say those words, but he had little choice at the moment. With every second that passed, Charity could die.

She glanced around, her gaze pensive. "I understand. But I only want to talk to you. Perhaps I'll come back next week."

"You can definitely do that. But ma'am, if you're in a dangerous situation, I beg you to get out of it. I can give you the numbers of some shelters in the area. You shouldn't stay with someone who harms you."

She nodded with a frown. "I'll come back next week. May I just use your restroom first?"

"Absolutely." He showed her where it was and then headed to his office. He had phone calls to make and a rescue mission to organize. Any other day, someone like Jasmine would take priority. But Charity's abduction took priority at the moment. He only wished the woman would talk to Lynn.

The landscaper was behind this? The man had mentioned Austin Johansson to Joshua just to throw him off his trail. How could he have fallen for it?

"Joshua, we have a problem," Lynn said from the front.

"One minute." He ran the man's information through the computer. He had no prior record. There was nothing that would have made people suspect him.

"I really think you should come now," Lynn said. Her voice cracked with tension.

"I've phone calls to make. Are you sure you can't wait?"

"There's a bomb in the lobby, and it's going to blow in less than a minute."

CHAPTER 43

Charity tugged on the chain again. There was no use—it was too tight to slip off and too strong to break.

She crawled forward, her fingernails clawing the supple ground as she tried to get the cup of water. Her reach was about four inches too short.

She didn't bother to crawl back. She lay there on the ground, the dirt gritty under her cheek. Her head swam from dehydration, from the elements, from desperation.

Don't give in to despair, she told herself again.

But the emotion was right there, on the cusp of her consciousness. It would be so easy to embrace it, to wallow in it.

No, she couldn't think like that. Joshua would find her.

But how? She still had no idea where she was. She was in the middle of the woods. Based on the canopy of trees overhead, the place wasn't visible from the air. She couldn't see any roads or structures in the distance. She was essentially in the middle of nowhere.

Tears tried to push their way out.

Finally, she forced herself to sit up. It took all her strength to keep herself that way without something to lean on.

How long would her body last like this? Without food? Water?

"You should just stop fighting," someone said behind her.

Charity flinched and swung her head back.

Claudia. Where had she come from? She wasn't supposed to be back until tomorrow morning. That's what she'd said.

"I have an update for you."

Her throat went dry. "About?"

"Joshua Haven. The police station just exploded, and he was inside."

A small cry escaped Charity. She didn't believe her. She couldn't. This was just another attempt to strip her pride. "You're lying."

"I'm not. I told you that we needed to eliminate him."

Someone who was that cold and that calculating would go to extreme measures to get what they wanted. Charity shook her head. How could she have fallen for all of this? "You *were* the one who set my house on fire."

Claudia's smile slipped. "I never wanted to hurt you."

"Then why did you do it?"

"Father thought fear would drive you to obedience."

Anger simmered in Charity. "I could have died."

"But you didn't. You proved you were strong."

"And your father kidnapped me? He left me in the woods. I just don't understand why. I don't understand how this all fits together." Charity'd had plenty of time to think about it while she'd been here in her cage.

"He believes fear is a great motivator. With fear, you'll be more inclined to do what he wants. He wanted to scare you. It was only another test."

"A test?"

"We weren't sure how we would get you here. He almost brought you that night, but he decided it was best if we waited. He wanted you to come to us. To come to *me*."

Her head swam. Charity was at the mercy of a

psychopath. Nothing Claudia said was logical.

"Did you kill Roberta Whitaker also?"

Claudia shrugged. "She came here. She realized what had happened. Andrea was alive then, and we couldn't risk her being taken away. She was part of our family by then. Father even allowed her out of this enclosure. He trusted her, like he trusts me."

A small cry escaped. This was a nightmare, pure and simple.

Poor Andrea. She'd lived here for so long. She must have been so scared.

But dwelling on that now would do her no good. She had to focus on surviving right now. "Can I have some food? Please."

"It's not time yet."

"Why not? Do you want to kill me?"

"We have to come to an understanding," she said softly.

"There's no way I can get away. Not with this chain around my ankle."

"It has to be a matter of choice. Can't you see? Everything is a choice."

"She's right, you know." A man stepped from the shadows. Charity stared at him a moment, feeling certain she'd seen him before. But where? He had long hair and wore a white T-shirt with jeans.

"You have to want to obey," he said, standing stoically in the background. "It won't work any other way."

"Who are you?" Charity asked, fear spreading through her chest until it reached her toes, her fingertips.

"You can just call me Father."

"You're not my father," she told him, her gut turning with disgust.

"No, but I will be."

Charity continued to study him, knowing she'd talked to him before. That's when it hit her. "You were cutting the grass at Daleigh's house the other day. You stopped me and said I'd been treated unfairly by the town."

A slight smile feathered his lips. "That's right. Did you know I also used to work for the school system? I was cutting grass there on the day you and Andrea decided to walk home. I'd just been waiting for the right opportunity to bring Andrea here. You both practically handed it to me."

Charity narrowed her eyes. "You've been watching me around town, also. I thought you were admiring Daleigh, but you weren't." He'd been the man wearing a baseball cap and sunglasses.

"I was simply learning your behaviors, your patterns, your routines. There was nothing to be alarmed about."

"I'm locked up in a cage, and you're telling me there was nothing to be alarmed about?" Her voice rose with outrage.

"You're feistier than I thought you would be. You gave up so easily that day in the woods when I grabbed Andrea."

"You never wanted me anyway."

He shook his head. "No, but I knew Andrea would come back for you. That's why I grabbed you first when I had the chance."

A cry caught in her throat. "I loved Andrea."

He smiled but his eyes were empty. "Now you get to take her place."

***

Joshua and Lynn got out of the building just in time. Pieces of debris lay all around them—bricks, cement blocks, plaster, and wood particles. Smoke rose around them, filling their lungs. A crowd had already begun to gather.

Thank goodness it didn't appear that anyone else was hurt.

Had Jasmine left that bomb there? It had to have been her. Was she involved in this the whole time?

"What do we do?" Lynn asked, grit covering her face.

"Are you okay?" He gripped her arms, helping her to her feet. The explosion had knocked them to the ground.

She nodded. "I think so."

"Lynn, I need you to call the chief and let her know what happened. I have to go find Charity."

Isaac's patrol car squealed onto the scene, and Joshua ran toward him.

"Isaac, I need your car." Joshua's was under a pile of rubble, and he didn't have any time to waste. "You've got to manage this scene. I have to go find Charity."

"You know where she is?" Isaac asked.

"I think so. The chief is trying to gather a team to head there. I'm going to go first."

"If you think that's best."

Joshua hopped into the car and pulled on his seat belt. Before he could squeal away, someone knocked at the window. Ron Whitaker.

Joshua put his window down. "I don't have time, Ron."

"Let me go with you."

"I'll do better on my own."

"Don't head out without backup. I promise; you can depend on me."

After a moment of thought, Joshua unlocked the door. "Get in."

As soon as Ron was secure, Joshua took off down the

road, headed toward Larry's house.

"What's going on?" Ron asked.

"I think I know where Charity is being held."

"What's your plan?"

Joshua gripped the steering wheel. "I don't have one except to find her."

Ron reached into his belt and pulled out a gun. "I'll be there to back you up."

"That gun is not a good idea."

Ron scowled. "I was with the police here for ten years. I know how to handle this."

"Have you had anything to drink?" Joshua asked.

"Nothing. I've been doing better. Just like I said I would."

Joshua slowed as he neared Larry's property. He didn't want to announce their arrival. The safest bet would be to stay in the woods and see what they could find. Joshua prayed that his moves would be the right ones and that Ron would be a help instead of a hindrance. There was too much at stake to mess this up.

Joshua pulled off into a patch of gravel, trying to conceal the car. Before he cut the ignition, his phone rang. It was the chief.

"Where are you?" she demanded.

"I'm headed out to Larry's. Isaac is watching over the scene at the station."

"Don't make any moves without backup. Do you understand? You don't know what kind of situation you're in. I'm not going to lose one of my officers. It hasn't happened yet, and it's not going to happen today."

"I have backup, Chief."

"Who? You said Isaac was at the station."

"Ron Whitaker."

"He's not a police officer anymore."

"But he's backup."

"Joshua . . ."

"We don't have time here, Chief. Charity's going to die if I don't find her soon. I can't let that happen. Not on my watch."

***

As people in desperate situations were prone to do, Charity began making a mental list of everything she would do if she ever got out of this prison.

The first thing: she'd truly stop letting her fears hold her back. Her fears about love. About hate. About the future.

If she took away those anxieties, she'd have no reason not to move back to Hertford. She'd have no reason to be away from Joshua. She could start again, find a new job in this area, and give life here in North Carolina another chance.

The question remained, however: Would she ever have a chance to do those things?

She didn't know the answer.

Her ankle was sore from the cuff she had around it. A thunderstorm brewed in the distance. A chilly wind had already picked up. Charity's legs were so welted with bug bites that there was hardly one smooth surface of skin there.

Lord, I believe You are a compassionate God. Please help. If You can't change my circumstances, change my heart and give me understanding and comfort. Please.

Just then she caught sight of someone coming toward her in the distance. She straightened, moving toward the fence. Who was it? Claudia? Larry?

But, as she watched, she squinted. It was neither. A woman she'd never seen before came toward her.

She wore khaki pants and a cotton top, and her salt-and-pepper hair was pulled back in a braid. A bruise covered her left eye, and her lip was crusty as if it had been busted.

The woman didn't say anything. She moved quickly and unlocked the gate. Then she rushed inside. Her fingers trembled as she released the cuff from around Charity's ankle.

"Run," the woman whispered.

This was the woman who'd called Charity. But who was she? Why was she helping her?

Charity stared a moment, wanting to say something.

"Run," the woman whispered again.

Finally, Charity nodded. "Thank you."

Without wasting any more time, she took off in the opposite direction from the one she'd seen Claudia and Larry approach from. She ran without stopping, without looking, without giving herself time to fear. She knew she just had to get as far away as possible.

CHAPTER 44

Joshua surveyed a house in the distance. He remained behind a tree, watching the place carefully for any sign of life.

A few minutes later, Larry Davis stepped out and stood on the porch. He stared into the distance, unmoving.

What was he doing? Did the man know he'd been discovered?

Ron remained beside him, acting surprisingly competent. Joshua still didn't know if it was the best idea for Ron to be with him, but it was too late to go back now.

Larry let out a cackle. It started as a low rumble and hung in the air, growing with time. The sound turned Joshua's stomach. A moment later, the man stepped back inside his house.

"You think he knows?" Ron asked.

Joshua shook his head. "I have no idea. But look at the truck in the driveway. It matches the kind we're looking for, based on the tracks we found where Charity was abducted."

Just then, someone else stepped from around the back of the house. A woman with a Dalmatian.

"Andrea . . ." Ron muttered.

"It's not Andrea, Ron. It's someone who looks like her. They found Andrea's body, remember?"

"How can she look so much like her?" Ron studied her, grief watering his eyes.

"Maybe she shares part of her DNA," Joshua suggested.

"Part of *your* DNA."

Ron cut him a sharp glance. "You mean . . . ?"

"You're not the poster boy for faithfulness. How do you know this woman isn't your daughter?"

Ron let out a small grunt. "What if Andrea's abduction was all my fault, someone getting revenge on me for my mistakes?"

"You can't think like that, Ron. Especially not now. I need you here with me and in the right mind-set. Let's not have another tragedy."

Ron grimaced and shook his head. "I treated Charity so poorly, Joshua. It wasn't fair."

"You're going to have the chance to tell her that. Hopefully soon." Joshua looked away from Ron for long enough to check on the girl. She watered some plants outside, the Dalmatian walking along beside her.

Interesting. So that was how Buddy Griffin was set up. These people must have, at some point, bought a Dalmatian from him. In that process, they'd figured out he'd be a good scapegoat. These people were master planners, able to frame more than one person in order to take suspicions off themselves.

"Everyone else should be here soon," Joshua said. "I think we should check out the rest of the property."

"I've got your back."

Just as Joshua looked up and spotted a camera located high in a tree, a gunshot rang out.

Joshua looked at the house again and saw Larry standing on the porch, a rifle in his hands. Things were about to get even more dangerous than before.

***

Charity heard the gunfire. Was someone shooting at her?

It sounded far away. As long as she kept moving away from the sound, she hoped she'd be okay. That was the only thought on her mind: keep moving.

She knew her feet and legs were bleeding, but she didn't stop. Not this time. She knew her life depended on escaping right now. Otherwise, that cage would be her death.

She'd rather take her chances out here in the woods.

If Joshua had been correct, this property was located between Edenton and Hertford. The total distance was probably fifteen miles. Certainly she'd run into something in between. She had to believe she had a chance.

Another gunshot rang out. What was going on?

Who was that woman who'd let her escape? What had happened to her? What would happen to her now when Father Larry realized she'd been the one to let Charity out?

A fence appeared in front of Charity, halting her in her tracks. A fence? Did it surround the entire property?

The structure was probably seven feet high and had barbed wire at the top. She'd never get over it. She had to find a gate, some way around it.

Her heart pounded in her ears, both from the exertion of her run and from the adrenaline that burst through her. She'd been so close to getting away.

Of course these people had thought ahead. They'd planned everything, hadn't they?

Which way should she go, to the left or the right?

In her mind, the right would lead to the road—or possibly back closer to her human kennel. The left would lead to the river. Were there any openings? Was climbing this even a possibility?

There was nothing to grab onto to get to the top. And, even if she did, the barbed wire would slice through her skin.

In a split-second decision, she followed the fence to the left, praying there was a break somewhere.

Movement in the distance caught her ear. Was someone following her?

Tension pinched at her spine. Was that a wild animal? Or was it Father Larry? Claudia?

She moved faster. But as she traveled farther, she still didn't see any openings. Was she just looping back around to where she started? Was there any way out of here?

Tears threatened to push their way out.

She heard another gunshot. This time, it was closer.

People yelled, but she couldn't make out any words.

Anxiety tried to squeeze at her throat. What was going on?

"You'll never get out, you know," someone said.

Charity paused and turned around. Claudia stood there, that psychotically carefree expression on her face.

"You found me," Charity said, her voice trembling as every other part of her froze.

She took a step closer. "I'm sorry Jasmine let you out. She shouldn't have. Father will make sure she's disciplined for her actions."

"Who's Jasmine?" Charity continued to inch along the fence, trying to put as much distance as possible between herself and Claudia.

"She's my mother."

"Why don't you call her Mother, then?"

"Father said Jasmine is a better name for her."

How messed up were these people? She'd never

willingly become a part of their clan. Never. "Claudia, I don't want to go back."

"But you must. You're a part of the plan."

"You leave sometimes. I saw you in the woods and in Edenton." She glanced around, looking for something to defend herself with. A stick or a rock . . . anything.

"Father trusts me. But Edenton was an accident. I didn't know you'd be there. I only approached you from the woods."

"How'd you know about puddle jumping?" Charity tried to keep her talking as she searched for a weapon.

"Andrea told me."

Charity saw a stick. It was three feet away, probably. She had to somehow grab it. "She told you she liked Dalmatians also?"

"Of course. She told me everything. Anyway, Father gave me a task."

"To lure me here?"

She nodded. "Exactly."

"Does Jasmine ever get out?"

"Only to do Father's will." She reached out her hand. "Come back with me. Let's make this easy."

"No. I don't want to go back."

Something changed in her gaze. "Then we'll have to do this the hard way."

***

"Come out or Jasmine dies," Larry said.

Joshua watched in horror as the man dragged Jasmine onto the porch. Larry had been coercing her into his dirty work all along, hadn't he? She was probably talking about herself when she came into the station, but also trying to warn him about Charity. He felt certain about it.

"Jasmine . . ." Ron muttered.

"You know her?"

"You could say that." Ron shook his head. "Everything is starting to make sense now. We had a . . . fling. I really messed things up, didn't I?"

Joshua turned his attention back to the situation at hand. He didn't have time to counsel Ron at the moment.

"Don't hurt her," Joshua called.

Larry glared. "Come out, then."

Joshua glanced at Ron. The best case scenario was that Larry didn't realize Joshua had back up.

"I'm coming out now," Joshua said.

He stepped out of the woods and onto the patch of land between the trees and the house.

"Put your gun down," Larry ordered.

Slowly, Joshua lowered his weapon to the ground.

"You'll never get Charity back, you know. She's mine," Larry said. "You should have just left it alone. No one else would have gotten hurt."

"I can't do that. Charity is important to me."

A bullet whizzed through the air. Before Joshua realized what was happening, Larry grabbed his shoulder, his face twisting with pain. A spot of blood appeared there.

Before Larry could harm Jasmine, Joshua lunged toward them. He pulled Jasmine out of the way and grabbed Larry's gun.

Moving quickly, he cuffed Larry, despite his protests and cries of pain.

"Are you okay?" he asked Jasmine.

She nodded, tears streaming down her face.

"Where's Charity?"

"I told her to run," she whispered.

"Run where?"

"She's back there somewhere. But Claudia went to find her. I'm sorry."

"Ron, take care of him. Can I trust you to do that?" The man was with the person who'd killed his wife and daughter. The situation wasn't ideal, to say the least.

"Yes, you can. I give you my word." Ron stepped toward Jasmine and put a hand on her elbow. The woman seemed to melt toward him.

"I have to go find Charity." Joshua took off into the woods. A quarter of a mile back, he found what looked like a cage. His heart slammed into his chest. Was this where Charity had been kept? What had they done to her?

Voices in the background made him pause. Someone was coming.

He ducked behind a tree and waited. A moment later, Charity came into sight. The woman who looked like Andrea—was Claudia her name?—clenched her arm.

"You could have avoided all of this," the girl said, almost in a singsong voice, one that made Joshua wonder if she was in her right mind.

Charity was wearing a strange cotton outfit. There were scratches on her arms and legs and dirt on her face. Her hair looked tangled, and her skin was pale.

Anger surged through him.

"I'm going to have to put you back in here until Father decides what to do with you," the woman said.

"No, you can just let me go. You don't have to do this, Claudia. There are other ways."

The dog walking beside Claudia suddenly barked—right in the direction of Joshua.

Claudia looked around, suspicion clouding her gaze. "I don't like the sound of that. We need to move fast."

As they reached the cage, Joshua stepped out. "Don't do it."

Charity used his unexpected appearance to her advantage. She pushed Claudia into the cage instead and slammed the door, clicking the padlock in place.

"What are you doing?" the woman demanded. She grabbed the rungs of the fence and pressed her face against them. "I don't belong here."

"No one does," Charity said.

The next instant she was in Joshua's arms. She collapsed, just as Chief Rollins appeared in the distance.

***

Three days later, Charity was released from the hospital. Joshua had been by her side as often as possible, but the two of them still hadn't spoken of anything beyond the investigation. Charity had been weak and had to have an IV and antibiotics for an infection that had set in around her wounds. Otherwise, she was okay.

She was exceedingly happy to be leaving the hospital. Joshua had offered to drive her back to Daleigh's place. Tomorrow, she needed to leave and head home to Tennessee.

The ride to Hertford was quiet, and they chitchatted about the weather and things of no consequence. Charity hated feeling the awkwardness between them.

At the porch, Joshua finally turned toward her. "Can we talk?"

She smoothed a wayward hair back. "I'd love to."

They walked to the pier and sat in the Adirondack chairs

there. She waited for Joshua to start.

"I'm sorry, Charity—"

"Don't be." She stopped him before he got too far. "You were just doing your job. I felt betrayed, but that didn't mean you'd actually betrayed me. Emotions can be funny things. I talk about them for a living, but sometimes when my own are right in front of me, I can't recognize them."

"I'd venture to say most people are like that."

Charity swallowed, feeling like there was a brick on her chest. So much had happened and they had so little time to talk about it all.

After a moment of silence fell, she asked, "Did anyone ever find Mr. Johansson, by the way? I never heard an update."

Joshua nodded. "He came out of hiding. He was camping in the mountains, apparently. He thought for sure he was going to be arrested for abducting Andrea. All these years he'd feared he was on the police watch list, mostly because of threats Ron Whitaker made toward him."

"Ron Whitaker . . . I guess I can't talk poorly about him, since he did risk his life to save me." She frowned, realizing some relationships were beyond repair.

"He's misguided, and he has a lot of faults. But he has some goodness inside, too. I'm hoping he'll tap into that."

"What about Claudia and Jasmine?"

"They're both getting help. I don't think they'll face charges, but both of the women are going to need counseling and help reintegrating into life away from that compound. They'd been programmed to believe a lot of lies."

"With some help, I believe they can change." *Look at me. I overcame the odds too.*

"Get this: Ron Whitaker is going to help pay for their therapy. He's actually been in contact with both of the women quite a bit. I think he's trying to make things right."

Maybe there was hope for the man.

"Did the coroner ever say how Andrea died?"

"Pneumonia. Without proper medical treatment, her body shut down. Otherwise, she appeared unharmed."

"That's a relief, I guess. I just hate that she had to suffer."

Charity realized they were avoiding talking about the giant invisible boulder between them.

"So you're leaving tomorrow?" Joshua said.

Charity licked her lips. "I am."

"You should have seen the town come together for you, Charity. You would have been touched." He glanced at her, the moonlight hitting his face and making it glow.

"The people here surprised me. I may not have seen what they did when I was abducted, but I've realized there are a lot of good people here. I'm just sorry I've been blinded all these years."

"I'm glad you have some answers, some of that closure you were seeking."

"I've never quite had the perspective that I had when I thought I was going to die, Joshua," Charity started, glancing down at her dress. "I had some spiritual realizations and some relationship ones, as well."

"And?"

She stood and walked toward the water, unable to sit any longer. Instinctively, Joshua seemed to appear behind her. When she turned, she found herself in his arms. "And I realized just how much you mean to me. There's never been anyone like you in my life, Joshua. I don't want to lose that."

His eyes turned from glimmering pools of confusion to bright with hope. "I was hoping you might say that. Charity, since the day I met you, I haven't been able to stop thinking about you. You make me want to believe in forever again, and that's not something I ever thought I'd say after my divorce."

"I can't tell you how happy it makes me to hear that." Her smile slipped. "But I do have to go back to Tennessee."

"I'm willing to give this a try if you are. We can take it day by day. We'll figure things out."

"I think that sounds like a great idea, Joshua. One of the best I've heard in a long time."

With that, his lips brushed hers. He pulled her into a long kiss, one full of promise and hope.

EPILOGUE

Charity squeezed Joshua's hand as she watched Ryan and Daleigh Shields take their first dance as a married couple. Charity had come into town for the wedding—and to see Joshua. The ceremony had been beautiful.

Jars filled with lights hung around the perimeter of the dance floor, a singer crooned ballads on a makeshift stage, and sweet tea was in abundance. Stars shone overhead, as well as a full moon. Charity couldn't imagine the night being any more perfect.

Ryan and Daleigh looked so incredibly happy together. At one time, Charity would have never been able to imagine that for her own life. Now, with Joshua by her side, it seemed like more of a possibility all the time.

As the reception lingered on, Charity stepped back and smiled. Weddings were beautiful things, and she knew Daleigh and Ryan would be happy together for a very long time.

A few people stopped by to say hello, and Charity chatted with them for a few minutes. Charity wasn't sure if everyone else truly accepted her more now or if she simply accepted herself. She'd been so overrun with guilt that she couldn't see clearly.

She only knew that she was happy to put that part of her life behind her.

"Charity?" Joshua asked, squeezing her hand.

She glanced up at him. "Yes?"

"I love you."

A huge grin stretched across her face. "I love you, too . . . more than anything."

She stood on her tiptoes and reached up to plant a kiss on his lips.

His arms seemed to instinctively wrap around her waist. "Do you have to go back to Tennessee tomorrow?"

She stepped out of his embrace and took his hands into hers. "I actually wanted to talk to you about that."

His smile slipped. "Okay."

"I was thinking of moving back to this area. I wanted to hear what you thought of the idea."

His eyes widened before his grin appeared again, wider than ever. "I think that's an excellent idea. In fact, I've been talking with the county sheriff, and we've agreed it's a good idea to hire a victim advocate for this area. Your name was thrown out there."

"I guess as police chief you have a little more pull now, huh?"

His arms went to her waist again. "As a matter of fact, I do."

"Daleigh mentioned that I might be able to rent her old place, now that she's moving out. At least until I figure out something more permanent."

"Funny that you mentioned that, because there's something I wanted to talk to you about." His eyes danced with happiness. "You know that offer you got on your property?"

"I do." She hadn't had time to hear any of the details. The paperwork was taking a long time to process. Plus, too many other things had been going on.

"It just so happens that I'm the one who made that offer," Joshua told her, his eyes glimmering in the moonlight.

This time, Charity's eyes widened. "Are you serious?"

He nodded, a grin pulling at his lips. "I have visions of building a new house there. There will be plenty of land, ample peace and quiet, and not a lot of drama."

"That sounds like a wonderful idea, Joshua."

Before he could respond, a little boy took off across the grass and threw his legs around Joshua. "Daddy!"

Charity smiled down at Rider. She'd been able to meet him once before, and she already knew that the little guy was a jewel. He was full of laughter and love and childhood wonder. And he was handsome to boot, just like his father.

"Hey, buddy." Joshua picked him up and swung the boy around. "Where did you wander off to? I thought you were with Mrs. Sarah."

"I was dancing with Mrs. Daleigh." Rider turned toward Charity. "Can we dance, too?"

"I'd love to," Charity told him, her heart warming at the thought.

Joshua and Charity exchanged a smile. As quickly as he appeared, the boy scrambled from his father's arms and headed back toward the dance floor. "Until then, I'm doing the waltz with the flower girl."

Charity chuckled. "He's quite a charmer. Just like his dad."

Joshua took her hand again. "Charity, I know it's too soon to jump into anything. But I just want you to know that I see my future with you. I *want* my future to be with you. I think Rider would like that also."

Joy exploded in her heart. Each wave brought more delight and satisfaction—satisfaction that she never thought she would get to experience. "I want the same thing, Joshua. More than I could have ever imagined."

"You're okay with coming back here?" Joshua asked.

She nodded, not a doubt in her mind. "I am. I'm ready to move on. I realize that there are a lot of good people here, people who never turned their backs on me. I just couldn't see it through my pain."

He brushed his lips against hers. "I love you, Charity White."

"I love you too, Joshua Haven. Now and forever."

###

Other books in the Carolina Moon series:

Home Before Dark (Book 1)
Nothing good ever happens after dark. Those were the words country singer Daleigh McDermott's father always repeated. Now her father is dead, and Daleigh fears she's returned home too late to make things right. As she's about to flee back to Nashville, she finds a hidden journal belonging to her father. His words hint that his death was no accident. Small town mechanic Ryan Shields is the only one who seems to believe that Daleigh may be on to something. Her father trusted the man, but Daleigh's instant attraction to Ryan scares her. She knows her life and career, however dwindling it might be, are back in Nashville and that her time in the sleepy North Carolina town is only temporary. As Daleigh and Ryan work to unravel the mystery, it becomes obvious that someone wants them dead. They must rely on each other—and on God—if they hope to make it home before the darkness swallows them whole. *Home Before Dark* offers a blend of Nicholas Sparks meets Mary Higgins Clark, a mix of charming small town life in North Carolina tangled in a gripping suspense.

Wait Until Dark (Coming Late 2015)

Standalone Novels:

Dubiosity
Savannah Harris vowed to leave behind her old life as an intrepid investigative reporter. But when a friend raises suspicions about two migrant workers who've gone missing

from the sleepy coastal town Savannah calls home, her curiosity spikes.

As ever more eerie incidents begin afflicting the area, each works to draw Savannah out of her seclusion and raise the stakes—for both Savannah and the surrounding community. Even as Savannah's new boarder, Clive Miller, makes her feel things she thought long forgotten, she suspects he's hiding something too, and he's not the only one. Doubts collide in Savannah's mind: Who can she really trust?
As secrets emerge and danger closes in, Savannah must choose between faith and uncertainty. One wrong decision might spell the end...not just for her, but for everyone around her.

Will she unravel the mystery in time, or will doubt get the best of her?

The Good Girl
Tara Lancaster can sing Amazing Grace in three harmonies, two languages, and interpret it for the hearing impaired. She can list the Bible canon backward, forward, and alphabetized. And the only time she ever missed church was at seventeen because she had pneumonia and her mom made her stay home. But when her life shatters around her and her reputation is left in ruins, Tara decides escape is the only option. She flees halfway across the country to dog-sit, but the quiet anonymity she needs isn't waiting in her sister's house. Instead she finds a knife with a threatening message, a fame-hungry friend, a too-hunky neighbor, and evidence of...a ghost? Following all the rules has gotten her nowhere. And nothing she learned in Sunday School can tell her where to go from there.

Death of the Couch Potato's Wife (Suburban Sleuth Mysteries)
You haven't seen desperate until you've met Laura Berry, a career-oriented city slicker turned suburbanite housewife. Well-trained in the big city commandment, "mind your own business," Laura is persuaded by her spunky 70-year-old

neighbor Babe to check on another neighbor who hasn't been seen in days. She finds her neighbor, Candace Flynn, wife of the infamous "Couch King," dead, and at last has a reason to get up in the morning in suburbia: murder. Someone's determined to stop her from digging deeper into the death of her neighbor, but Laura is just as determined to figure out who's behind the death-by-poisoned-pork-rinds.

The Trouble with Perfect
Since the death of her fiancé two years ago, novelist Morgan Blake's life has been in a holding pattern. She has a major case of writer's block, and a book signing in the small mountain town of Perfect sounds like just the solution to help her clear her head. Her trip takes a wrong turn when, on her way there, she's involved in a hit and run—she's hit a man, and he's run from the scene. Before fleeing, he mouthed the word "help." She plans to give him that help, but first she must find him. In Perfect, she finds a town that offers everything she's ever wanted. But is something sinister going on behind the town's cheery exterior? Was she invited as a guest of honor simply to do a book signing? Or was she lured to town for another purpose—a deadly purpose?

Other Books by Christy Barritt:

The Squeaky Clean Mystery Series:

Hazardous Duty (Book 1)
On her way to completing a degree in forensic science, Gabby St. Claire drops out of school and starts her own crime scene cleaning business. "Yeah, that's me," she says, "a crime scene cleaner. People waiting in line behind me who strike up conversations always regret it."

When a routine cleaning job uncovers a murder weapon the police overlooked, she realizes that the wrong person is in jail. But the owner of the weapon is a powerful foe . . . and willing to do anything to keep Gabby quiet.

With the help of her new neighbor, Riley Thomas, a man whose life and faith fascinate her, Gabby plays the detective to make sure the right person is put behind bars. Can Riley help her before another murder occurs?

Suspicious Minds (Book 2)
In this smart and suspenseful sequel to *Hazardous Duty*, crime scene cleaner Gabby St. Claire finds herself stuck doing mold remediation to pay the bills. But her first day on the job, she uncovers a surprise in the crawlspace of a dilapidated home: Elvis, dead as a doornail and still wearing his blue suede shoes. How could she possibly keep her nose out of a case like this?

It Came Upon a Midnight Crime (Book 2.5, a Novella)
Someone is intent on destroying the true meaning of Christmas—at least, destroying anything that hints of it. All around crime scene cleaner Gabby St. Claire's hometown, anything pointing to Jesus as the "reason for the season" is being sabotaged. The crimes become more twisted as

dismembered body parts are found at the vandalisms. Who would go to such great lengths to dampen the joy and hope of Christ's birthday? Someone's determined to destroy Christmas . . . but Gabby St. Claire is just as determined to find the Grinch and let peace on earth and goodwill to men prevail.

Organized Grime (Book 3)
Gabby St. Claire knows her best friend, Sierra, isn't guilty of killing three people in what appears to be an eco-terrorist attack. But Sierra has disappeared, her only contact a frantic phone call to Gabby proclaiming that she's being hunted. Gabby is determined to prove her friend is innocent and to keep her alive. While trying to track down the real perpetrator, Gabby notices a disturbing trend at the crime scenes she's cleaning, one that ties random crimes together—and points to Sierra as the guilty party. Just what has her friend gotten herself into?

Dirty Deeds (Book 4)
"Promise me one thing. No snooping. Just for one week."

Gabby St. Claire knows that her fiancé's request is a simple one that she should be able to honor. After all, Riley's law school reunion and attorneys' conference at a hoity-toity resort is a chance for them to get away from the mysteries Gabby often finds herself involved in as a crime scene cleaner. The weeklong trip is a chance for them to be "normal," a word that leaves a bad taste in Gabby's mouth.

But Gabby finds herself alone for endless hours while Riley is busy with legal workshops. Then one of Riley's old friends goes missing, and Gabby suspects one of Riley's buddies might be behind the disappearance. When the missing woman's mom asks Gabby for help, how can she say no?

Secrets abound. Frankly, Gabby even has some of her own. When the dirty truth comes out, the revelations put everything in jeopardy—relationships, trusts, and even lives.

The Scum of All Fears (Book 5)
"I'll get out, and I'll get even."

Gabby St. Claire is back to crime-scene cleaning, at least temporarily. With her business partner on his honeymoon, she needs help after a weekend killing spree fills up her work docket. She quickly realizes she has bigger problems than finding temporary help.

A serial killer her fiancé, a former prosecutor, put behind bars has escaped. His last words to Riley were: *I'll get out, and I'll get even*. Pictures of Gabby are found in the man's prison cell, and Riley fears the sadistic madman has Gabby in his sights.

Gabby tells herself there's no way the Scum River Killer will make it across the country from California to Virginia without being caught. But then messages are left for Gabby at crime scenes, and someone keeps slipping in and out of her apartment.

When Gabby's temporary assistant disappears, Gabby must figure out who's behind these crimes. The search for answers becomes darker when Gabby realizes she's dealing with a criminal who's more than evil. He's truly the scum of the earth, and he'll do anything to make Gabby and Riley's lives a living nightmare.

To Love, Honor, and Perish (Book 6)

How could God let this happen?

Crime scene cleaner Gabby St. Claire can't stop asking the question. Just when her life is on the right track, the unthinkable happens. Gabby's fiancé, Riley Thomas, is shot and remains in life-threatening condition only a week before their wedding.

Gabby is determined to figure out who pulled the trigger, even if investigating puts her own life at risk. But as she digs deeper into the facts surrounding the case, she discovers secrets better left alone. Doubts arise in her mind and the one man with answers is on death's doorstep.

An old foe from the past returns and tests everything Gabby is made of—physically, mentally, and spiritually. Will her soul survive the challenges ahead? Or will everything she's worked for be destroyed?

Mucky Streak (Book 7)
After her last encounter with a serial killer, Gabby St. Claire feels her life is smeared with the stain of tragedy. Between the exhaustion of trying to get her fiancé back on his feet, routine night terrors, and potential changes looming on the horizon, she needs a respite from the mire of life.

At the encouragement of her friends, she takes on a short-term gig as a private investigator: a cold case that's eluded investigators for ten years. The mass murder of a wealthy family seems impossible to solve but quickly gets interesting as Gabby brings more clues to light. Add to the mix a flirtatious client, travels to an exciting new city, and some quirky—albeit temporary—new sidekicks, and things get really complicated.

With every new development, Gabby prays that what she's calling her "mucky streak" will end and the future will become clear. But every answer she uncovers leads her closer to danger—both for her life and for her heart.

Foul Play (Book 8)
Gabby St. Claire is crying foul play, in every sense of the phrase.

When crime scene cleaner Gabby St. Claire agrees to go undercover at a local community theater, she discovers more than backstage bickering, atrocious acting, and rotten writing. The female lead is dead and an old classmate who's staked everything on the musical production's success is about to go under.

In her dual role of investigator and star of the show, Gabby finds the stakes rising faster than the opening night curtain. She comes face to face with her past and must make monumental decisions, not just about the play but also concerning her future relationships and career.

Will Gabby find the killer before the curtain goes down—not only on the play, but also on life as she knows it?

The Sierra Files

Pounced (Book 1)
Sierra is used to fighting for the lives of innocent creatures. But when a killer puts the lives of her own cats on the line, her crusade becomes personal.

Animal rights activist Sierra Nakamura never expected to stumble upon the dead body of a coworker while out filming a project. She definitely never expected to get involved in the investigation. But when someone threatens to kill her cats unless she hands over the "information," she becomes more bristly than an angry feline.

Making matters worse is the fact that her cats—and the investigation—are driving a wedge between her and her boyfriend Chad. With every answer she uncovers, old hurts rise to the surface and test her beliefs.

Saving her cats just might mean ruining everything else in her life. In the fight for survival, one thing is certain: It's either pounce or be pounced.

Hunted (Book 2)
Who knew a stray dog could lead to so much trouble?

Newlywed animal rights activist Sierra Nakamura Davis is coming face to face with her worst nightmare: breaking the news she eloped to her ultra-opinionated tiger mom.

Her perfectionist parents have planned a vow renewal ceremony at Sierra's lush childhood home, but a neighborhood dog ruins the rehearsal dinner when he shows up toting what appears to be a fresh human bone.

Between the dog, a nosey neighbor, and an old flame turning up at all the wrong times, Sierra hunts for answers. Surprises abound at every turn as Sierra embarks on a journey of discovery that leads to more than just who did the crime.

Pranced (Book 2.5, a Christmas novella)
Sierra Nakamura Davis thinks that spending Christmas with her husband's relatives will be a real Yuletide treat. But when the animal rights activist finds out that his family has a reindeer farm, she begins to feel more like the Grinch.

Even worse, when Sierra arrives, she discovers that those very reindeer are missing. The community is depending on the creatures to spread holiday cheer at the annual light show. Plus, Sierra fears the animals might be suffering a far worst fate than being used for entertainment purposes.

Can Sierra set aside her dogmatic opinions to help get the reindeer home in time for the holidays? Or will secrets tear the family apart and ruin Sierra's dream of the perfect Christmas?

About the Author:

USA Today has called Christy Barritt's books "scary, funny, passionate, and quirky."
Christy writes both mystery and romantic suspense novels that are clean with underlying messages of faith. Her books have won the Daphne du Maurier Award for Excellence in Suspense and Mystery, have been twice nominated for the Romantic Times' Reviewers' Choice Award, and have finaled for both a Carol Award and Foreword Magazine's Book of the Year.

She's married to her Prince Charming, a man who thinks she's hilarious--but only when she's not trying to be. Christy's a self-proclaimed klutz, an avid music lover who's known for spontaneously bursting into song, and a road trip aficionado.

When she's not working or spending time with her family, she enjoys singing, playing the guitar, and exploring small, unsuspecting towns where people have no idea how accident prone she is.

Find Christy online at:
www.christybarritt.com
www.facebook.com/christybarritt
www.twitter.com/cbarritt

Sign up for Christy's newsletter to get information on all of her latest releases here: **www.christybarritt.com/newsletter-sign-up/**

If you enjoyed this book, please consider leaving a review.

Made in the USA
San Bernardino, CA
03 November 2015